HIGH LEAD AND LOW DEEDS

HIGH LEAD AND LOW DEEDS

JUSTICE BEGINS™ BOOK THREE

MICHAEL ANDERLE

LMBPN Publishing
PMB 196, 2540 South Maryland Pkwy
Las Vegas, NV 89109

Version 1.00, December 2021
ebook ISBN: 979-8-88541-000-7
Print ISBN: 979-8-88541-001-4

THE HIGH LEAD AND LOW DEEDS TEAM

Thanks to the Beta Readers
Larry Omans, Kelly O'Donnell, Rachel Beckford, Allen Collins,
Kit Mitchell

Thanks to the JIT Readers

Dorothy Lloyd
Dave Hicks
Wendy L Bonell
Diane L. Smith
Deb Mader
Jeff Goode
Zacc Pelter
Kelly O'Donnell

If I've missed anyone, please let me know!

Editor
The Skyhunter Editing Team

DEDICATION

*To Family, Friends and
Those Who Love
to Read.
May We All Enjoy Grace
to Live the Life We Are
Called.*

— Michael

CHAPTER ONE

Dr. Gaje "Gage" Gurung's eyes bulged as the pain shot up his leg, but other than that, he didn't react in any obvious way. People had often told him that he was good at hiding his emotions. "Stoic" was the English word that best described him.

The Westerners also said he was polite. He didn't consider himself any more or less polite than the average person should be, but he was willing to accept the compliment.

"Careful!" the other man chided him. "You need to stretch the ankle *slowly*. Go through one little part of the motion at a time, and feel your way through it. Don't skip any steps. There are no shortcuts, get it? Physical therapy is nothing to screw around with, bud. This is how you get better. This is how you walk again, so you can finally put on the uniform."

Gage inhaled through his nose before breathing out of his mouth, allowing his face to settle into a relatively calm grimace. "Yes, I understand. Thank you, Dr. Costa." Looking down at his leg, he started the process over again—rotating his foot and limbering it up.

His overseer watched him and shook his head. "I told you to call me Dante."

Gage chuckled. They got along pretty well, but he'd fallen into the habit of calling his new friend "Dr. Costa" whenever they were discussing the subject of his ankle. When talking about other things, it was easier to use his name.

The two men had shared a small house in the Atlantican hills for the last five weeks. Daria Barruk, the ex-smuggler and current Executioner had procured the place for them through her old underworld connections once Gage had agreed to join her fledgling organization.

The problem, of course, was his ankle. He'd fractured it during a tumble down an excavation shaft, then made it worse by participating in an armed brawl.

So Daria had ordered him to heal up under the care of another doctor, albeit one of the medical variety. Dante Costa, the American.

The house was little more than a cottage. It was quaint and cozy enough although it had that antiseptic lack of personality characteristic of residences not yet lived in. Like essentially all buildings on the island of Atlantica, it was new. The timber was fresh and bright, and the furniture mostly plastic or stainless steel stuff. Gage found it odd and ugly, but it served its purpose well enough.

They conducted their basic exercises and almost everything else in the central living area, which wasn't expansive but provided sufficient room. Later they would move outside—once Gage felt up to moving around enough.

After stretching, they moved on to having Gage stand, shift his posture, do basic strength training, and practice walking around in circles. It was still stiff and sore and stabbed him with sudden jolts of agony when he got careless, but his ankle was far better than it had been a month ago.

Dante had yet to say as much outright, but Gage suspected that his recovery period was nearing its end. Soon, he would be able to begin his duties as Atlantica's third Executioner.

As he continued his slow, shuffling movements around the periphery of the living room, forcing himself gradually to walk with a more normal gait, something occurred to him. He snapped his face toward the doctor. "Leopard moray eels, or dragon eels, display what exceptional ability?"

He used the voice he always employed when posing a question like that, disguising his British-tinged Nepali accent with his best imitation of an American television host.

Dante's rather handsome, olive-skinned face at first fell slack in confusion. Then he blinked, and his expression brightened. He snapped his fingers. "Ah, yes. The ability to change their sex in response to a lack of suitable mates."

Gage chuckled. "Most impressive. How did you know that one? I thought that at last, I would've stumped you for good."

Dr. Costa adjusted the lapels of this jacket and beamed. "I once dated a gal who ran an aquarium in New York. She was full of... interesting... information. Quite the character."

"Hmm, yes." Gage took another step, wincing slightly, but he was getting a better feel for managing his movements. That included how to tolerate the types of pain that were simply the result of his muscles needing to adjust and how to avoid the kinds that indicated he was doing something truly wrong. "Why did you date her?"

Dante held two hands out in front of his chest, palms turned upward, each in a broad cupping motion. "Oh, you know. She had assets."

Gage moved on, biting his tongue while nodding in appreciation. "I see. Why did you *stop* dating her?" He was getting into the groove of walking by now, and was confident that he could go a long way without hurting himself, provided he didn't get startled or do anything clumsy or stupid.

His new friend shrugged. "She was crazy as hell. Also I, uhh, had problems of my own at the time. You know."

In point of fact, Gage *did* know. As the two men had talked more and begun to trust one another, Dante had shared the single biggest tribulation in his life. The thing that got him in so much trouble and lurked at the root of most of his failures, difficulties, and close calls.

Morphine.

Treating Gage in this remote hamlet was partly a way for him to get away from Atlantica City, with its many insidious temptations. The island had no real laws to speak of. Plenty of people were looking to make a quick fortune by any means available. If you could pay for it, you could find it for sale.

Gage nodded. "Yes. Things don't always work out with women. Or with, well, many other endeavors in life. We are fortunate to be here now. Things could've been far worse."

He moved on, his stride becoming smoother the more he practiced, and when the ankle pained him or felt stiff, he paused to stretch or massage it under the doctor's watch.

Dante muttered, "I guess so. I'm better off here than I might've been back home after everything that happened. What about you? Didn't Daria say there was this mysterious group of people who were going to come after you or something? The Miracle Cabal or some shit like that?"

Gage frowned. "Yes. The Coven of Miracles was their name. She feels they'll seek revenge upon us for interfering with their operation. They needed a great deal of Atlanticore to complete whatever they were planning.

"Daria buried it all, along with the archaeologist Dr. Limbu. I worked under Limbu, and it's too bad that things turned out the way they did. Still, she was mad. And corrupted by greed and ambition."

"Yeah." Dante pulled out a small comb and ran it through his wavy dark hair. "Greed and corruption usually cause that to happen, don't they? Plenty of it back in New York and New Jersey.

"At least back there, it was all the usual stuff. Gambling, prostitution, extorting politicians, fixing boxing matches, et cetera I don't understand what half the corruption here is all about. Magic crystals? Ancient civilizations? Come on."

By now, Gage had completed a lengthy cycle in one direction. He stopped and turned, preparing to walk back the way he came, now counterclockwise around the room, to help his foot adjust to the slightly different angle.

"Atlanticore is not *magic*," he pointed out. "We weren't able to finish our research. It's a mineral with properties that go beyond what modern science understands. The Atlanticans of the distant past had truly incredible technology."

Dante laughed. "I know that, man. Just kidding. Well, I know the 'it's not magic' part. The rest is new to me. And pretty damn interesting, now that you mention it. More interesting than moray eels that can change sex. You never talked about all that in much detail. I would be curious to hear more. You know, when you feel up to it."

Gage began his walk in the other direction. The mild difference in his weight distribution made him wince for a moment, but he adjusted to it after the first three or four steps. "We can discuss it sometime." He sighed. "I suppose I haven't felt very much like talking about it because of the disappointment and loss that go with it."

He paused, focused on his movement, and decided whether to say more. His friend gave him time, saying nothing and watching his foot and ankle instead.

Gage opted to go ahead and speak. "Coming here and being able to study Atlanticore and the ancient ruins so recently found in the wilderness was a great dream of mine. I didn't begin to study archaeology until I was...older than most who begin their university educations. I'm glad I did it, regardless. Yet I worried that I might not have time to participate in such an important dig."

"Understandable," Dante commented. "Take it easy there, bud.

You're doing a lot better these days, but you don't want to come down with too much pressure on the front of the ankle. Let the foot roll off the floor, heel to toes."

The Nepali glanced at his feet and did as the doctor instructed. "Of course. I know that you had dreams, too. Mine would've been to continue the dig and to have the people I worked with still alive.

"Dr. Limbu ruined it all. She and many other people died in the fighting that broke out, and we could only save the lives of the rest by blowing up the excavation shaft and promising to leave it in peace forever. Now, no one knows how long it might be until we discover another site like that."

Dante adjusted his position, the better to watch Dr. Gurung as he made his circular progress around the room. "I get it. I mean, it sounds like you and Daria stopped things from ending up even worse, but still a complete disaster. Why aren't you going back into archaeology? Why the hell are you joining the Executioners instead?"

Gage breathed in and out as he strode. As much as he liked Dante, the man was blunt. He made few efforts to phrase things in gentle ways or be diplomatic in his manner of asking questions.

"I don't know," Gurung admitted. "I have several ideas, and I've been thinking about them. Perhaps it's time for me to find a way to speak them in words, rather than allow them to stay as only ideas in my head."

Dante added with a sour smile, "Yeah, might be. By the way, no offense. I'm not questioning your judgment. I'm curious. You know me."

"Of course." Gage chortled. "Yes... I have my reasons. Daria Barruk helped save my life. I feel that I'm obligated to her, and she asked me and said that I would be a tremendous help to her. She is highly persuasive."

He stopped, resting, and looked up at the doctor. Dante waved for him to keep moving.

"Yeah, makes sense considering her background. She's not too bad-looking, either. Heh, heh."

Gage confessed, "True. Although there is nothing, ah, of that nature between us. We worked together, fought together, and became friends." He swallowed. "That's not all. I think my other reason for taking her offer is because I don't want to think about what happened.

"Getting back to where I was would take a great deal of time. I also have a degree in Applied Engineering, but that is boring. I miss some of the adventures that came with my military service. So, I am here."

"Here, taking it easy in a cabin, eh?" Dante quipped.

Gage snorted. "Ha, ha. This is not *easy*, anyway. You push me hard. But I think I will see action soon."

"Yeah, probably," the doctor agreed. "You've made good progress. And... Oh, Janet is here. Take a break. I'll go let her in."

It was impossible not to notice how Dante perked up at realizing the nurse had arrived. He practically sprang from his vantage point by the big easy chair toward the front door, tearing it open as the car outside purred to a stop.

Janet Feng was a stunningly beautiful Chinese-American woman in her middle or late twenties. Daria had produced her through her contacts to assist the two men in the process of Gage's gradual recovery. She lived in a small village that acted as a suburb of sorts to the northeastern portion of Atlantica City. The drive wasn't far despite the cabin's relative isolation. Janet typically came in every day except Sunday, which she took off unless there was an emergency.

Gage felt like sitting down but decided to stay on his feet. It would help strengthen his ankle. So he stood and waited as Dante escorted Janet into the cottage.

The young woman was wearing the standard white outfit of

her profession with a light jacket over it, and she wasn't wearing a hat. Her black hair was rather short, stopping a centimeter above her shoulders, and it curled around her face on both sides like a hood. It had taken a good two weeks before Gage had noticed, to his embarrassment, that the girl had a pink scar running down the left side of her jaw. The haircut was undoubtedly a way of hiding it from the world.

When she saw Gage, she gave him a warm smile. "Hello, Dr. Gurung. I hope you're doing well." Although she'd lived the bulk of her short life in the United States and her English was excellent, she retained a vestigial North Chinese accent.

"Most well, thank you." He nodded. "The same to you. We've completed my walking around the room."

Before the nurse could say anything, Dante interjected, "Hey, now, I never said you'd finished. Ha, just kidding. Do one more round while Janet gets ready, and we'll call it good."

Gage pretended to grimace in anger, but he didn't mind. "So be it. You seem to enjoy this too much, Dr. Costa."

Dante gave a fake evil laugh as Janet, half-smiling but looking faintly exasperated with the banter between the two men, took off her shoes and jacket and went to the tiny kitchen table to set down her bag and take inventory of her materials. Gage also assumed she would make a pot of tea—something which Dante, being American, was largely indifferent toward but which Gage appreciated immensely.

While the nurse did her thing and Gage progressed with his final circle around the living room, Dante quipped, "I suppose I do enjoy doing easy stuff like this more than all the garbage I was into before. Not that the operation on your ankle was all *that* easy, but at least I get to relax up here. Working for that gang was a little too much excitement for me. Mr. Katakura thought he had to *leverage* me into doing this shit. Ha! It's a piece of cake, really."

Gage nodded as he came to the end of his brief revolution, then sat, at last, in the big easy chair. Janet would be unwrapping, massaging, and rewrapping his ankle so standing would've been counterproductive.

Then he thought of something. "I will be better soon, yes? What will you do afterward, Dante? Does Ty have another job for you?"

Dante's face darkened. "I'm not sure. Probably. Maybe. He hasn't mentioned it. He might let me go free." He hesitated. "In that case, I don't know what to do. Not sure if I want to go back to Atlantica City what with all the, y'know, temptations.

"I could go back to America if I could get some fake ID papers, maybe. I could move on to Europe. If I'm lucky maybe some rich prick at one of the country villas out here will hire me as their physician. Who knows."

Gage nodded. He'd grown to like the young Italian-American doctor. Parting from him would be unfortunate, and he didn't like the thought of him getting back into trouble.

After his de facto exile from the United States, Dante had ended up forced to act as a medic for a violent gang of arms dealers. Little by little, Gage had learned most of the details of the situation as they'd grown more familiar with one another. When Ty Katakura had taken the gang on, clashing with them immediately and killing more than half of their members, it was little more than luck that had saved Dante from being gunned down alongside his employers.

Luck and a bit of bravery. At first, Gage had been skeptical about the doctor's story about what had finally transpired. Still, men who lied about such things tended to brag about them. The fact that Dante had been hesitant to discuss it vouched for his honesty.

During a ferocious battle against the gunrunners' main cell, one of the boss' chief lieutenants got the drop on the Executioner and probably would've killed him. Dante sprang into action, picked up a fallen handgun, and unloaded it into the man's head. Ty had been stunned and had decided to spare Dante's life on the condition that he returned the favor.

After Daria had wrapped up her operation and disclosed that she knew a man with a broken ankle, both of them had ended up at the little house in the hills.

"Hey," Dante remarked, "at least I won't have to listen to you and answer your questions about eels. Or questions about, let's see here...TV dinners, internal combustion engines, Batman, sedimentary rocks..."

Janet was ready. "Please, gentlemen, allow me to begin my work without the distractions of your endless chit-chatting."

Dante rolled his eyes where Gage could see it and she couldn't, but he shut up. Gage tried not to laugh. He liked both of them enough to refuse to take sides.

The nurse walked over to Gage, got down on her knees, and took hold of his gauze-wrapped foot as she had so many times before. A full cast was no longer necessary.

After unwrapping it, she cleaned the area with sanitary pads and began massaging it. The technique reduced the buildup of scar tissue around the initial fracture and Dante's incisions to reset the bone. Her hands moved with care and assurance. The pain flared up here and there, but otherwise, it was almost relaxing.

While Janet worked, Dante examined the ankle himself. "Looking a *lot* better, bud. I think you can probably return to duty in only a few more days. As long as you're careful, of course."

For the first time in too long, Gage was excited. "Yes? I have waited a long time now. It has been pleasant here, in a way. But I would like to return to work."

"Yes," Dante confirmed. His face had gone a touch slack. Something dark and sad lurked behind his eyes.

It was what they'd talked about a moment ago—the fact that

once Gage had fully recovered, the young doctor might have nowhere to go, nothing to do, and no one to help him.

Before Gage could say something, Dante shrugged, stood, and turned away. "Janet, I'm going to take the car down to the shop and get us something to eat. I'll be back shortly."

"All right, Doctor." She didn't look up. "Please be careful." She was undoubtedly worried about the car nearly as much as the man. It belonged to her, but they'd agreed that Dante could use it from time to time when necessary. Fortunately, he was a sensible driver. On Atlantica, licenses and insurance were nonexistent.

A couple of minutes after the car buzzed away, Janet paused and inhaled. "You should be good for a moment. Would you like some tea, Dr. Gurung?"

"Yes, please, and thank you." He smiled at her. "I would make it myself, but I think you are better at it."

She blushed, stood, and went to the kitchenette, where a pot was steaming on low heat, not far from boiling. A moment later she brought him a cup and saucer. He set it on the little table beside him, allowing it to cool and steep, and Janet returned to the kitchen area to sip from her cup before sanitizing her hands and preparing to re-wrap his ankle.

She didn't talk much, but it didn't bother Gage. He settled back into his chair, closed his eyes, and enjoyed the near-total silence. It was nice to be left alone with his thoughts. To recline and relax, without the noise of other people or the sounds of the city. Although, as he settled into a trancelike state of calm focus, he rediscovered a fact that he technically already knew.

The cottage wasn't silent at all. Neither was the wilderness outside. Once the usual cluttering sounds quieted, everything else came alive. He heard its chatter, its groanings, its symphony.

It wasn't a windy day, but there was a breeze outside. It rustled through the spaces between the hills or rushed around cliffs and crags on its course over the mountains and toward the Atlantic

Ocean to the east. Gage heard it move between each blade of grass, felt the way it buffeted the sides of the house outside, and sent the tree branches swaying above and to the sides.

The cottage itself had a voice as well. It spoke in low, creaking whispers as its new foundations settled into the ancient earth. Insects burrowed in the ground below the base of the walls. Mice and other small creatures scrabbled around, looking for a way in, although Daria had said the place was well-constructed to keep out unwanted visitors.

Above the walls where bugs and rodents crawled, birds lighted on the branches of trees or nestled in the crooks to build or tend their nests. Some went out on limbs to sing to one another, whether mating calls or threats and warnings to others who might infringe on their territory.

Taking shape amid the subtle natural cacophony was another sound, soft but too regular to be part of the others, which sounded a great deal like the heavy, booted feet of a large man moving slowly closer to the cabin.

From behind.

Gage sat up straight and opened his eyes. Dante had left through the front door. The footsteps approached from the opposite direction, away from the road and toward the narrow ravine between the hills behind the cabin. There was nothing that way aside from a vague rocky path that led down to the temperate jungle wilderness beyond.

The footfalls didn't sound like Dante's, either. Though tall, he moved with a light, springy, somewhat swaggering gait. Whoever approached now did so with a heavy, deliberate plod, like the advance of a glacier.

It was all wrong. Everything about this was wrong, and it set off all Gage's alarms and warnings. It prodded him within the sensitive spots in his mind that had developed throughout the long years of the Second World War, and had been further cultivated by his travels to strange and dangerous places in the two decades since.

Janet had turned away from whatever she was doing a moment ago and gently moved closer to Gage. It looked as though she might sit next to him with her tea, perhaps to strike up a conversation, but more likely to do nothing but rest, drink, and relax in peaceful silence. She noticed the look on his face and the shift in his attitude.

"Dr. Gurung," she began quietly, her eyebrows rising in concern.

Gage reached down by his side and wrapped his fingers around the handle of carved water buffalo horn attached to the weapon at his hip. A kukri, the big forward-curving knife of his native country, lay in a leather holster. He stood with surprising speed and drew the blade.

Janet froze, and her mouth dropped open. The beginnings of a scream formed in her throat. Gage clamped a hand over her mouth in time to stifle the cry of alarm.

"Please, be quiet," he whispered. His eyes darted around the little house, while with his right hand he brought the kukri up to chest level, the tip of its blade pointed outwards.

Janet relaxed, but only slightly. She had grasped quickly enough that Gage's sudden aggressive demeanor wasn't directed at her but still shook with fear at whatever else might've brought about the total change in his demeanor.

The cottage fell quiet again. Gage listened. Outside, the footsteps had stopped...then they resumed, moving toward the house and up the hill before circling the northwest corner where the back door lay.

It would be a direct assault, then.

Gage pivoted and pushed Janet toward the northeast corner of the interior main room, where she could crouch behind a chair and table. It wasn't much, but it would get her out of the way.

"Oh!" she gasped as she stumbled against the wall.

"Stay down. Whatever you do, keep down." Gage turned toward the back door, wishing he had his old Webley service revolver—but willing to face down whatever came through the door with a knife alone if that was what it took. His people had never backed down from a fight.

Then with a thunderous *bang*, the wood around the doorframe near the knob splintered and the entire thing fell off its hinges.

Standing there with blazing eyes was an enormous man, so big he nearly looked like he wouldn't fit through the doorway. He held a submachine gun high at his shoulder, its barrel aimed at Dr. Gurung. Gage saw his finger beginning to squeeze the trigger.

There was no time. There was no time to charge him, no time to dive or roll out of the way. Gage did the only thing he could think of. He screamed the war cry he'd used so often in his military days and threw the knife.

CHAPTER TWO

The kukri was universally regarded as an excellent melee weapon. Close combat experts and blade connoisseurs the world over had praised its status as a model edged weapon when used as intended. Its broad, thick blade, aggressive recurve, and general shape and design, especially when made of high-quality steel, placed it among the royalty of the world's edged weapons.

Of course, its association with the Gurkhas, known as both fearsome and fearless, had greatly bolstered its reputation. The pride of Nepal. The deadliest soldiers of the British Empire.

All of this assumed that its wielder would use the kukri to hack and slash. Its design was never suitable for a throwing weapon.

The enormous man snarled with a savage mixture of free-floating rage and mirthless enjoyment and stomped over the threshold as the Gurkha knife spun toward him. He didn't see it until it was too late—but Gage's aim and balance had been off.

Flying end over end in a zigzagging, diagonal course, the blade missed its chance to strike the attacker's chest, neck, or face. Instead, its point buried itself in the man's bulky shoulder.

Not deep enough to cause serious injury, but enough to stick in place.

Gage's eyes widened in horror. The man flinched, but it was no more than a muscular reaction with no sign of pain or fear. The assassin, whoever he was, had all but ignored the knife. Whether through battle-lust and adrenaline, or thanks to drugs, he barely felt it.

He opened fire.

Janet screamed, crouching farther into her space in the far corner, trying to make herself invisible or to sink through the floor. She was smart. Some civilians were foolish enough to panic and stick their heads up, taking a bullet for their trouble.

Gage couldn't move out of the way as fast as he would've liked. His ankle hampered him, refusing to work as it had before his injury, while he twisted aside and ducked behind the couch.

Bullets sprayed to his sides, over his head, and ricocheted off the floor near his feet. Either the attacker was a poor shot to begin with, or the kukri had, if nothing else, interfered with his marksmanship. Chunks of lead tore holes in walls, chairs, and tables or ricocheted off the floor, drawing sparks, dust, and steam where they struck. The noise was painful, almost deafening.

As Gage moved across the floor, seeking the minimal and probably insufficient cover provided by the big easy chair, there came a lull in the gunfire. His ears rang and throbbed, but he faintly made out a raspy curse in what might've been Russian.

Gage's eyes fixed on the assailant, and for a brief instant, he was able to form a clear visual and mental picture of the man and how he was armed and outfitted.

His initial impression of overwhelming size had been correct. The attacker had to have been around seven feet tall, perhaps even *over* seven feet, and he had significant bulk as well. It was impossible to determine exactly what his body looked like—if he were muscular, fat, or trim—due to the heavy greatcoat he wore.

Atlantica's weather, strangely for its northerly latitude, tended to be mild or warm nearly all year, so the man must've been sweltering in such an outfit. However, it provided him with extra protection and perhaps camouflage.

Additionally, the man had reddish-brown hair, greenish or hazel eyes, and a large nose. His skin was pale and his features European. His jaw and chin were covered by a short but scruffy beard, slightly redder than the hair on his head.

In his huge hands, the weapon he held appeared to be a Soviet PPS-43, a simple stamped-metal submachine gun developed midway into the Second World War and intended as a replacement for the better known, more expensive, and faster-firing PPSh-41. The 43's rate of fire was still more than fast enough to devastate a single opponent or a small group of people at close to moderate range.

It fired the 7.62 x 25 Tokarev cartridge, a relatively small round but a high-velocity and eminently deadly one. Gage had seen pistols and submachine guns chambered for it before. He'd briefly been in Manchuria toward the end of the war, where the Russians had used it to execute Japanese troops who refused to surrender.

Now, it was about to be used to execute him. The assassin had paused for less than a second after his sudden realization that a large knife had embedded itself in his shoulder. He shifted the gun, holding it one-handed. As massive as he was, it could almost be mistaken for a long-barreled handgun in his grip.

Gage was about to leap and roll toward the alcove near the small foyer where his revolver lay hidden under an old coat, heedless of the risk of damaging his still-tender ankle when something else happened.

A tall, dark, and slim figure appeared behind the attacker. In the growing shadows as the day became dimmer and more overcast, it took Gage an instant or two to recognize Dante Costa.

The American doctor flung himself at the huge man's flank and reached up to seize the protruding handle of the kukri. He yanked down on it, dragging the blade through flesh and sinew beneath the greatcoat's thick fabric.

The assailant grunted and squeezed his eyes shut, gritting his teeth behind his coppery beard. The pain was getting to him for the first time. He'd shifted his submachine gun to the other hand, but it nonetheless sagged in his arm as the shock of the knife wound went through his whole body.

Gage's brain went into overdrive. Everything was happening too fast for him to know what to do. His relative disability and the fact that he'd rather stupidly thrown away his only weapon hampered his instinct to charge forward and attack. Plus there was Janet to consider. She still crouched in the far corner, sobbing in terror.

The big Russian recovered from the jolt of agony almost immediately. He whirled, roaring and cursing incoherently, and somehow grabbed Dante despite his injury and holding onto his gun. Then he threw the doctor into the house. Dante tripped and tumbled across the floor, vanishing into the short hallway beyond where Janet hid that led to the bathroom and bedroom.

Then the hitman squeezed off a final barking volley of fire before it went dry. With the general confusion and his right arm injured, his aim wavered, and he mostly blew holes in the walls to either side of the hall, failing to hit Dante. One of the bullets struck only a foot or so above Janet's head.

The empty magazine fell to the floor, and in a flash, the giant somehow had another in his hand. Gage did a split-second calculation. With his ankle below full functionality as it was, there was no way he could make it to the alcove and retrieve his gun before the attacker could open fire again. Either he, Dante, or Janet would die. Perhaps all three.

His only option was to charge.

He howled a raw, high-pitched cry and flung himself at the

huge man, bounding with his good leg to make up for the smaller strides he had to take with the other. One hand clawed for the gun to knock it aside while his other reached for the kukri still stuck in the man's upper shoulder area, which now streamed blood down his coat. His whole upper right sleeve was stained a dark brownish-red.

At the moment Gage charged, the Russian had been facing the hallway, apparently expecting Dante to pose more of a threat while he reloaded. Yet Dante hadn't emerged. Although Gage crossed the floor faster than expected in his desperation, the hitman was faster.

The huge assailant snapped back around, and his thick, long leg lashed out. The treads of his boot took Gage in the chest with a powerful thumping blow that sent the much smaller man flying backward to sprawl on the floor.

Then the Russian turned again to the hallway. He advanced toward it two steps, trying to get a bead on the fallen doctor to finish him off. Dante Costa was nowhere in sight. At some point during the chaos, he'd scrambled off.

The giant man spat a string of words in his native tongue as he tore the kukri from his shoulder. It came loose in a spurt of blood, and he tossed it aside. It clattered against the floorboards and skidded into the foyer, far out of anyone's immediate reach. Then he switched his PPS-43 to his left hand again, holding it like an oversized pistol.

Gage rolled over and used his knees and hands to brace himself and rise to his feet. His ankle flared with pain, slowing him, but he was able to favor his leg enough to get up before the Russian could simply perforate him with bullets while he lay helpless on the floor.

The assassin had noticed and turned toward Gage. The submachine gun trembled in his grip as though eager to deal out death.

With his focus totally on the attacker, Gage didn't see where

Dante reappeared from. The doctor was simply back, armed with a baseball bat and swinging it in a downward diagonal arc toward the attacker's gun hand.

It connected with a loud *crunch*. The solid wood smashed the man's knuckles before moving on to the firearm itself and knocking the weapon from the giant's hand. He dropped it, and it clattered toward the middle of the floor.

Dante shouted, "Get her out of here, Gage!" He stepped forward as the attacker swiveled toward him while moving backward. "This is how we played baseball in my neighborhood, you oversized bastard. You know anything about fucking *baseball?*"

He feinted at the Russian's head, and the big man took the bait, raising his hands to protect himself. Instead, Dante swung the bat into his injured shoulder. The man cried out in anguish, and the blow had enough force behind it to drive him stumbling back toward the wall as well, despite his bulk.

The way to the front door was clear.

Half-jogging and half-limping, Gage ducked behind Dante as the American advanced on the Russian and the two of them disappeared into the hallway in a tangle of violence. He reached the far corner, found Janet's wrist, and heaved her up to her feet. "Come. We must get you out."

She stared at him and didn't protest as he led her along, moving as fast as he could through the small living room, around the corner into the foyer, and opening the front door. He practically shoved her out before slamming it shut behind her and had to hope she would have the good sense to stay outside and out of the fight.

A heartbeat after the front door *banged* shut, Dante exclaimed, "Oh, *shit!*" Then there was a tremendous *crash* of wood and plaster splintering.

Gage groaned and hobbled fast enough to call it a jog back into the living room. To his shock, there was a human-sized hole in the interior wall that separated the living area from the hallway.

Their unnamed enemy had stepped through it and was dragging the stunned and bloodied Dante through to finish him off. At his feet, the baseball bat lay in two pieces as though the massive Russian had broken it over his knee. His strength must've been incredible.

Gage scanned the floor. The fallen submachine gun was closer than his kukri was. He lowered himself into a painful crouch, seized it, and sprang back up to spin toward the assailant and squeeze the trigger.

Nothing happened. Dante must've jammed or damaged it when he knocked it out of the Russian's grasp. There was no time to diagnose the problem because the big man's muddy hazel eyes moved toward him.

Gage threw the gun as hard as possible, aiming for the assassin's head. The frame struck him behind the ear, halfway toward his crown, rattling his skull and opening a cut that bled a brighter red spot amid his auburn hair.

The Russian turned and dropped the half-conscious Dante to the floor. His beard bristled, and his eyes practically shone with a fury that had deepened, turning cold instead of hot.

Gage staggered forward a couple more steps, bent over, and felt the comforting solidity of his kukri's horn handle once more in his grasp. By the time he straightened and pivoted toward his foe, the bigger man was already in motion. They waded straight into one another.

This time, Gage was ready for the kick. The giant's foot struck thin air as the Gurkha stepped nimbly around it, ignoring the burning pain that arose in his ankle. The kukri became a bolt of lightning in his hand, striking to and fro, its edge nimble while its thick, heavy spine gave it added cutting and hacking power.

The Russian was fast and strong but not fast enough. The

blade opened deep cuts on his hands and arms. His heavy coat and modified body armor beneath it protected him from fatal wounds, but the attrition of a dozen slashes to his extremities was beginning to take its toll.

When Gage moved in for the kill, hoping to get a clear strike at the man's throat or inner thigh, a sudden backhand strike caught him in the head above the eye. The Russian's immense knuckles and the force behind the sheer mass of his hand drove Gage back, stunning him.

Then Dante was back on his feet. Cuts from wood splinters or sheer impact lined his face, and there were bruises on his hands and arms. He grasped the lower, thinner half of his baseball bat, which now ended in a sharp, jagged point. He snarled in wrath and drove it into the back of the giant's right thigh.

The impact and the damage to his muscles and tendons caused the Russian to drop to one knee, robbing him of the initiative to finish Gage off. His face contorted with pain and frustration.

Gage knew he might not get another chance. He sprang up and forward, kukri in hand, and swiped the blade upward. When standing, the man was so tall that his neck and head were almost out of reach since Gage was a short man. On one knee...

The broad knife's flashing strike split open the skin along the assailant's jaw and cheek. The cut trailed down to his neck but missed his jugular. The man let out a wounded roar so loud it seemed to have a force of its own. He clutched his ravaged face with bloody hands, sprang to his feet, and bulled his way through the massive hole in the wall he'd made.

Gage and Dante rose. Both struggled against their injuries as they moved toward one another.

"Here." Dante gasped. "Take my arm. We're going after that hulking bastard together." Fortunately, he'd offered his right arm, meaning that Gage could take it with his left and keep his good hand free to fight. The kukri remained in his trembling grasp, covered with blood and bits of fabric from the Russian's coat.

The two sweat- and blood-covered men leaned on one another, gasping for breath and maddened with battle rage, determination, and fear for Janet as they stumbled through the living area and around the corner to the tiny foyer. While Gage stood with his knife ready, Dante opened the front door.

Outside, it had begun to rain heavily. They hadn't noticed in the rush of the fight. The sky had turned dark and threatening, the color of ashes, and the air *hissed* and whispered as gray sheets of water fell upon the trees, rocks, and dirt, turning it to mud.

Neither their attacker nor the nurse was anywhere in sight.

Gage thought fast. "He has fled. He has given up. See if you can trail him—and find Janet. I'll go to the car and use the radio to call Ty and Daria."

"Yeah." Dante grunted. "Yeah, good idea. Be careful, bud." He let go of Gage's arm and turned away, making a broad circle around the corner of the cottage, seeking tracks in the softening earth to indicate where the Russian might be going.

He also cupped his hands around his mouth. "Janet! Where are you?" He repeated the call every few seconds.

Gage limped toward the vehicle, moving as rapidly as possible on his injured ankle. His long convalescence had kept him from intense physical activity, plus he was in his middle forties, so the battle had taken a lot out of him. The vicious warrior within him had never gone away. However, his body wasn't in optimal condition for this level of exertion. His breath came in hard gasps, and the many bumps and twists of the struggle plus his minor injuries all pained and weakened him.

He opened the driver's side door and sat heavily in the seat, allowing his legs to lift into the air to spare them any pressure against the ground. Then, with his left hand, he hauled the half-lamed one up and over into place. He was about to set the kukri in his lap to use both hands when someone grabbed the side of his pants near his left calf.

His right hand shot out, the blade whistling. He bit off a strangled cry as he stopped himself. The kukri hovered in midair, vibrating in the rain as his hand shook.

It was Janet. She'd been hiding under the car and was trying to get his attention as she crawled out. If Gage had been a fraction of a second slower in checking before he completed his swing, she would've lost her hand at the wrist, with the fingers probably remaining locked around his pant leg.

He exhaled and made himself relax. "Miss Feng. I wish you'd said something. Here, let me help you up." He set the knife down at his side—it was still within easy reach if the huge Russian were to appear again—and used both hands to pull the nurse out into the open. Her face, hair, and white clothing were all smeared with mud, although the rain began to wash it away at once.

The woman's lips moved as though she were trying to say something but was still too deeply shocked to speak properly. Gage didn't know much about her personal background. It was clear that she had no experience with violence. He felt only sympathy for her and wished that they could've spared her the whole thing.

Dante appeared around the cabin's other corner after circling the house. He stopped in his tracks when he saw Janet, then sprinted across the yard toward the car. "Janet!" he called. "Is she okay?"

Gage wondered if *any* of them were okay, given how much damage he and Dante had taken in their fight against the assassin. "Somewhat," he said. "I don't think she's seriously hurt."

The handsome young doctor reached the vehicle's side and at once took the nurse in his arms, reassuring her and checking her for wounds, despite being in worse shape than she was.

Gage left the two of them alone for the time being. He

doubted the Russian would return, but it was better not to assume they were safe. He switched on the radio within the vehicle—provided by Daria and Tyler once they decided that Janet's car would be the primary mode of transportation to and from the cottage—and dialed it to the Executioners' frequency.

Once the static cleared, he began, "Mayday. This is Gage Gurung. We've sustained an attack. All three of us are alive, but we've taken injuries. Nothing that will be fatal, I think. The assassin has fled. We don't know if there are others nearby. Over."

He waited for a little over a full minute and was about to repeat his message when there came a brief crackle from the other end.

"I'll be able to meet you in minutes." Ty grunted. "I want to know everything that happened. More than anything, I want to know who attacked you. And why. But mainly *who*. Over."

The cold determination in his voice would've been frightening if he'd been anything other than a friend.

Gage nodded. "We'll tell you everything. Is Daria all right? Over."

"She's busy. Stay where you are and stay vigilant. Pay attention to your surroundings and have your gun on you. Not nearby, but *on your body or in your hand*, period.

"With a doctor and a nurse there I'm sure I don't need to give you any medical advice. I'll be—wait. New development. Head to Daria's room in the city. You know the one I mean. You can drive, right? I'll meet you there. Out."

Dante had checked Janet for serious damage and seemed confident that she was mostly unharmed, aside from her obvious mental and emotional devastation. He squeezed her shoulder and leaned toward Gage.

"So, he kept saying 'more than anything.' Did I hear that right?"

Gage nodded. "Yes, he wants to know who attacked us."

"Who?" Dante scoffed, laughing crazily into the wetness and wind of the storm around them. "*More than anything*, I want to know *what* attacked us. I didn't know they grew humans that big."

CHAPTER THREE

Since Gage's left ankle was the one healing, he could still drive. He wasn't sure he would've trusted either Dante or Janet with the task. Dante had suffered a severe battering, might have a few broken bones, and had lost enough blood to feel somewhat light-headed. Janet was still recovering from the psychological trauma of what she'd seen and experienced.

Still, he wasn't looking forward to the task. At least the drive into the city wasn't too far.

As they passed out of the hills and into the village where Janet lived, she spoke for the first time since they'd pulled her out from under the car. "Where are we going?" Her voice sounded oddly distant, as though it came from much farther away than the back-seat. Gage wondered if she hoped they'd drop her off at home.

Dante reached back and patted her hand. "To a hotel. One that's run by our friends, right? We'll be safe there. I promise."

"Okay." Janet drifted back off.

Gage drove faster than usual, but he didn't rush or do anything stupid. Getting into an accident would be far worse than being two or three minutes late, and the last thing Janet needed was a destroyed car.

Past the village, they came to the outskirts of Atlantica City. A year ago it had consisted of little more than a few buildings beside a dock and some vacant lots carved out of a scrubby coastal plain. At present, it was well on its way to becoming a bustling modern metropolis, and sections of it had advanced to the point of being relatively indistinguishable from any other major world city.

The hotel Daria used was near the city's center, in the upscale business district. The place itself was, if not top of the line, at least considered fancy and luxurious enough to be tolerable by any "respectable" guest. At first glance, it appeared to be around six or seven stories tall. It was a large building, but the various skyscrapers that had gone up around the city already and others still being constructed dwarfed it.

As Gage pulled the car around to the far side of the building, where there was an open air parking area as well as a covered, two-story garage, he saw a distinctive armored military truck resting toward the rear of the open lot. There was an empty spot not far from it, so he pulled the car in there and was unsurprised when a familiar figure opened the driver's side door of the big truck and hopped down to the pavement.

Ty Katakura didn't waste time with pleasantries or formalities. He strode directly across the concrete toward them, closing most of the distance before Gage could shift the car into park and get the door open.

"All right," Ty barked, "can all of you walk? I can help anyone who can't, and I can get someone to help the rest of you if need be. Daria isn't here, but we have the run of the place with her permission. She'll be along later if she can manage it."

Gage lifted his legs out as Ty examined him, Dante, and Janet. "My ankle took several bad twists during our fight. I believe I can walk. Janet is having trouble. With her mind—she isn't badly hurt. Dante? How are you?"

The doctor had hastily bandaged himself during the drive

there with stuff from the car's first aid kit. "I'm fine. A bottle of red wine wouldn't be a bad idea. It helps replenish blood cells. I lost quite a bit, I think."

Nodding, Ty first helped Gage up and made sure he could stand. Then as Dante clambered out his side, Ty reached into the back seat and gradually pulled Janet into the open air. She wasn't precisely catatonic, but she'd gone into a withdrawn state of extreme passivity.

Nonetheless, when urged forward, she could walk okay while staring blankly ahead. Dante took her arm and led her behind the other two. Out in front, Ty supported Gage with his arm as the Gurkha limped toward the front entrance, which led to the hotel's lobby.

As they moved, Gage took note of his new companion's appearance. It looked as though Ty had finally cut his hair short again. Despite his military background, he tended to neglect it until it hung over his eyes in a shaggy black mop. Otherwise, he was the same lean and rough-edged young man as ever.

Entirely of Japanese descent, he'd come to Atlantica for the same reason so many other people had—out of desperation. To escape trouble, debts, limitations, and bad memories best forgotten. The United States, his country of birth, hadn't treated his family well despite his and his father's service in America's wars.

On Atlantica, though, he'd become somewhat of a living legend in only a short time. His exploits as the first Executioner had made him one of the most respected—and feared—people on the entire island.

Today, like most days, he wore the armored uniform of his office over a simple outfit of combat-ready trousers and jacket, along with rugged but high-quality boots and gloves. His AR-10 rifle didn't hang over his shoulder. He'd probably left it locked up in the trunk. At his right and left sides, he wore a holstered 1911 pistol and a sheathed wakizashi, part of a set of functional and authentic samurai swords provided by the Executives. He'd strapped the tanto dagger that came with the set to his right calf.

When they entered the lobby, the concierge saw Ty and recognized him, perking up at once. "Sir. How can we help?"

Ty waved. "We're going up to Daria's usual room. We'll sort out the paperwork later. Keep an eye on our vehicles and don't let anyone in who isn't one of us, Daria, or anyone approved by us."

"Of course." The man allowed them to pass the desk toward the elevators.

Moments later, Ty opened the room, which was moderate-sized, comfortable, and well-furnished, with two beds. They laid Janet on the far one beside the window, reassuring her that everything would be all right. Then Gage and Dante sat on the bed nearer the center of the main floor. Ty pulled out a chair but didn't bother to sit yet.

There were two ice packs already languishing in the in-room freezer. Tyler took them out and tossed one each to Gage and Dante. The latter almost certainly could've used more like four or five of them to himself, but to his credit, he didn't complain. He only held the pack on one wound for a few minutes, then shifted it to others as needed.

Ty was bursting with obvious impatience. He gave the two men only a minute or two to settle in and ice their wounds while he paced back and forth, his hands clasped behind his back and his jaw set in a tight grimace.

Then he began.

"All right, tell me what happened. Everything, starting at the beginning, and I especially want details on who these people are and what the hell they were doing. Anything that could help us find them, not to mention find out why they wanted you dead."

Gage drew a deep breath and recalled how he'd heard the assassin approach outside while he was relaxing with his tea after Dante had left. He described the experience as well as he could, pausing at the part where the gigantic man burst through the door.

Dante interjected, "Yeah, this guy was enormous. I'd guess seven feet tall, maybe more like, say, seven-foot-two or something, and had to weigh three hundred pounds at a minimum. Age, uh, it was hard to tell, somewhere between thirty and forty-five, I think. Gage, did you recognize what the hell language he was speaking? White guy, red hair and beard, so something European, I think."

Gage squinted. "I believe it was Russian or a related language such as Ukrainian or Bulgarian."

Ty missed a step in his pacing and squeezed his hands together behind his waist as though he were itching to draw a weapon. He didn't look at either man. "Any official insignias on him?"

"No," Gage said. "He wore a large and heavy coat, such as the Russians often do, but there was nothing like that." They all realized at once what the Executioner was getting at, what was on his mind.

Ty nodded. "Of course not. Nothing to identify him as a Soviet agent. Of course, it's *possible* that he's some Russian who defected and now works for...for God knows who. The same smugglers I've been fighting for months, maybe.

"If he *did* have a Soviet insignia, that would be suspicious because it would probably mean that someone was trying to frame the USSR for their actions. Usually, the Russkies aren't stupid enough to put a goddamn KGB logo right on the chest of someone who's carrying out a covert job for them in another country."

Gage recalled that Ty had once said he didn't consider himself much of a detective. Yet he seemed to be picking it up rather nicely. His mind found it easier to see the layers of deception at work in these sorts of things. Still, Daria was the better of the two at subterfuge and diplomacy, so Ty likely hoped she would show up soon so he could ask her input.

Dante snorted. "You never can tell what's going through the mind of a fucking Communist, but why would the Soviets want Gage dead? Or, uh, me, for that matter. Or maybe Janet?"

Ty looked at them. "You mean you couldn't tell who he was targeting? Did it seem like he was prioritizing one of you or the other? If he had a mission to kill one specific person, he probably would've tried to do that first and only fight the rest of you as needed before getting out."

Gage shook his head. "No, he simply attacked whoever was closest to him. He tried to shoot me at first. Then he tried to beat Dante to death. We both fought against him, so he fought back. He didn't attack Janet, but that might be because I hid her in the corner right before he came in. So he might not have seen her at all."

Ty rubbed his chin. "I see." His dark eyes narrowed as he examined first the short archaeologist, then the tall doctor. "Is there anything you're not telling me? Anything I should know about why someone would be after either of you—or both of you?"

It took Gage a moment to realize that Ty was suspicious of them. He didn't believe their story, or at least it had occurred to him that something was wrong, or that they must know more than they did about the attacker's motives.

"Whaaaat?" Dante protested. "No, sir. I had no idea who this guy was, and I don't think Gage did either. Maybe the same assholes I was with when you found me hired him to take me out and Gage was in the wrong place at the wrong time.

"Or maybe it's that Miracle Workers' Union or whatever it is that Daria mentioned, who were trying to rub Gage out, and I was the one who got in the way. The damn guy didn't say anything in English, and he ran away after Gage split his face open so it's not like we had much of a chance to ask him anything."

Ty rolled his tongue around his teeth as he considered the man's words.

Dante added, "Oh, and we haven't been dealing dope out of the cabin or anything like *that* either, if that's what you're thinking. It's been practically a vacation for both of us, to be honest. Not so much for poor Janet."

He looked at the young woman and took her hand. She seemed calmer but still was in no hurry to interact with the rest of the world yet.

The Executioner studied Dante's face, then turned to Gage. "What do you have to say, Gurung?"

The Gurkha shrugged. "I have no more to say. I quite honestly know nothing. It was all very strange. We are people with enemies, yes, but there was no way to find out who this man was working for."

Ty paused, then shook his head. "Yeah, okay. You guys don't know a damn thing. This is good insofar as it means you probably didn't bring this on yourselves by doing anything stupid. The bad part is, we have no idea why it happened. At least a gigantic redheaded Russian with a scar down his face is going to have more trouble hiding than someone a little more normal-looking."

"Okay," Dante grumbled, wringing his scab-covered hands, "so what do we do next? Hide out here until the problem goes away by itself? Hire a bunch of mercs to sweep the island for Russkies? Let you go beat people up until they talk?"

Ty, who appeared to be in no mood to joke around, didn't bother to answer the latter portion of the question directly. "I'm going to call Eleanor Cervantes, my contact with the Executives. She can usually get us what we need, whether supplies or information. Or extra help.

"What I'm going to ask her for is some security personnel

who can watch over you three here at the hotel. Then I'm going to start looking into who's behind this attack. Maybe Daria too, depending on how much else she has going on. Any objections to that?"

"No, sir," Dante piped up at once. "I'm pretty sure we could both use a nap, after all that. Maybe a nice big meal or three, as well."

Gage smiled. "No, thank you. That will do. As Dr. Costa says, we should rest."

Janet said nothing. She was examining one of the potted plants on a nearby end table. Although she did incline her head a bit toward Ty when he spoke, his forceful and authoritative voice tended to capture people's attention.

Ty nodded. "All right. I'm leaving to make the arrangements." He glared briefly at Dante. "For now, I'm glad that none of you are injured any worse and that you'll all recover shortly. Like we agreed."

He turned and marched toward the door, adding over his shoulder, "I'll be in touch. Call me if anything happens."

Then he flung open the door, stepped out into the hallway, and was gone.

The instant the latch clicked, Dante scrambled over to Gage and put his hands around the man's injured ankle, feeling it to ascertain its condition.

"Ah," Gage stammered in surprise, "I believe I am mostly all right? Thank you. I put too much pressure on it, and it took several twists. I don't think it broke a second time if that's what worries you."

The physician's lean face went through a short series of contortions as he continued his examination, at first seeming frightened that they'd lost all their progress over the last weeks, then looking hopeful before finally settling into a kind of grim resignation.

"Well, it's worse than it was a few hours ago, that's for sure. I think Lady Luck was mostly on your side, bud. I'm leaning toward prescribing an extra week of recovery time to be safe. You didn't crack the bone in half or anything. If I can get us to a proper X-ray, we can be certain. As long as we keep it tightly bound and avoid anything as exciting as what happened earlier today, we'll be good."

Gage nodded. He couldn't help noticing the way Dante said *we*. "Are you afraid of what Tyler would do if I broke it again?"

"Yes, of course. Or Daria. Or both of them. She threatened to shoot me if I made your leg worse instead of better. That's possibly the better option though—compared to Ty gutting me with his sword."

Gage frowned. "I don't think they would do that. You're trying your best, and I will vouch for you if it comes to that."

His friend cast him a half-embarrassed look of gratitude. "I appreciate that. I truly do. There is one other little problem." He took his hands away from Gage's beleaguered ankle and sat back on the bed, rubbing his eyes with his knuckles.

"What?" Gage asked. He was curious. His immediate suspicion was that Dante referred to what they'd discussed earlier at the cottage—his uncertain fate once Gage had fully mended.

He was wrong.

Dante cleared his throat and cast his eyes downwards. "I, ah... I might know something, after all. About what happened earlier, and why. Fuck. I should've said it. I didn't know how that guy would react to it. The great and terrible Executioner Katakura has a bit of a reputation for, you know, shooting first, stabbing second, and never getting around to asking questions until the blood gets cold."

That much was true, Gage had to admit. "Yes, well. I've killed men over the years when it was necessary. Yet you trust me. Tell me, and perhaps we can come up with a way to, um, to make use of this information without angering Mr. Katakura."

Dante picked up the ice pack, now barely cold, and put it

against a nasty bruise on his side above the hip where the Russian had dragged him over the edge of the shattered wall. "Yeah, that's the idea. Okay, so the gunrunners I was embedded with before Ty plucked me out of that whole lifestyle? Those guys had connections overseas. I mean, they have to. Gunrunners always do, right? Well, they did a lot of business with the Soviet Union, or occasionally its satellite countries."

Gage nearly winced. That was exactly the sort of thing Ty wanted to know about. He wouldn't be happy to discover that Dante had withheld it.

"The Commies," Dante went on, "provided tons and tons of armaments, a whole bouquet of them, to these guys I was with. Of course, there are two sides to every deal, you know? So what *they* got out of it was the privilege of getting some of their agents snuck in here on Atlantica. The Western countries mostly have been trying to squeeze those bastards out, naturally. But *everyone* wants in on Atlantica these days. Everybody eventually comes looking for their piece of the pie."

Janet turned her head to look at the two of them, but her stare was still vacant. Gage began to wonder how long it would take her to recover. He turned his eyes back toward the doctor.

"It makes sense," the former Gurkha agreed. "I do not understand. Why would you be so worried to tell all this to Tyler? He wanted to know about such things. I should think he would be happy to hear it so he can investigate more effectively."

Dante sighed and looked at the ceiling. "When Katakura pulled me out, we did this whole debriefing session where he grilled me up and down about the arms dealers and the extent of my activities and what I knew about their operation, et cetera. Well, I never mentioned the Russkies." He scowled at the plaster.

"Why not?" It was making more sense to Gage now. The gist of it was that Dante feared Ty would punish him for not divulging everything sooner. He sensed there was still more to it.

Folding his hands behind his head, Dante expounded,

"Because for one thing, I didn't want to incur the Soviets' wrath. Those pricks send their guys all over the planet to hunt down people who piss them off. Remember when Stalin had that guy track down Trotsky in Mexico and stab him in the head with an *icepick?* Jesus Christ."

Gage did vaguely recall hearing about that, though at the time he'd been more focused on his farm back in the mother country and hadn't paid a great deal of attention to global political affairs. The Second World War had given him plenty to think about, and at the time, he craved simplicity.

"I see. That's an understandable reason. Especially, well, after today. What else?" He shifted his ice pack to his ankle. He'd been holding it variously against his face where the Russian had back-handed him or his chest where the man had kicked him.

Dante sat up straighter. He was beginning to recover a little of his customary swagger. "Second, Ty only asked me about what *I* was doing for the gang. I never interacted with the Soviets or treated any of their guys, nothing like that. I heard about it, is all. I guess I figured that if Ty didn't specifically ask, there was no reason for me to mention it."

Gage couldn't help wondering if they might've averted the horror of what had happened earlier if Dante hadn't been so tight-lipped. "There is a reason for you to mention it now. Please, when Tyler returns, I think you should tell him. I will be by your side. I promise.

"He will not kill you simply for making a small error in judgment. Still, with both of our lives threatened like this, we must tell the Executioners. Otherwise, they will waste their time while those responsible for this attack run free. What if they encountered Janet by herself?"

Dante paled at the mention of such a prospect. He looked down at the nurse with eyes that suddenly brimmed with emotion. Then he turned back to his friend.

"Okay. You're right. I'm not exactly looking forward to this, though." He found his comb, which had somehow remained in his pocket despite the altercations, and ran it through his hair. If he was going to face down the first Executioner's fury, he might as well look good for the occasion.

They sat in silence for about three minutes. Then footsteps approached their room, and Ty opened the door, striding in. "The security team is on their way, ETA twenty to thirty minutes," he reported. "Four guys for now. Later, if we get a better idea of what we're dealing with and there isn't as much danger, we might scale it down to two.

"All of them have been vetted by Mac. Senior Officer MacLeod. I can't remember if I ever introduced either of you two to him. He's trustworthy, and he knows what he's doing. So you'll be in good hands."

Gage nodded. "Excellent. Thank you, good sir. What about Executioner Barruk?"

Ty crossed the room and planted himself back in the same chair he'd used earlier. "She's investigating a series of murders. Pretty serious stuff, so I can't pull her off that for the sake of personal favoritism. It's going to be up to me to go after your big Russian friend."

"Well, from what I've heard, you're usually able to take care of these things by yourself."

Ty smiled grimly. "Usually, yeah. If you guys are okay and don't have anything else you need, I'm going to get on it as soon as the muscle arrives."

Dante had been silent since Ty had returned. Gage prodded him with his elbow. Ty noticed at once and fixed his eyes on both of them.

It was clear that there was no use in delaying any longer. Dante scooched off the bed and stood to his full height. He might've looked average, even puny, next to the titanic assassin, but for the moment, he was the tallest man in the room.

"There is something else," he stated. "Executioner, I apologize for not mentioning this earlier."

Ty leveled his gaze at him and went still. "Oh. Speak."

Dante drew a deep breath and repeated everything he'd told Dr. Gurung, including his reasons for holding back until now. Gage watched them both and nodded here and there to corroborate Dante's story.

Tyler listened without interrupting, holding himself like a statue and remaining in a state of calm, focused, and deeply unnerving silence. When Dante reached the end of his spiel and stopped talking, Ty gave a slow, deliberate, single nod. Then his arm shot out, and his fist clocked the doctor across the jaw.

Dante staggered back a step as his head turned from the force of the blow, but he didn't fall over, sit, or try to get away. He gritted his teeth, breathed in and out, and turned back to the other man without trying to return the favor—although his hands had nevertheless balled into fists.

"All three of you almost died today because of your reluctance to tell the truth. That *bothers* me, Dr. Costa," Ty declared in a disturbingly soft voice.

Dante grunted. "Yeah, I know. I was there."

Gage raised a finger. "Now, now, Executioner Katakura. Please consider. How could Dante have prevented this by mentioning that the gang did business with the Soviets? He didn't know any of the details. All of it was secondhand information. He couldn't have pointed you toward any individual suspects. The only people he could've identified were other members of the arms-running gang. You executed all of them if I recall."

Ty's face snapped toward the Gurkha, and his black eyes were blazing with sudden fury. For a moment, Gage thought the man was going to strike him, too.

He snarled, "You seem to think you know a hell of a lot for someone who only became an Executioner for the health benefits."

Gage felt a twinge of anger in his gut, but he knew what was going on. In his frustration and desire to protect his friends, Ty was taking out his anger on the very people he was trying to help—he wanted Gage to get angry at him so his feelings could be "justified" by the reaction. Hotheaded younger men often did such things.

Gage chose not to take the bait. Instead, he stared back at Katakura with a steady and neutral expression, leaving it on him to react next.

Ty's eyes drifted downward, and he exhaled. The bristling posture he'd adopted softened. "Sorry," he muttered. "I have a lot going on right now, and I'm not as even-tempered about this as I should be. Before I heard from you about what happened earlier, I was in the middle of looking for some kids. I haven't found them yet."

Dante squinted. "What, newborns? Who the hell brings children to a lawless place like Atlantica?"

"That is exactly what I was wondering myself," Ty snapped. "No, they're older, but still kids. A pair of twins. I don't know what their parents were thinking. Being angry at them... isn't helping me find their children.

"*Now,* you two tell me about all this happening. Bad enough you're in danger, but I might have to deal with the goddamn Soviet Union on top of everything else. Things on this island could get even worse if we get drawn into the Cold War."

Gage and Dante exchanged a glance. They hadn't known each other all that long, and they came from extremely different backgrounds. Yet there was a curious degree of understanding between them, a sense that they were on enough of a similar frequency that it wasn't always necessary to speak to agree.

Gage said, "Dr. Costa has cleared me to begin my duties very soon, perhaps in a week, but I can walk now as long as I'm careful. Dante will be out of work once I fully recover. So, perhaps we can help with this."

Ty blinked. "Oh? How?"

Dante snapped his fingers and put on one of his more charming and confident smirks. "You keep looking for those poor kids. Since we were the ones that the big-bastard Russkie was trying to kill, we'll get a handle on him and his bosses."

Tyler looked them both over. It was impossible to guess what he thought precisely. Gage's best estimate was that he took their battered physical condition under advisement and evaluated whether they were fit to do a damn thing.

"The Soviets already have a handle on you, from the sound of it," he quipped. "They got about halfway to finishing the job. If that guy had focused on one of you at a time, I'd probably have less company right now. You're lucky he divided his time and only half-killed the both of you."

Dante scowled and was about to make an intemperate remark, so Gage spoke first.

"Yes, but we're now aware of this threat. We'll be ready. With your security friends watching our backs—and Janet—it will be easier."

Dante cooled off and, with a sympathetic look, added, "Neither of us wants children to suffer. If you split your attention between jobs, that might happen. So, it would make sense for us to take part of the load. Either take us up on the offer to deal with the Russians ourselves, or we can pick up with looking for the kids while you deal with the new problem. What'll it be?"

Ty grimaced, and his eyes went distant. "I already promised those dumbass parents that I would find their kids. So, I'll have Eleanor touch base with you two so you can start sorting it all out on your end. She'll get you weapons, supplies, all that kind of stuff, and she might be able to track down information that will point you in the right direction. I'm going to warn you, so listen closely."

Neither of them spoke as the Executioner lowered his voice.

"You need to be careful. You need to assume that any wrong

step you take could be your last, and prepare accordingly. I want you to keep in touch with Daria or me, through Eleanor if need be. If you stumble across anything major, you reach out to us for backup."

Once again, the archaeologist and the physician locked eyes for a second before looking back at Ty.

"Agreed," Gage said.

CHAPTER FOUR

Janet Feng awoke. She instantly tensed, not because anything was immediately wrong, but because she had a pleasant, relaxing dream—and by contrast, there was no way to tell anymore what the real world might have in store.

She used to believe that the world wasn't quite such a bad place. Until...

She rubbed her eyes in the darkness of her room, wherever she was. The terrible day, the attack on the little cottage by the monstrous man with the gun... She didn't know how long ago it had been or how much time had passed since the last thing she could remember. It might've been ten in the evening of the same day, or it might've been a week later. Her sense of time had grown vague and indistinct.

The bed beneath her was soft and comfortable, and a single sheet plus a blanket of moderate thickness covered her. She was warm but not excessively so. She looked around, trying to ascertain where she was.

It appeared to be a hotel room. A hazy memory came to her of Dr. Costa mentioning a hotel, a place where they would be safe.

She was uncertain when that had been or if this was the same establishment he had in mind.

Neither Dante Costa nor Gage Gurung was anywhere in sight. Neither was the man who'd tried to kill them.

She tried to relax. She couldn't dispel the dread and unease that had engulfed her the instant she'd awoken and now clung to her mind the way the humidity did after a rainy summer day. Although she still felt somewhat tired, as though her mind was too dogged and oppressed by worry to have recharged itself during whatever amount of slumber she'd had, the thought of going back to sleep seemed ridiculous. Perhaps impossible.

Instead, Janet kicked off the covers and swung her legs aside, sitting up in bed and allowing her eyes to further adjust to the interior gloom.

She stretched and yawned. She was still wearing her white nurse's uniform, strangely enough, but not her jacket or shoes. Whether she'd taken them off herself, or Dr. Costa or someone else had done so for her, she had no idea.

The room was adjacent to a small bathroom. Another door in the center of the wall seemed to lead to another room, perhaps part of a suite of two. On the other side of it, someone was talking.

Janet tensed again. She didn't recognize the man's voice. Whoever he was, he at least sounded like an American or a Canadian, so he couldn't have been the hulking Russian who'd broken into the house with a machine gun. The person on the other side of the door had a rather harsh and brusque way of speaking, though. Based on the tone, she automatically thought of a military officer or policeman issuing orders, but his diction was more casual.

She got to her feet and slowly moved toward the door. The words spoken were indistinct at first, but they took shape as she got closer.

"...can thank the Executives for this. All I did was cart it over to you. Ought to be enough to get you through what lies ahead, though."

Then the voice of Dr. Gurung responded, and for an instant, Janet relaxed.

"Ahh, yes, most excellent. I do believe I went to war in Asia with less firepower than this." He chortled, and there came a couple of *clanking* and rustling sounds.

Next came the voice of Dr. Costa. "Medical supplies, good. We're both pretty beat up still, so I'll probably have to re-patch the stuff I patched earlier as a consequence of *any* serious action. That's always fun. Not to mention if one of us gets a busted chair leg through the gallbladder or something ridiculous like that."

Janet frowned. It struck her as odd that Dr. Costa could talk about something so awful in such a flippant tone, as though the notion of being impaled were no more than a joke to him. Her fingers went involuntarily to the scar along her jawline.

"Well," the third man shot back, "hit 'em with this first, and they won't get a chance to use their precious chair leg, will they?"

Again, a metallic rustling sound.

"Oh, hey," Dante piped up. "Is that an Ithaca 37? I always wanted one of those. An old guy in my neighborhood back home chased more than a few wise guys out of his flower shop with one. Heh, heh. Wait. Did you *confiscate* this? From my former employers, I mean."

"Yes, I did." Something in the grim tone of the unidentified man's voice made Janet's blood run cold. She knew for a fact, without having to hear anything else, that he was a killer.

"I'm sure you'll make better use of it than they would. As for the 1911, do you know how to use one of those things? Good gun, but unless you know how to operate the slide and all the safety features you might be better off with a revolver. I have a couple of good .357 Magnums if you'd prefer."

"No, no, I handled a .45 before. Wasn't as nice as this one. More like yours there. A beater," Dante said.

The third man let out a dry chuckle. "Plenty of ammo, too. Here. Don't carry so much that you can't run if you need to. Practice reloading fast. Anyway, I need to get going. Eleanor says she might have a lead on those kids. You two will be mostly on your own for a little while. Talk to Eleanor if you need to. Even if Daria and I are busy, she'll find a way to help you."

The three men exchanged goodbyes, and a pair of footsteps walked away, fading out after a door opened and shut.

Janet realized she'd been holding her breath. She let it out. Then her hand found the doorknob and slowly, making as little noise as possible, she turned it and eased the door open a crack.

In the room beyond, Dante and Gage sat in chairs that they'd set up on either side of the foot of a bed. Scattered atop the sheets was a profusion of weaponry, along with pieces of gear and rigging for transporting it all, plus boxes of ammunition and various other equipment.

Dr. Gurung had been sliding a forward-curved, broad-bladed knife, like the one he'd pulled out when the giant assassin had first appeared, into a leather sheath. Then Dante leaned toward him. "Here. Put your foot out."

"Of course." Gage extended his bad leg. The physician wrapped a brace around it, checking the exact position and wrapping it tight enough to keep his ankle from moving around too much but not tight enough to cut off circulation. With that done, Gage sheathed a second kukri before turning his attention to a strange-looking rifle and an old top-break revolver.

Dr. Costa, too, was deep into the process of arming himself to the teeth. Janet knew very little about guns. She could recognize and distinguish the basic types but generally couldn't identify a particular make or model. The nurse had a rudimentary understanding of how they worked and the differences between calibers and so forth. Her father had an old Mauser C96 Broomhandle left over from the Japanese invasion and the

Chinese Civil War, and it was the only firearm she had any real familiarity with.

Still, it looked like Dante was equipping himself with a shotgun of some sort, one of the ones that had only a single barrel, and if she wasn't mistaken, had to be pumped between shots. There was also a big silver pistol, one that Americans liked, and a mass of different shells and cartridges lying around the bed in distinct piles.

It was therefore strange to see Dr. Costa also packing a first aid kit with medical paraphernalia, all the basics he would need to quickly but effectively treat any number of wounds, plus a few more advanced or esoteric implements. Oddly, she didn't see him packing any painkillers aside from pills. From what she recalled of their work together, he disliked morphine and wouldn't allow its use in his practice.

Weapons and medicine—instruments of death and healing side by side. It was surreal to her, borderline comical yet also chilling. She wondered if Dante specifically expected to be wounded or to have to injure others.

What were they doing? She ruminated on the question. It made sense that they would arm themselves for defensive purposes in case the gigantic killer from the cottage came back for them.

Everything about the two men's demeanor and the amount of gear they were handling suggested they were about to go on the *offensive* instead.

Her heart skipped a beat. Did they intend to pursue some kind of vengeful rampage? Men had a way of getting themselves killed when they succumbed to that mindset. Sometimes, they got others killed too while they were at it.

Then her reflections were interrupted when the lamp between the pair flickered.

Dante was looking down at a forceps and roll of gauze. He muttered, "Thanks, Thomas Edison. Prick."

Gage chuckled, but there was a sardonic edge to it that differed noticeably from his usual good-natured humor. "Did you know that Edison used to stage animal electrocutions as a way of trying to discredit Tesla's Alternating Current systems? I read about that in university during my third year of engineering."

As the small man spoke, he loaded cartridges into a small cylindrical speed loader, the faster to reload his revolver should he need to do so in the heat of combat.

Dante snorted, but his mouth smiled. "I didn't know that, but I believe it. Edison was an asshole."

"Absolutely." Gage laughed. "At least the light bulb hasn't flickered again."

Shrugging, Dante pointed out, "I think we can attribute that to the manufacturer, instead of the guy who originally invented the concept decades ago."

The other man paused a moment in contemplation. "This is fair; this is fair."

Janet marveled at the contrast between the two. They were, at first glance, incredibly mismatched. There was no reason to assume they belonged in the same building, let alone sitting side by side and joking around like old friends who'd grown up together.

Dante Costa was a relatively young man, especially for a medical doctor. Janet had politely refrained from asking his age, but he couldn't have been older than thirty and perhaps a couple of years younger than that.

He was tall and svelte and had the air of a man who knew that his good looks were worth preserving and showing off, so he took care of himself and his appearance. He was quite handsome with a well-shaped if severe hatchet face. The overall impression he gave off was very much in line with his Italian heritage, though his eyes were a light greenish shade that contrasted strikingly with his black hair.

Gage Gurung was about as different as could be conceived.

He was short and stocky, not fat, but growing noticeably rotund about the midsection, with thick limbs. He was at least fifteen years Dante's senior, and what remained of his hair had mostly turned gray.

Despite the glasses over his brown eyes and his mild demeanor, the faded scars on his face, neck, and hands suggested his background as a fighter in wars. Being from the highlands of Nepal, where the influence of Tibet overlapped with that of India, his appearance seemed almost a blend of different Asian features. He might be able to pass for a resident of several different lands.

Both were capable of great violence. They seemed familiar and comfortable with the substantial and deadly arsenal lying before them, neither more nor less so than they were with silly jokes about intellectual matters from their days as students.

Then, at nearly the same instant, both men grasped that someone was watching them. They turned their heads toward the door separating the suite in almost perfect unison.

"Miss Feng," Gage greeted her, smiling warmly and nodding. "It is good to see you up again. We are fine, mostly. You are safe here. I hope you rested well."

She blinked, about to return the greeting with something appropriately polite, but Dr. Costa had pushed back in his chair the second he saw her, stood, and was coming over with a concerned look. Janet's cheeks flushed hot with embarrassment at having eavesdropped and suddenly becoming the object of their attention. Still, she made no move to escape.

Dante planted himself before her and took her hand. "Janet. How do you feel? We were worried about you. You barely spoke or did anything for so long. You were in shock, of course. But it passes. Can you talk?"

She opened her mouth and searched for her voice. "Yes, I can. How long was I asleep? I can't remember much since we...since we left the cabin. It's all indistinct in my mind."

The doctor nodded, took her by the shoulder, and guided her back through the doorway into her room, leaving Gage behind with his guns and a new armored uniform. On the shoulders of the chest piece was a distinctive symbol of a skull and sword.

Once they had relative privacy, Dante explained, "You were borderline catatonic for several hours. We decided it would be better for you to have a separate room, so we relocated to a suite where we could be close to help if anything happened, but you'd still have your space.

"We put you to bed around nine or ten at night. I checked on you twice, but I don't think you stirred much all night. Or all morning. It's currently a little past noon."

She frowned. She'd been out for longer than she would've guessed. There was some reassurance, though. She hadn't damaged her memory so badly that she'd lost track of any significant amount of *waking* time. If entire days had elapsed without her recalling it, something would've been seriously wrong.

"I see, yes," she began. After a glance toward the suite door, she implored, "What is going on? Please tell me. Why do you have so many weapons, and who was that man who brought them?"

Then she bit her tongue. Without intending to, she'd admitted to listening in on their conversation with the man in question.

Dante didn't seem fazed, though. "That was Tyler Katakura. You've heard of him, I'm sure. He's supervising our protection for the time being."

Janet's eyes widened a little. "Oh. That makes sense. I know that Dr. Gurung mentioned becoming an Executioner, but I never thought much of it. It's difficult to imagine him doing the same sorts of things as..."

Then, unwanted, an image flashed in her mind. Gage Gurung, screaming and bloody, wielding his kukri at the Russian assailant twice his size.

"Yeah, well." Dante interrupted her brief flashback. "Gage is a tough guy, more than you might think. He was a Gurkha and fought in the war. That's a good thing, considering what's going on right now.

"I'm sorry, but some nasty people are coming after us. Me and Gage, I mean. We don't think they want to hurt you. They probably have no idea who you are. Still, the two of us are going to conduct a little investigation into how to make it all stop."

Janet arched an eyebrow. "'Investigating' requires that many guns?"

Dante laughed. There was a definite sarcastic bent to his mirth, but it didn't seem directed at her.

"Of course," he confirmed. "On Atlantica, handy tools like those are sometimes necessary for things like investigations, negotiations, trips to the store, and so forth. It's a side effect of not having actual laws."

She stared at him blankly, not sure whether to join in the joke or chastise him for making a joke about it to begin with.

He noticed, and his mood shifted at once, becoming somber again. "Janet," he remarked, voice softening. "I'm sorry about this, really I am. I should never have allowed you to get wrapped up in my mess. None of what's happened is your fault, and I would never want you to pay the price for it. When Tyler Katakura 'hired' me—and you—to help him take care of Gage, no one ever expected it would bring this sort of trouble to your doorstep."

Janet was mildly surprised by his sincerity. It appeared that his flippant comments were simply a façade to protect his self-image, whereas now, she saw the real Dante. "Don't apologize I should've known that taking a strange job like this would come with risks and complications." She sighed. "I didn't imagine the complications would include a machine-gun-toting ogre coming to kill us."

Dante nodded in a grim, regretful way and gave her shoulder a light squeeze.

"What are your plans? What will you do next?"

The tall physician looked off to the side. He wasn't examining anything in particular but simply gazing into the distance while his mind sought a good way of answering the question.

"You remember that some gunrunners press-ganged me into acting as a medic for them, right? Well, Ty killed most of them and drove the rest into hiding. Good for disrupting the illegal arms trade on Atlantica. Not so good for finding out more about their deals with the Soviets.

"I happen to know a little something. At least one of them, a guy working with the Russians, escaped and has gone to ground. Probably hopes that if he keeps his head down, Ty's sword will miss it. I think I know someone who might know where that individual is hiding. If we can find him, we might have a good chance of flushing out the bastards and wrecking whatever their scheme is."

Janet turned it over in her brain. It was good to know that Dante *had* a plan and that he and Gage were taking steps to resolve the situation. But...

"What am I supposed to do?" She looked up at him, caught his gaze, and knew that she was pouting. She almost couldn't help it, though, and it often got a reaction from men. "Sit here and wait for things to happen to me?"

She got the tone and expression exactly right—the perfect blend of concern, self-pity, defiance, and sympathy.

Dante reacted at once with a warm, reassuring smile. "It's too dangerous for you to get involved, Janet. If nothing else, because they might use you to get to me. It's not your fight. They might come after people I know for the sake of drawing me out."

Janet's blood ran cold. She hadn't quite thought of it that way. At worst, she'd wondered if simply being around Dante meant that more assassins would show up and she might get caught in the crossfire.

The physician nodded at the other doorway leading out to the hall. "There's a security team here to watch over you while we're gone. Good, tough men. Ty trusts them, so I do too. You'll be well protected. Hopefully, this will only be for a few days. Then it will be over, and you can walk away from all of this with some extra hazard pay, right? Then forget you ever took the job."

She took Dante's hand in hers and protested, "What if I don't want to forget every part of the job? It…it hasn't all been bad."

Dante started as though the abrupt display of affection stunned him. He blinked and his mouth opened and shut, but no reply was forthcoming. Then he pulled away, his cheeks taking on a pinkish hue beneath his olive tan and his whole demeanor growing sheepish.

Janet hadn't expected him to react that way. She tilted her head, gazing at him in confusion, and tried not to look as hurt as she felt.

"Dammit," Dante muttered under his breath. He cleared his throat and raised his voice but kept looking only at the floor. "Tonight. I'll try to check on you tonight, one way or another. In person, if I can, but it might be over the radio or the phone."

He turned and headed back toward the inter-suite door to rejoin his friend and finish his preparations.

Janet bowed her head and looked away. "I understand, Dr. Costa."

CHAPTER FIVE

Gaje Gurung read the note in his hand for the third time to ensure that his mind was processing everything correctly and he hadn't missed anything important. He could barely believe it, but he was a scientist, and all the evidence he needed to draw his conclusion was right there.

With a sour grimace, he folded the piece of paper and slipped it into his pocket. At that same instant, the elevator reached the bottom of the shaft. His stomach drifted down before righting itself within his body. There was a pleasant *ding,* and the doors opened.

Dante asked from beside him, "Well? What did it say?"

Gage sighed. "It said that the Executives have decided to standardize our vehicles, and they're beginning with the name. Each will be called an... *Autocutioner.*"

Dante stared slack-jawed at him for about two full seconds. Then his lips trembled as he made a loud sputtering sound that transformed into peals of laughter.

"Autocutioner!" he exclaimed, wrapping his hands around his midsection while his whole body heaved. "Holy shit! That's great. Oh, man. Who thought that up? Ha, ha..."

The concierge gawked at them as they passed. It must've been a most unsettling sight, Gage thought—two mismatched men in body armor, bristling with weapons, one of whom limped, and one of whom had apparently taken leave of his sanity.

Gage flashed the man behind the desk an awkward smile and picked up his pace, confident that Dante would notice and be able to keep up with ease given his longer legs. That was if he weren't too oblivious due to being consumed with mad cackling.

The good news was that the brace around Gage's ankle combined with a couple of aspirin and a small shot of whiskey meant that he could walk faster than he expected with only a slight interruption of gait. Still, moving near maximum speed was only to get him out of the hotel post-haste.

The front doors appeared in front of him, and he pushed through, with Dante trailing close. The other man's laughter had descended to a semi-normal register. Once out on the sidewalk, with the streets of downtown Atlantica City stretching before them, Gage slowed his pace.

He moved deliberately, with a confident stride that suggested he knew where he was going and had every intention of getting there. It occurred to him, in a way, that he was mimicking Dante's rather swaggering way of moving.

Dante took a cue from Gage's steady amble and toned it down a notch. Ahead of them was a cluster of five or six youths, rough sorts with sallow faces and beady eyes. They took one look at the pair and parted at the center to allow them through. Gage gave them the slightest nod of acknowledgment as he walked through. The group reformed behind them after they passed.

Something was different. He was now an Executioner. Everyone would recognize the symbol on his uniform, the fear and respect it commanded.

Dante didn't have a uniform, exactly. He didn't wear the skull-and-sword since neither Ty nor Daria had recruited him into the order. Nonetheless, he had the same type of high-quality armor and gear as his friend.

The vest they both wore was of cutting-edge Atlantican design. It was stronger than the flak jackets commonly used in most militaries but not as heavy or bulky as the serious plate armor worn by certain special units. It wouldn't stand up to multiple shots from a powerful rifle. Still, it offered excellent protection against pistol rounds, buckshot or birdshot, and all but the most accurate and dedicated of knife strikes.

Both men were also heavily armed and wore their weapons openly. Gage had heard it said that a warrior was sometimes better served by deception. In certain circumstances that was undoubtedly true, situations in which stealth was paramount and enemies or potential enemies needed to be off-guard until the time came to kill them.

For now, it was better to be intimidating. Atlantica needed to learn who they were and what they stood for.

Gage had received an AR-10 rifle, much like Ty Katakura carried. It came with a sling, and he carried it with one hand on the pistol grip, barrel aimed downward while allowing the sling on his shoulder to support the rest of its weight. His Webley revolver rode holstered at his hip. Two kukris—his old one he'd had since he was a boy, along with a new one Ty had brought him as a token of the Executives' goodwill—were sheathed and crossed over one another at the small of his back.

Dante wore dark clothes to go with his black armored vest. For his primary weapon he carried an Ithaca 37 pump shotgun, also slung on his shoulder, and a bandolier of 12-gauge shells— buckshot and slugs—crossed his chest. A new and rather shiny Colt 1911 pistol and a collapsible baton rode on his belt, and atop the bandolier, his medical bag hung across his chest.

Other pedestrians strolled by on the other side of the street, as well as people gathered in small groups around corner lamp posts or cars parked along the curb. Most of their eyes were drawn toward the two dangerous-looking figures as they passed. No one spoke or jeered or approached them, but all recognized what they were seeing. Men on a mission. No one to trifle with.

Gage was vaguely embarrassed by the whole thing. Being ostentatious or intimidating wasn't generally his way of approaching the world.

Dante seemed to enjoy the opportunity to amplify his swagger. Yet, of the two, he had less experience with combat and violence. Judging by the good fight he'd put up against the towering Russian, he was far from helpless. Gage had gathered that he'd been in fights and handled guns before, during his long period of less-reputable activities in both America and Atlantica.

They advanced across the asphalt, and an approaching car slowed to let them walk by before picking up speed rapidly and buzzing off into the distance. Then they stood beside Gage's new ride, the so-called Autocutioner.

Dante leaned over and spoke softly into the shorter man's ear. "So, I overheard the part about how Atlanticore crystals power all you guys' vehicles. Is that true? I gotta see."

Gage half-frowned. "We're in public. It might be best not to let people see something so valuable. They did tell me the hood stays locked... Hmm.' He pulled his keys from his pocket and found the one associated with the truck's hood.

"Okay." Dante shrugged. "I'll act as your lookout, and block the engine compartment from sight if anybody's around. What do you say? Deal?"

Gage sighed and put the key into the slot. "Yes, that should work. To be quite honest, I'm curious to inspect it myself." He glanced around. No one was close enough to see much, and Dante's tall frame was between the vehicle and the small group of loiterers across the street.

As he opened the hood, a soft blue glow greeted him, and he nodded in satisfaction.

In the center of the engine compartment, a surprisingly jagged and irregular cluster of azure Atlanticore sat in a leaden cradle, attached to a complex matrix of wires and cathodes that funneled the unique mineral's incredible power into the rest of the vehicle.

Gage blinked. He'd been studying Atlanticore and its mysterious properties before Daria came along and changed his life. Yet how the crystals could generate so much energy over so long a time was still poorly understood. They'd even discovered crystals that must've lain dormant for thousands of years in a buried ruin but still powered the strange devices left behind by the ancient Atlanticans.

Dante kept his position to interfere with the loiterers' line of sight but shifted and gave a low whistle of appreciation. "Damn. Looks like a giant Christmas decoration or something. Well, Christmas decorations are usually green or red, but whatever. Nice, though. How's it work?"

"I don't know," Gage admitted. "Atlanticore generates something very similar to electrical energy, but we don't comprehend all of its properties yet. This will be my first time driving this truck. Now, let us go, please."

Dante didn't object. Gage closed the hood, made sure it was locked to guard against thieves, and circled to climb into the driver's side. The physician joined him as his passenger.

The truck itself was like one of the more compact ones used by the U.S. Army and other militaries. It was about halfway between Ty Katakura's behemoth and Daria's small one, which was barely more than a regular pickup truck. He wondered why the Executives hadn't standardized a single vehicle model for them all. The Executioners were still a young organization. Despite all their money, perhaps his benefactors had to make do with whatever was available.

Gage sat and stared at the controls in front of him. The steering wheel, the slot for the engine key, the gear shift, the signal bar, and various other dials, switches, readouts, and levers. For a second or two, his mind went blank as he struggled to remember everything he was supposed to do.

"Hey, Gage, can you drive a truck like this? It's not too different from a car."

Scowling, the Gurkha shot back, "Of course I can, yes." He exhaled. "The last time I drove a vehicle such as this was during the Second World War. Twenty years ago. I was driving a Japanese fuel truck toward a plane trying to take off. I'm surprised it worked."

Dante stared at him blankly for an instant before his eyes widened and his jaw went slack. "Uhh, you know, I can drive if you want, okay?"

"No, no." Gage waved him off. "It will come back to me...soon. Here."

Muttering to himself, he started by putting the keys into the ignition and checking all the controls, determining what each of them did and where it was before he shifted out of park. There was also the matter of maneuvering a much larger and heavier vehicle than Janet's car.

He drew a deep breath. "All right. Let us go." He shifted into gear, looked behind him and checked his mirrors, and kept his face stoic as the truck lurched onto the road. His foot felt strange on the gas pedal, and they jerked forward, slowed nearly to a stop, and jerked again as he picked up speed.

Dante's mouth wrinkled in dissatisfaction, but once they got going, their course became smooth enough that he refrained from making any uncalled-for remarks.

Instead, he told Gage where to go. "Head east. The place we're looking for is at the edge of downtown Atlantica metro, the rougher part of town. There's a guy who should be there. Questioning him might throw a lot of light on our current situation.

He's the ex-boyfriend of one of the gunrunners I worked for. No guarantees, but he might've heard something."

Gage nodded. He thought about asking if the gunrunner in question was a man or a woman but decided it was pointless. In his native Nepal, strict laws governed the people's sexual behaviors. Since traveling abroad—and especially since coming to Atlantica, where there were no rules to speak of whatsoever—his horizons had broadened considerably. Plus, judging people for things that were none of his business wasn't part of his nature.

"It's interesting that everyone needs companionship, even dangerous criminals, yes? People who are trying to do better with their lives, too. Surely you understand." He glanced over at Dante, gauging his reaction.

The physician shifted his posture and avoided eye contact; his aura of confidence dimmed a little. "What are you talking about, man? We've got a job to do. If there's something important I need to know about, just say it."

Gage hesitated. Since it was so evident that he'd made Dante uncomfortable, he would have to proceed with caution and make it clear that he only wanted to help and offer friendly advice.

"Dante," he began in the softest voice he could muster. "I might be older, and I might come from a different origin than yours. But I see things, and I understand some of how the human heart works. Perhaps I'm not always right. Still, I've seen the way you look at Janet. I can tell that the two of you care for each other... although you—both of you—struggle to express it and make your true wishes known."

The truck rattled down the streets, taking two turns that brought them farther east and southeast, toward the transitional zone between downtown and the slum-like area that had sprung up near the docks. It was usually considered the seediest and most dangerous part of the city.

Gage hadn't spent much time there, but he could tell simply by looking at the place and feeling its overall character, noticing the way the sallow-faced hoods who lounged at the mouths of alleys looked at him as he drove past.

Dante chewed on his friend's words, unsure how to respond. He started to say something no fewer than three times. In each instance, he made a faint gasping sound, spread his hands, and allowed them to drop to his lap as his attempt at speech gave way to a fading sigh. It reminded Gage of a boat's outboard motor beginning to fire only to fail after the first buzzes and rumbles.

"Perhaps," Gage suggested, "I'm not so observant as—"

Dante interrupted him, suddenly rediscovering his voice. "No. No, you're right. You *do* see things. I guess that, well, ever since Janet and I started working together to take care of you at that place in the hills, I started…I don't know, looking at her differently, talking to her differently. Like, it made my day when she showed up, and something was missing when she didn't.

"Seeing her almost get killed was rough. I took it pretty hard." He sighed. "I suppose that means I'm developing feelings for her. No point in beating around the bush about it."

Gage nodded. "What do you think about that, friend?"

"It felt wrong," Dante added in a surprisingly sharp voice. "Felt wrong to act on it, to do anything. I'm not sure exactly how she feels. You know how women are. You can't tell what they're thinking half the time, and the Chinese aren't all that expressive. At least not compared to Italians, right? Even if I could tell she wanted me, like no shadow of a doubt, I don't think it would be…fair."

His voice trailed off, and he looked out the side window at a sidewalk. Although fairly new, it already sported a couple of cracks. Gage let him brood for the moment.

Once he'd collected his thoughts, Dante added, "Because of what's going on now, and because of the past. We're in a dangerous situation. No offense since I like you and all, but I agreed to treat you because I didn't have much choice.

"Now we have goddamn Soviet agents after us. We shouldn't

drag her into that. Not to mention, if she and I ended up together, she would have to deal with my past. All the shit I did when I was younger that I'm not proud of. The fact that I'm a damn morphine addict. Recovered so far, but still. It's too much for someone else to have to bear."

"Hmm." Gage wanted to show that he was listening and understood, but he couldn't jump right in with useful commentary yet. Dante had given the matter some thought on his own, and shooting him down and telling him he was wrong would be unwise and unfair.

Dante looked back at him. "So, what do you think, bud?"

"It seems like the kind of thing the other person should be able to decide for themselves." Gage looked ahead, focusing on the road. They couldn't have been far from their destination. "If you have feelings for her, it should be her decision if she wishes to bear all that or not." He shrugged. "I might be too old to give such advice to a handsome young bachelor."

Dante tilted back his head and laughed. "Good one! Handsome. What bullshit won't you come up with next? Makes me feel a little better though. Oh, turn right here. We're almost to the place."

Gage signaled and swerved the truck onto the appropriate street. Although his friend tried to make light of the whole situation, the pain and uncertainty beneath his cocky veneer were obvious.

Dante was so wrapped up in his thoughts that he barely reacted when they arrived at the locale they sought. It was undoubtedly a modern building but cleverly designed to resemble an ancient Greek or Roman holy site, complete with faux marble columns and nude statues out front. A sign hovering next to the structure and above its parking lot read "Temple of Aphrodite" in vaguely Latin-styled letters.

Gage pulled past the sign and found a parking space near the far end of the lot, beside a couple of nondescript concrete walls, where they would hopefully attract as little attention as possible.

"This is it, yes?" He glanced at his friend.

Dante nodded. "Yep. I know it well."

"Aphrodite," Gage mused, combing through his reservoir of knowledge. "The Greek goddess of love and beauty." Then he frowned. "Wait. What, ah, what manner of place is this, exactly?"

CHAPTER SIX

"Oh, it's a brothel." Dante casually stretched his arms. "Kind of a mid-tier one. Halfway respectable by brothel standards, but not top of the line. What did you expect?"

Gage shrugged as he pulled the key from the ignition and opened his door. "I don't know what I expected. It doesn't matter. I must say, it appears to be an interesting place. The decor is nice."

Dante laughed, opened the door on his side, and hopped down to the pavement. "Yeah, it's not too bad. The guy we're looking for is a prostitute who works here. At least, he did last I heard, which was before I got sequestered with you up at that cottage. If he's not here, we'll have to look elsewhere. Let me do most of the talking, okay?"

Gage agreed. He climbed carefully down from the truck, favoring his leg. Once he was standing, he could walk somewhat more normally. He double-checked the truck to ensure everything was locked up securely, then followed as Dante led the way toward the "temple's" grand entrance.

It occurred briefly to Gage that some of the patrons, the staff, or random onlookers might become alarmed by the sight of two men in armored vests and dressed for war who'd come to ask questions. However, Atlantica had no laws against prostitution. If an Executioner showed up, it was either to help resolve a conflict or to track down an individual or group who'd done something far worse than solicit the usual services of a semi-respectable brothel.

Still, the two of them drew a great many wide-eyed stares. People gave them a wide berth. Gage wondered if performing the investigation incognito might've been a better idea. There was a real possibility that seeing him and Dante approach in so obvious a fashion, some people might pass the word along. Anyone who might help them would flee before they could garner any useful information.

As they passed under the carved arch and between the fluted columns, Gage nearly stopped in his tracks. One of the statues standing beside the front doors wasn't a statue. It was a woman standing on a pedestal and coated with brownish metallic paint, the better to resemble a bronze sculpture. She was naked, although the paint concealed the finer details of her nudity.

"Welcome to the Temple of Aphrodite," she said to the two men as they passed. It looked like she greeted everyone, probably startling a few of them, before resuming her act as a nonliving object.

Gage was too surprised to react much at all, but Dante quipped, "Thanks." Then he pushed open the right-hand door, holding it for Gage as they entered the establishment's main floor.

The decor within was about what Gage expected based on the exterior and the place's overall aesthetic theme. It wasn't overly ornate, but there were more faux marble fluted columns within, along with a combination bath and fountain in the center. Men and women languished or fondled each other on various couches hung with draperies. Most of them spared a cool glance for the two newcomers before returning to their debauchery.

The place doubled as a bar and restaurant of sorts since waitresses held trays piled with drinks and snacks as they moved through the groups of people to the couches. Appropriately enough, the beverage of choice seemed to be red wine. The servers wore skimpy togas that provided the bare minimum of coverage to be "clothed" at all.

There were also a few others, both male and female, acting as "living statues." Some of them seemed to be there for decoration more than anything, but judging by the way a few patrons sidled up and talked to them, they, too, might've been part of the available roster of prostitutes.

A waitress saw Dante, smiled, and let out a cheerful "Hello!" before moving past. At first, Gage thought she was simply polite, but her manner was noticeably *familiar.*

She wasn't the only one. All sorts of people throughout the brothel, whether customers or workers, recognized the tall American physician.

Dante returned their greetings with nods or the occasional "Hi," but otherwise, he kept moving slowly toward the rear of the main lobby area.

Gage shook his head, bemused. Part of him was mildly disgusted since the idea of paying for sex had never appealed to him, but another part of him was amused and faintly awed by the sheer gaudiness and decadence of the place.

That made him wonder why everyone seemed to know Dante so well.

A thick-waisted john with a hat askew on his head and a flagon of wine in hand saw the doctor and announced in an unnecessarily loud voice, "Hey, Dr. Costa! Looking good in the new getup, buddy."

Dante looked a tad embarrassed and annoyed. He didn't visibly flush, but a barely perceptible cringe in his demeanor suggested that he hoped the man wouldn't see or interact with him. "Thanks. I have stuff to take care of. Take it easy."

The stocky man chortled as they walked past and busied himself flirting with a young lady on a nearby couch.

An alcove toward the rear of the main floor looked like it led to an office or another room beyond. An expansive hardwood desk blocked it from the rest of the lobby. Gage guessed the wood was teak, judging by the light orangish color and familiar texture, but he couldn't be sure.

A woman sat behind the desk in a high-backed, throne-like chair covered with deep red leather. Her face and demeanor were severe, and she was around Gage's age, making her significantly older than most of the workers. Yet she retained most of the attractiveness she'd undoubtedly had in her youth.

Her garb wasn't as borderline scandalous as the others, but it was still revealing enough to determine that her body remained well-kept and alluring. Her brown hair was piled atop her head and held in place with silver pins.

Dante turned his face to Gage and whispered, "That's Ms. January, better known as Juno. She's the madame here."

Gage had assumed as much. He'd never visited a house of prostitution, but he understood that older, more experienced women usually managed them.

As they drew closer to the desk, Juno's eyes fixed on Dante, and a big smile spread across her face. It reminded Gage of the Cheshire Cat he'd seen in an animated film. She leaned forward in her chair and braced her elbows on the desk's surface, resting her chin in her hands.

"Looks like you're moving up in the world, Dr. Costa. That getup couldn't have come cheap. Although it looks like you've been in a fight recently, or perhaps an accident. That's unfortunate. What can we do for you today?" Her voice was a low purr, but it had a curious quality of cutting through background noise with ease.

Gage looked back and forth between Dante and the madame, trying to guess how well they knew each other. He was curious.

Dante ignored his friend for the time being. He returned the woman's smile. "Thank you, ma'am. I'm holding up fine. I hoped to see Jubal if he's available." He was using his "professional" voice, the generically American manner of speaking he employed when engaged in official business or trying to impress someone, instead of his more organic New York accent.

Rather than saying anything in response, Juno glanced down at her desk. She consulted a schedule or ledger that she probably updated throughout the day to keep track of her employees. Then her face froze and her eyebrows arched as though she'd suddenly remembered an important piece of information that had nothing to do with the schedule sheet.

"Yes," she stated, in a softer voice than she had spoken with thus far. "Personal arrangement for our little Icarus, I'm sure. I expected as much. Go ahead, Doctor. You know where he is." She flourished a hand, and her bracelet of pearls made a gentle rattling sound.

Dante bowed his head. "Thanks again, Juno. Ma'am." He turned away.

Juno looked at Gage next, capturing his eyes with her gaze and widening her eyes slightly as though waiting for him to speak. She'd probably figured out that he was with Dante but was still willing to treat him like a regular customer.

He only nodded to her with a faint, polite smile and fell behind Dante as the tall physician ambled into the wide hallway beyond the madame's desk. It led away from the brightness and bustle of the lobby and toward the brothel's more private quarters. Red curtains hung, and half-columns jutted from the walls between doors that opened onto areas where presumably the kitchen and winery were located.

Toward the end of the hallway was a grand staircase that split in two halfway up. It curved around to either side of the building to end at balcony hallways with lines of rooms on the second and third floors.

When they were about halfway to the first of the steps, Gage could no longer contain his curiosity. He cleared his throat. "It seems that you know the woman and that man with the hat. It is, ah, good that you have friends here."

He winced as soon as the words left his mouth. The goal was to ask how and why Dante was so familiar with the staff and clientele here, but without making it sound like he was implying or assuming anything that might embarrass his friend.

He failed since Dante gave him a sharp look over his shoulder and snorted. "Hah! Yeah, yeah, I get it. You wonder what an upstanding citizen like me is doing with so many acquaintances in a place like this. Well, if you want to know, I'll tell you. You might not like the truth, though. Not because it's juicy, but because it's pretty fucking boring."

Gage blinked. "I, ah, did not mean to—"

"Sure, whatever." Dante talked over him, not giving the older man the chance to get a word in edgewise. "It goes back to when the gunrunners 'recruited' me and made me work as their doctor.

"This guy we're looking for, the one who escaped the Katakura Sword of Justice or whatever, his name is Pietr Urlicht. He was a moderate-ranking sort, did a lot of middleman stuff, including bossing me around. Well, after a while, he trusted me enough to give me personal jobs as well as stuff for the gang."

They reached the staircase. It was wide enough to walk side by side, and Gage came up on Dante's left once it was clear that he was veering right. That way, the physician could speak to him more privately rather than having to call over his shoulder. It was hard on his ankle, though.

Dante went on. "So Pietr brought me here, you know, as a doctor, to look after his boyfriend, Jubal. Or Icarus, that's his working alias at this particular establishment. Well, I guess I did a good job, and word got around because pretty soon, I was tending to damn near everyone who worked here. I treated their venereal diseases and shit in addition to more prosaic stuff like colds, pneumonia, and bruised knees.

"Then the johns noticed and were asking me for under-the-table consultations and paying me off the books for prescriptions and stuff. So yeah, that's why everybody knows me. I'm a familiar face."

"Ah, yes." Gage nodded. His skin tingled, burning faintly with mild shame. He hadn't accused his friend of anything, and it would've been none of his business no matter what, but he still felt as though it were ungracious of him to have suspected anything but the truth. "That does make sense."

His ankle protested the labor of climbing the stairs, and he drifted gradually behind as Dante kept the same speed. It looked like they would bypass the second-floor landing and proceed to the third.

Then something occurred to him. "Dante. What if Jubal doesn't wish to help us? He might be scared to do so after what happened to those men in the gang. I believe others might consider him, um, an *accessory*, I think is the term."

Dante suddenly noticed that Gage was having trouble keeping up with him. He paused, and once the Nepali reached his side, he slowed his gait as they climbed. Gage didn't ask for help. He could manage. It simply took him longer than it would've if his ankle were fully functional.

"Well, we'll have to see," Dante grumbled. "Pietr and Jubal always had a...tumultuous relationship I guess you could say. Last I knew, they hadn't spoken much lately, but a lot has happened since then. It's been a good month and a half since I saw Pietr, so who knows. Hopefully, Jubal will be in a good mood while also losing any particular loyalty he has to Mr. Urlicht."

They reached the top landing, where the stairs gave way to a broad veranda-style corridor overlooking the lobby, with a line of doors and rooms to their left. Gage stopped and bent to adjust the brace on his leg. It had come loose during the ascent.

"Yes, we must hope for the best. But I must ask. What will we do if this man Jubal doesn't cooperate?"

Dante frowned. "I have no intent or desire to *force* the information out of him if that's what you mean." He turned away and slowly strolled down the passage.

"Not even for Janet's sake?"

Dante stopped, and Gage again wondered if he had made an error in how he said things. His English was fairly good, but some of the nuances of the language still escaped him at times. There were also the issues of tone and unspoken assumptions, which varied from culture to culture. Where Westerners were concerned, he was most familiar with Britons. He had less experience with Americans, or Canadians, or people from elsewhere in Europe than the United Kingdom. Not all Westerners were the same.

As such, Dante might've thought Gage was trying to make a fool of him by "catching" him in some small act of hypocrisy. Such was not Gage's intention. His motives were genuine.

The taller man's voice was mostly neutral but had a demanding edge. "What do you mean? How would it help her for us to rough up a hooker? I don't see it." He shook his head.

Gage finished tightening the brace and stood straight. "You said earlier that people are coming after us, and as long as they think we're a threat, they'll try to use Janet against us. Or hurt her to draw us out."

Dante almost missed a step, but this time he kept walking, albeit at a slower pace. It appeared that he was thinking it over.

"No," he stated after a moment's pondering. "No, I'm not going back to doing that sort of stuff." His voice was low. He hadn't so much announced his position as simply exhaled it.

They continued past several doors. Jubal's room seemed to lay somewhere in the middle or farther part of the hall.

Gage inquired, "What kind of stuff? I don't understand." He had his suspicions but didn't think he should say them aloud.

Dante sighed. "It's the dark side of my profession, at least when you work for the bad guys. When you know how to heal, you learn a lot about hurt. Knowledge of the human body and how it works. What its weaknesses are.

"The not-so-good people who paid for my education back in the States? Sometimes they needed to make somebody hurt a lot. Without them being in much danger of dying. See? I don't have to be any clearer about it, do I? I hope not because it's an ugly business and I don't want to talk about it."

His shoulders had slumped while he explained it all, and he no longer attempted to make eye contact.

Gage thought back to the war. To all the violent, brutal, and bloodthirsty things he'd done as a Gurkha. Some of it people had called heroic after the fact, some they hadn't. All had involved him inflicting pain and death on other human beings. Most of it, he didn't regret. Under the circumstances, it had seemed to be necessary.

He hadn't *enjoyed* it, either.

"I understand," he told his friend. "Please believe me when I say that I know some of how you feel. I was a soldier, as you may remember. They gave me many medals and told me I should feel proud of them.

"With each new one I received, I began to wonder if I deserved them. Some things I did, I think that perhaps they should've given me a bullet instead. Such thoughts still occur to me from time to time. It has been that way for twenty years."

He reflected upon the first incident to flash within his memory, a battle in the Philippines when his unit attacked a small Japanese fort. The mission's success had required stealth and surprise. Gaje Gurung had been among those who went in first to neutralize the guards and throw open the gates so their comrades could storm in and defeat the enemy before they had time to react.

Gage had come across two young men, barely twenty from the look of them, lounging near the rear entrance. He'd somehow managed to hack his kukri into the lungs of the first one while he kicked the second into a wall to stun him until he too could be killed. The latter guard had recovered with astonishing speed. Although he tripped and crawled through the gate, his arm outstretched, one trembling hand reaching for the alarm.

Leaving the first man gasping and choking to succumb to his wounds, Gage had pounced after the second. He came upon the boy a second or so before he could hit the alarm. The young man had turned to look at him, his face contorted with terror, his eyes moist, and blubbered something in Japanese.

Gage recalled having a split second's worth of hesitation, of pity for his adversary and horror at what he had to do, but the mission was too important for such things. So he'd brought the blade of his kukri straight down onto the guard's head, splitting open his skull and killing him instantly. Gage sometimes wondered if the boy would've agreed to run away without saying anything if Gage had spared his life.

Probably not. Imperial Japan was a ruthless society that didn't permit its warriors to surrender, flee, retreat, or bargain with the enemy. If by some chance Gage had spared him, and he'd run off, his superior officers would likely have scooped him back up and had him executed for cowardice or dereliction of duty.

Still...the faint twinge of regret, the doubt about whether he'd done the right thing, had never gone away.

"I know," Gage repeated. "We do terrible things, sometimes. Still, we must seek to live better lives and do good where we can. Such is the burden of...thoughtful, but perilous men."

Dante Costa said nothing. A vague shift in his demeanor told Gage that he'd heard and acknowledged his partner's words. For the time being, he had nothing with which he was willing or able to reply.

He stopped in front of a particular door that looked no different from the others. He waved at it with a faint shrug. "This is it."

CHAPTER SEVEN

Gage stood by, forcing his mind back to the task at hand, banishing the unwanted and unpleasant thoughts of either his or his friend's past actions. There might've been some value in remembering such things. To dwell on them to the point that they infringed upon the present was beyond pointless.

Dante stepped toward the door and rapped his knuckles on the surface three times.

From within, a low and muffled voice said, "Please go away." There was an unusual quality to Jubal's speech. Gage couldn't tell if it was due to him having an unfamiliar accent, or because the prostitute was eating something or had a shirt over his head, or something else.

Dante glanced back at Gage with a narrow-eyed look of exasperation. Then he reached down and tried the doorknob. Finding it unlocked, he twisted it and pushed the door open, stepping over the threshold in the same motion. Gage went in behind him and stepped sideways to get out of Dante's way while covering his flank.

The chamber within was about what Gage would've expected—comparable to a hotel room but with the characteristic

Hellenic flourish present throughout the establishment. It looked comfortable and lived in, not as gaudy or luxurious as anything in the lobby, but hardly bare or austere. The bed was messy, its covers scattered halfway across the floor.

Near the rear was a dresser and toiletry stand, arranged diagonally against the corner. It held a gilt-edged oval mirror mounted on a swivel stand. A young man of about twenty-two or twenty-four stood with his back more or less to the two visitors, but since he was looking at himself in the mirror, they could see his face on its surface. He could also see them.

Jubal let out a sharp sigh of annoyance but didn't bother to turn around. "I'm not available right..." he cut himself off, and his words trailed away as he focused on the pair within the reflection. His glare of irritation gave way to confusion. "Doc, what are you doing here?"

Gage studied the young man as Dante took a step farther into the room. Jubal's ethnic background was difficult to determine on sight, but he had a slim, boyish frame and was hairless aside from the black braids atop his head. He wore no shirt or shoes, only loose-fitting white cotton pants. His skin was an attractive dark golden color, and he had a narrow nose and full lips. His relative beauty would probably be acknowledged as an objective fact even by those who had no interest in men.

His voice, however, was surprisingly deep. Gage decided that the accent was probably African. He couldn't pick out which country or region the boy might hail from, though.

Gage glanced to the side, toward the bed. For the first time, he noticed a pair of white wings mounted on the wall over the bed. They were fake, made on a wooden frame of some sort, yet the feathers attached to the frame appeared to be real. He guessed that they were from swans or some other famously elegant bird. He didn't know much about wildlife beyond his firsthand experience, but that would be his best guess.

"Hi, Jubal," Dante said in a soft voice. "I needed to talk to you about... Are you all right?"

Hearing the sudden note of concern in his friend's tone, Gage examined the young male prostitute more closely. He realized that Jubal had been dabbing makeup onto his face, foundation or concealer, to cover up a patchwork of ugly purplish bruises.

Jubal turned his face away from the doctor and the mirror in a vain last-ditch effort to hide his injuries, but it was too late. Dante had seen. He strode across the room to Jubal's side and reached out to touch his cheek, examining his face, then his arms and upper body.

Gage didn't feel it was appropriate for him to get too close yet, but he took one further step and saw Dante turning up Jubal's wrists. Those, too, were badly bruised, as though someone had grabbed him hard and pulled him around or held him in place while Jubal struggled against them.

Dante frowned as he examined the markings. Then he looked at the young man's face. "Pietr?"

Jubal's eyes glistened as they welled up with tears, and he turned his head away with a sharp motion. He also snatched his forearms back from the physician's grasp. Facing the wall, he hugged himself and allowed his shoulders to slump.

"It, well..." Jubal's deep voice caught in his throat. "It sounds like he wasn't lying about everything, at least."

His words came out in a series of short gasps. He was trying to master his emotions, working hard at not breaking down and crying. He succeeded...but Gage had no idea what he was talking about, and he didn't think Dante did, either.

Jubal continued, "It doesn't change a thing. It changes nothing. But he didn't lie. At least the last thing he said to me wasn't complete bullshit. That counts for something. That is...better than nothing." He swallowed a growing lump in his throat.

Dante squinted, but his face had fallen in concern and dismay. "Jubal. What does that mean?"

The boy didn't answer. Judging by the way his mouth contorted and the way he rubbed his arms and pouted at the wall, it seemed that he wanted to say more, but he wasn't sure if he should or could.

Gage glanced backward and poked his head out the doorway. No one else was around. No one was coming. Satisfied that they were safe, he closed the door to offer them more privacy and security. Then he turned back toward the two younger men who stood beside the mirror.

Dante decided to try a different approach to the issue at hand. "What happened with Pietr? When did you see him last, and what did he say and do? Think back to the beginning, and tell me all of it, step by step. Remember, I'm here to help."

The silence within the bed chamber became stuffy and oppressive, as though the lack of sound had substance unto itself —like humid fog during a heatwave or smoke during a fire.

Then, at last, Jubal drew a deep breath and began his story. It was difficult for Gage to understand him, particularly with his odd accent and lack of enunciation, but he caught most of it.

"Pietr came in a few days ago," the boy mumbled. "I hadn't seen him for weeks before that. Two or three, maybe even four weeks. I think no more than a month. He looked terrible.

"It was as though he'd been sleeping rough. Catching two hours here and there, sleeping in the street or on floorboards, that sort of thing—if he'd been sleeping at all. He looked older than he should, with big dark bags under his eyes, terrible. I was worried about him."

Dante nodded. None of what Jubal had said so far came as any great surprise. Ty Katakura had hounded the arms dealers with relentless persistence ever since he'd so thoroughly destroyed the core of their operation.

Jubal went on, "I asked Pietr what was wrong. He said that his old contacts were coming after him. Not only them. The Executioners, too." At that, he shot a sullen, suspicious look at the Executioner.

Gage stood and kept quiet. He wondered if his presence was inhibiting the young man from speaking openly. For the time being, he waited. If necessary, he could always offer to step outside and let Dante question the prostitute by himself.

Jubal kept talking. "He said he needed to leave Atlantica as soon as possible. He wanted all the money I had on hand. Insisted, demanded. Wouldn't take no for an answer. I, ah...at first I was okay with that. Because I thought he meant that he wanted the two of us to run away from this place together. If that were so, I would've. Maybe I'm stupid. But I would've."

"Fair enough," Dante commented, reserving judgment. He'd subdued his brash demeanor. As a doctor, he understood the importance of listening to others when they discussed their problems. "Go on."

Jubal turned halfway back toward Dr. Costa, perhaps a gesture of cooperation, although his eyes remained distant and unfocused while his mind dwelled on the recent past.

"So I began to get my things together. I don't own much. I wanted the things I cared about and the things I would need for a long trip. Pietr came up behind me. He grabbed me by the shoulders, spun me, and slapped me across the face. Then when I started to ask why he did that, he shook me and yelled at me that there was no time for fairy tales. That is what he said—fairy tales. He only wanted the money."

Jubal went on to describe how they'd fought, both protesting the other's words and intentions, shouting back and forth with greater volume and increasing anger, both becoming more and more desperate.

Jubal had insisted that he would follow Pietr anywhere—that he loved him and would be devoted to him. However, he wasn't about to give Pietr everything he'd scraped together since he'd come to Atlantica and let him run off with it alone, leaving Jubal behind.

Dante nodded. "Understandable. Then what? I'm pretty sure I can guess how he reacted." He crossed his arms.

The younger man nodded. "Yes. He did not take it well."

Pietr had become more hostile and violent with a kind of desperate impatience fueling his mounting aggression. Finally, he'd lost his temper altogether. He'd punched Jubal in the face and proceeded to smack and punch him further, throw him around the room, kick him in the ribs once or twice, and even struck him in the head with the young man's discarded shoe.

By then, Jubal was too emotionally ravaged and in too much physical pain to do much of anything, so he'd lain on the floor, gasping and moaning. His crazed boyfriend had ransacked the room, turning over furniture, pulling out drawers, and throwing things in heaps across the room as he searched for cash and valuables.

Jubal took a step away from Dante and looked back into the mirror's glistening surface. "Only a week before he returned, I'd moved most of my savings out of my room and into the safe downstairs. So there was not nearly as much money here as he thought he would get.

"He was in a hurry. He was too angry to think of something like that. I was fading in and out. I believe I lost consciousness at least once for a minute or two. Then..."

Once he'd found everything there was to take and stuffed it into his coat, Pietr had hurled insults and profanity at him, torn up one of his outfits, and kicked one of his chairs into the wall as the last sign of how mad he was. It seemed he was leaving his lover with something to think about.

At this point in the account, Jubal paused to half-choke on the emotions the memory dredged up. He sniffled. It took another half a minute or so before he could continue speaking and finish the story.

"Then he came back. He rushed into my room only a moment after he'd rushed out. He picked me up off the floor. Now, he was being gentle. Like he was helping me. He laid me on the bed, stroked my cheek and shoulder, and said he was sorry. Then he kissed me goodbye and left."

Jubal was weeping quietly. He'd managed to restrain himself from sobbing or otherwise sacrificing too much of his dignity, but he could do nothing to stop his eyes from tearing up and his nose from growing stuffy.

"That bastard son of a bitch," he concluded. Despite the harshness of his words, there was a strange lack of venom behind them, only sadness.

Gage frowned and shook his head. Clearly, Jubal had retained feelings for his lover despite all he'd described and was angry at him for leaving him in such a state of emotional confusion.

Dante was still contemplating how to respond to the whole thing, so Gage decided to step in. People had told him that he had a soothing voice. Like a grandfather, they'd said, even when Gage was still only in his middle thirties or so. That had been ten years ago.

"Jubal." He addressed the young man for the first time since Dante had opened the door. "There is nothing wrong with feeling the way you do. Pietr was the one who was wrong to treat you that way. I think you know that, even if you still love him, in a way. Yes, he wasn't lying when he said that many people are looking for him." He paused. "Some of those people have intentions toward him that are far worse than anything I mean to do.'

The boy cast a rather cynical eye toward the Nepali and snorted. "You're an Executioner. You kill people. What intentions could be worse than that?"

Dante and Gage exchanged a glance. The former's mouth had twisted into a grimace of frustration, but Gage was determined to be patient. "Where are you from, Jubal? I've been all over the world, but I'm afraid I don't recognize your accent."

Jubal rolled his narrow shoulders. "I am Amhara, from the highlands of Ethiopia. What are you, Indian? Turkish?"

"I'm from Nepal. I was a Gurkha," Gage explained. "It's true that I did many violent things during the war. I've tried to be peaceful since then. I don't like killing people. There are usually better ways to deal with problems."

Dante nodded. Seeing an opportunity, he looked at Jubal and added, "As to your question of what could be worse than death, well, I think you could answer that better than most. You know the type of people he was involved with, right?"

His tone was gentle, but the words themselves were a wake-up call. Jubal appeared to get the point. He perked up and stopped sniffling.

Dante went on, "The truth is, we aren't looking to kill him. He probably deserves it, but it's not what we're here for. We need him to answer some questions. He has information we can use to stop other people from getting hurt."

There was a moment of tense expectancy. Jubal was paying close attention to what the physician said while keeping one eye on the Executioner. There was a guardedness to him, even hostility, as though he was ready to argue with them or lie to them on Pietr's behalf.

It passed. In the space of a second or less, the resistance melted away. Jubal's shoulders sagged and he turned, facing the two men full-on, and sighed.

"Pietr didn't get the money he was looking for. Not from me. So he probably went to his cousin Vlad instead. Vlad runs a big drug operation here. He's the sort of man who would be able to loan money to his family if they needed it."

Gage nodded. Dante saw the gesture in his peripheral vision but kept his gaze focused on Jubal. "That makes sense. Do you know where we could find this guy? And how to approach him? Anything you could think of that might help us find Pietr through him."

He took out a pen and a scrap of paper as Jubal begrudgingly gave him an address along with rough directions to the place. It was near the southwestern fringe of the city, between the built-up area and the various slums and shantytowns that had sprung up in the hinterlands.

"Good," Dante said. "That will help. Again, how do we deal with him?"

Jubal scowled. "I don't know. I've never met him. Since he's a criminal, he probably thinks of everything in terms of money, power, and reputation.

"Your options are most likely to beg him for help in exchange for a favor, blackmail him with threats, or simply attack and rob him. He would understand those things better than a formal meeting and flashing your badge and credentials. I don't know anything about what sort of man he is or how likely he would be to kill you on sight."

Dante finished scribbling a couple of notes, then folded up the paper and returned it and the pen to his pocket. "Right, well, that's still good to know."

Muttering more to himself than to his visitors, Jubal added, "I think Pietr has always been like this with everyone. I don't know why I care. Everything was always complicated with him, from what he's told me. It sounds like he beats other people, or they beat him. I should've known..."

Gage shook his head and offered, "Sadly, some people don't seem to understand that life doesn't always have to be painful."

Dante snapped his fingers. "Yeah, speaking of which, let me write you a prescription." He pulled the pen back out and selected a proper piece of stationery from a pad on Jubal's tiny desk, then scribbled something.

"Some anti-inflammatory stuff. It will take care of most of the swelling and ease the discomfort while you recover. Go ahead and put it on my tab as long as they'll let you. I spoke to Juno on the way in and asked for you specifically, so you shouldn't have any problems getting them to take care of it. Besides, by now I'm sure she recognizes my prescription handwriting."

At that, Gage blinked. "I didn't think anyone was capable of 'recognizing' a doctor's handwriting when it came to prescriptions."

Dante snapped his head toward him. "Thank you, Gage, for your extremely useful input," he grumbled. Then he looked at Jubal, laid a hand on his shoulder, and added, softer, "Thank you for all your help. I'm sorry about what happened. Feel better. I'll check in with you again before long. And..."

Jubal had wandered over to sit on the edge of his bed. He raised his eyebrows, waiting for the last of Dante's spiel.

The physician's tone grew firmer, more authoritative. "Start looking for a way to get out of this line of work. There are other things you could do that would come with far fewer risks to your health—mental and physical. Doctor's orders." He handed the slip of stationery to the boy.

Jubal scanned it and gave him an odd look that was roughly an even mixture of smile and sullen jeer. "Well, thank you for the prescription, Doc. As for the second part...I'll think about it."

Dante nodded as he turned and walked toward Gage and the door. "You should. Goodbye, and good luck."

Gage said the same and gave the young man a short, respectful bow. Then he stepped out the door, pausing a couple of seconds as Dante came out after him. The hallway seemed bright and airy after the room's intimate stuffiness.

It took half a moment after the two men exited the private chamber for Gage to register that other people were coming up the right-hand branch of the great staircase, and it sounded like they'd already passed the landing for the second floor. *Several* people. It wasn't suspicious in and of itself, but the Gurkha felt faintly uncomfortable. Something deep in his gut twinged as though a sixth sense were warning him of danger.

Without consciously thinking about it, he lowered his right

shoulder to more easily shrug his AR-10 off his back and into his hands should he need it. His mind also fixated on the feel and location of his holstered pistol. And the twin kukris on his back.

Dante didn't seem to share his trepidation. The physician was probably wrapped up mentally and emotionally with the business that had taken place in Jubal's room and the question of what they should do next.

Gage was about to elbow his friend and whisper his concerns. Then he saw something familiar cresting the staircase—the piled-up brown hairdo of Juno, the madame. For a fraction of a second, he relaxed.

Behind Juno was a group of five men. Four in the rear, two at each flank. In front of them but behind the toga-clad woman was a figure from a nightmare. Seven feet tall at least, broad-shoul-dered, and with a huge square bearded face that was badly slashed and now looked held together with wire stitches.

Gage froze. The giant's hand wrapped around Juno's neck from behind. As he moved to grab Dante's arm, his friend stopped too. Both of them had seen what was approaching. Within the next half a second, their visitors had seen them too, and with hurried steps they stomped up the last of the stairs to the topmost landing.

The massive and hideous face of the mutilated Russian lit up as the crazed eyes focused on the two men. In his other hand he held another PPS-43 submachine gun—or perhaps the same one, if he'd somehow recovered it from the cabin in the hills after Gage, Dante, and Janet had fled. His arm seemed to move with a bizarre underwater slowness as he brought the weapon up.

Juno saw Dante and Gage at the same instant the five men did. Her eyes widened, and her mouth fell open. "Dr. Costa! They—"

The colossal hand clamped down, squeezing with vicious force and cutting off whatever she had been about to say. Only a strangled, wordless cry came out. Her shoulders hitched up, and her arms rose, clawing at the air as her head tilted to the side.

The big man bellowed something in Russian. His four comrades streamed around him, two on each side, brandishing weapons and baring their teeth.

Before Gage or Dante could act, before they could do anything to help or save her, the assassin hoisted Juno up by her neck, lifting her as easily as if she'd been a small cat, and hurled her over the railing.

The woman's scream was awful to hear. The hand squeezing her neck had damaged her throat in some way, so the cry of pain and terror came out as a gurgling, strangled squawk that nonetheless carried throughout the building's broad space.

Juno spun head over heels through the air, revolving twice in her descent before smashing face-first into the white tiles that covered the ground-level floor. The tiles cracked, and the woman crumpled into a broken heap, her blood already flowing across the floor. The patrons and workers nearby gawked in total shock.

The Russian's four henchmen were ready to open fire.

CHAPTER EIGHT

Without needing to discuss it, signal with their hands, or communicate in any way, Dante and Gage both decided on the same course of action at the same time. They dashed back toward the still-open door to Jubal's room.

Their timing was impeccable as the explosive thunderclaps of gunshots split the air to fill the makeshift temple. The deafening noise echoed off the faux marble, metal, and concrete of the building's interior and unleashed chaos and terror upon the whole place. Down below, people screamed, tipped over chairs in their haste to get out, and ran toward the exit—or at least toward cover.

The whip and *whiz* of individual bullets streaking through the air were still perceptible beneath the roar of many cartridges detonating at once. They cut through the atmosphere to *buzz* past Gage's and Dante's faces or tear up the rug and floor between their legs.

Dante was taller and had full use of both legs so he was ahead of Gage, but the Nepali moved faster than he would've thought possible. Adrenaline had already kicked in, protecting him from pain. The brace held his left ankle in the proper position to run on it if he had to without massive impairment.

As the two men sprinted toward their only available shelter, they saw a slight problem. Jubal had stepped out to see what all the commotion was, probably after hearing Juno scream as she plummeted to her death.

Gage saw him first. Dante had lost a second of response time as his mind struggled to decide what to do next—capable though he was, he couldn't take instant action under all varieties of stressful and chaotic situations. He was trying to unsling his shotgun and return fire against their assailants, running toward the room, and taking account of everything else that was happening. His brain got bottlenecked in confusion.

Gage shouted, "Jubal! Get back!" He spread his arms, keeping his back flat toward the Russian and his henchmen to present as wide a target as possible. He was wearing body armor. The young man wasn't.

Jubal froze, his dark eyes bulging in panic and his lips moving soundlessly in stunned horror. Gage covered him as two bullets struck him in the back.

He grunted, more from the thumping impact than from actual pain since his armor stopped the slugs. Still, they'd hit hard enough that the men must've been using rifles. Gage hadn't had time to see exactly how the others were armed.

At the same time the bullets hit, Gage brought his arms in to push Jubal out of the way, urging him to retreat to his room's relative safety. With the attackers barking and cursing behind him in between the roar of their guns, there simply wasn't time. Plus, lead filled the air.

Gage felt another bullet zip toward him, then past. His hands connected with Jubal's bare shoulders. The prostitute's face remained locked in a flabbergasted expression of terror. Dante was moving in to help shield him.

It took Gage a fraction of a second to realize what had

happened. The third projectile had zipped under his arm, passing through the space between his vest and his tricep. Jubal's bare side lay beyond.

The young man let out a hoarsely guttural yelping sound, a shriek that transformed into a ragged gurgle. A tremor went through his body and his muscles tensed. Blood flowed down his torso and spattered the carpet and tiles beneath their feet with glistening droplets of bright scarlet.

Dante exclaimed, "No!" He spun with ferocious speed, his shotgun in his hands and fired a quick blast at their foes. They saw it coming and dodged to the sides of the hall. Two of them pressed against the banister and the others piled against the opposite wall. Smoke filled the air as the buckshot passed mostly between them. A stray pellet or two might've nicked one of them, but they were too fast and too well-organized.

They weren't out of ammo yet, either.

Jubal crumpled in Gage's grasp, falling into him, then toward the wall as the small man heaved and dragged him over the threshold, spurred on by the rush of adrenaline. The brightness of the temple's main open area gave way to the dimmer, warmer tones of the bed chamber.

Gage pulled Jubal across the floor, heading for the bed, and noted the blood trail he left behind. Dante hopped in after them, his lips drawn back from bared and gritted teeth.

The gunfire outside died down. "Dante. He's hit." Gage gestured down at Jubal with his chin.

The physician dashed toward the wounded young man. "I know. Cover me! I can save him. I have to. Oh, God. I think they got his lung."

The gears and mechanisms of Gage's mind fell into place and performed their necessary functions. Reality seemed slower, and despite knowing that his heart rate had increased and his stress responses were active, he felt strangely calm. His body did what it needed to do.

The rifle that hung on his shoulder fell into his hands. He spared a glance back at his friend, kneeling to tend to Jubal, who was still alive but badly hurt. The bullet that had made its way through Gage's attempted defense had struck and shattered one of the boy's ribs and perhaps gone clear through him. He gasped and convulsed as he bled.

Outside, the hit squad advanced toward the room with heavy, deliberate, yet quick steps. It also sounded like they were reloading their weapons. Assuming that at least one or two of them had rifles, they probably could've fired through the walls and potentially hit their quarry. Gage estimated that they wanted to be more decisive, to know for sure that their targets were dead on sight.

Gage had no intention of giving them a chance. He flicked his eyes down to the gun in his hands and recalled what Ty had shown him of its functionality.

Never before had he operated an AR-10. It was a relatively new firearm, not introduced until around five years ago if he recalled correctly. Long after World War Two had ended and Gage handed back his old Lee Enfield rifle to the British government. Yet, its mechanisms weren't too complex. It still felt like a *rifle*. Ty had vouched for its quality, power, and reliability.

The one thing that had confounded Gage when Katakura had demonstrated the weapon was the selector switch. Gage didn't much like automatic firearms. He'd used submachine guns once or twice and found them inaccurate and inefficient despite their obvious value in laying down suppressing fire. In his opinion, turning a rifle into an automatic weapon was a mistake. Perhaps he was wrong. He was, after all, getting old.

Still, he'd left the rifle in semiautomatic mode. Twenty rounds without working a bolt still seemed to him like incredible firepower.

His hearing was still acute despite his ears ringing from the barrage the Russian and his men had laid down. Judging his targets by the sounds outside and moving down the hall, he raised the rifle to his shoulder, aimed, and squeezed the trigger twice.

Behind him, Dante half-sprang to his feet before shaking his head and returning to his work on Jubal. "Jesus Christ, what are you doing? You scared the shit out of me!"

Gage ignored him, but he hoped Dante hadn't been startled badly enough to make a mistake in his attempt to stabilize Jubal's condition. He focused on the two smoking holes he'd blown in the wall.

Outside, their adversaries barked in Russian, and feet *thumped* away from the portion of the wall he'd shot through. He'd failed to hit any of them with his attempt at blind fire, but he'd scared them enough to grant himself extra time to act.

He changed his mind about full auto. A glance at the rifle found the selector switch. He unloaded the rest of his magazine into the wall, praying that the rounds wouldn't travel far enough to hit any bystanders. He was pretty sure that everyone else had evacuated the building once the shooting started, anyway.

The gun roared, and its muzzle tried to climb in his hands, but he mostly held it down. His accuracy would've been poor if he'd tried to hit something specific. In this case, he only sought to drive the enemy back, to scare them away from the room so he, or possibly Dante, could mount an effective counterattack. A wild patchwork of smoking holes opened in the material between him and the hallway beyond, and the Russians cried out in alarm.

It seemed he wasn't the only one who realized they couldn't simply hide in this room.

"Go," Jubal gasped. "Go fight those bastards. I will be fine for a minute. I think."

Dante looked at him sharply. Then he stood. "Keep that rag on your wound and try not to move. Your lung isn't collapsing yet, but it might, and if it does, we're going to have serious problems. Right now, you need to stop the bleeding first and foremost."

Then, sucking in his breath, the physician took his shotgun in both hands and looked at Gage.

The Nepali had ejected his empty magazine and fumbled a new one into the well. His experience with box magazines on submachine guns meant that he understood the basic principle although the AR-10's specifics were new.

His eyes and Dante's locked. Gage nodded at one of the larger holes he'd shot in the wall. Then he looked at Dante and flicked his gaze toward the door. Outside, their enemies were regrouping and advancing again. Gage's volley probably hadn't hit any of them.

Dante nodded. He leapt toward the door at the same instant that Gage sprang forward and brought the barrel of his rifle to rest within the jagged opening in the wall. A man moved into his field of vision, but the thug saw him simultaneously and jumped back before Gage could fire.

Dante flung open the door and unloaded with two shells from his shotgun, his hand working the pump with surprisingly expert dexterity and ejecting the empty casings between shots. The blasts stopped the Soviets from returning fire...yet. Gage heard them rolling aside or hitting the floor, and they took a couple of random potshots in return. One blew a chunk out of the doorframe.

As the pair retreated into the room, with Dante adding fresh shells into his Ithaca to top it off, the potshots turned into a barrage.

"Down!" Dante shouted. Gage had already flattened himself on the floor. Automatic weapons thundered outside, and the wall and door gained still more new perforations.

Once the worst of it subsided, Gage ran his hands over his body, limbs, neck, and face to check for wounds. In the heat of battle, it was surprisingly easy to take a bullet and not even realize it at first. It had happened to him twice in the war.

Satisfied that he was unharmed, he glanced at Dante, who appeared to have been grazed across the thigh but was otherwise fine.

Jubal, on the other hand, was on the verge of losing consciousness, and his deep golden skin was taking on a distinctly grayish pallor. Dante hesitated, uncertain if he should stay in the fight or return to working on the young man.

Gage waved. "I will hold them off. Keep Jubal alive. We must either try to escape or defeat them all. We cannot stay here long." Outside, the Russians were once again advancing up the hall. A short burst of gunfire accompanied each person to keep their adversaries from stopping them.

Inhaling deeply, Gage crawled the short distance across the floor to the half-shattered door. It was shut but not latched. Still lying on his belly, he grabbed the lower edge and flung it open, aiming his rifle from the prone position and opening fire at once, now back in semi-auto.

A scrawny, unshaven Russian had been crouch-walking along the balustrade to get a bead on the doorway. He had one, but his weapon, an AK-47 rifle, had jammed. His eyes bulged in horror as Gage aimed at him. "*Nyet!*" he exclaimed.

Gage fired twice. Both rounds cut through the man's forward arm and into his chest, blowing red holes out his back and sending him rolling across the floor, dead by the time he came to a stop.

Then Gage pivoted, aiming his rifle down the hallway toward where the others should be. One was advancing down the other side of the corridor, hugging the wall where the doors to the other rooms lay. As soon as he saw Gage readjust his position, he knocked down the door to the adjacent room and disappeared into it.

That was bad. The man could simply fire at random through

the wall and potentially kill Dante and finish off Jubal. There were still three others to consider, as well.

It looked as though the bearded giant, as well as one of his other henchmen, had retreated to the staircase, taking up positions a few steps down from the landing to benefit from the added cover. Gage couldn't tell where the last man had gone. He might've fled to gather any reinforcements waiting outside. There was no way to be sure...so far.

Gage fired two shots through the door of the adjacent room, then three more toward the other men crouched beneath the stair landing. Then he flipped over and rolled back into the room as they returned fire.

Dante had laid his shotgun on the bed beside him and was trying to get Jubal to dry-swallow a couple of pills while he filled a small syringe with some kind of fluid from his medkit. Once Jubal managed to gulp down the painkillers, coughing and half-choking on them, he retained his hold of the needle in his left hand while drawing his 1911 pistol with his right.

Gage said to him, in a loud whisper, "There is one man in the room next door. It sounds like he's moving around. Is there some other way into these rooms? From the other side?"

Discouragingly, Dante reacted to the question by jerking in alarm. He almost lost his grip on his syringe. "Yeah. There's a sliding glass door in the back that leads out onto a balcony. All the rooms on this side of the second and third floors have them. The exhibitionist types like to go out there and cavort in the open air, hoping someone sees them. Now that you mention it, the distance between balconies isn't much."

He plunged the needle into Jubal's arm and injected the contents. Gage was pretty sure it was some kind of fluid replacement for all the blood the boy had lost. Then, before Gage could offer to check out the balcony himself, Dante tossed the needle aside, snatched up his Ithaca, and ran toward the rear of the chamber.

"I'll deal with it," the physician shouted. "Hold them off from this end!"

Gage muttered to himself and exchanged his half-spent magazine for a fresh one, turned back toward the door, and fired three shots through or around it when it seemed their attackers were about to try storming the room again.

CHAPTER NINE

Dante cleared the room in two seconds. Jubal had a dressing screen set up beyond the bed that hid the back door from sight. It was probably why it hadn't occurred to Gage or him that the goons might attempt a different approach.

He knocked the screen aside with the butt of his gun and heaved the sliding door open with his left hand. The balcony beyond was about ten feet by five feet and contained two divans and a small glass table, as well as an umbrella to ward off Atlantica's frequent rain. He looked left.

Sure enough, one of their foes had made his way through the neighboring room to the adjacent balcony and was preparing to leap the short distance across—it was about a yard and a half, far enough to give a man pause if he was in poor condition, but nothing too massive.

The man in question was a lean and sprightly Turkish-looking guy, probably from one of the Central Asian republics within the USSR. He'd slung his AK back over his shoulder and was crouched to spring. A knife was out in his hand.

"No. No, you don't." Dante raised the shotgun as the man jumped.

The Ithaca roared, spewing flames as it discharged its payload of double-aught buckshot and rocked back in Dante's firm grip. The blast hit the enemy square in the torso while he was airborne. The vicious grin on his face transformed instantly to a contorted expression of fear and alarm, and he squawked horribly, thrashing as he sailed across the short gap.

Being shot with eight or nine simultaneous projectiles ruined not only the man's jump but his entire life. He flailed uselessly and crashed into the side of Jubal's balcony, toppled back into the void between rooms, and hurtled down to *crunch* loudly against the pavement three stories below. There were no pedestrians around—everyone must've heard all the shooting and headed for the hills.

Dante allowed himself a split second of grim satisfaction at having so thoroughly destroyed his enemy. Then his mind fogged over and grew sticky and tangled. Too many things were happening at once.

He had to check on Jubal. He had to help Gage secure the front against the other three attackers. He had to make sure one or more of them didn't come out onto the balconies again and try the same thing as the Turkish guy. He had no idea which he should do first.

There was no time. He needed to make a decision *now*. The shooting had started again within the building.

"Fuck," he rasped and took a couple of hopping steps back toward the sliding door. Stopping there, he looked into the room to see how Gage and Jubal were doing, hoping he would be able to keep an eye on the neighboring balcony at the same time.

Jubal was half-sprawled on the bed and still breathing, at least. More holes were opening in the walls as peals of gunfire echoed out of the brothel and into the city, and Gage was attempting to return fire more or less blindly. He still lay prone on the floor. Dante wondered if—

He jerked his head aside and bent halfway over backward as

though playing limbo. His inattention had nearly led to his death, but his instincts and reflexes had saved him.

Another of the assailants had burst onto the next door balcony, armed with a pair of Tokarev pistols he fired in unison at Dante's head and throat. The bullets sailed past and over, one coming close enough to rustle his hair.

As he struggled to regain his position and raise his shotgun, he lost balance, and another pair of shots from the Russian blew off chunks of building materials from the wall next to him and raised a cloud of concrete dust, all of which flew directly into his face.

He expected to die. It made sense that this was the end, that his opponent had got the drop on him, combined with a little luck, and that the Tokarevs would blow his head off. If he was fortunate, the Russian might shoot him in the torso, and his armor would give him another chance.

Neither of those possibilities was what happened.

The nondescript man on the other balcony dropped his pistols and leapt across the space. He landed hard and stumbled into one of Jubal's divans, which scraped and crashed aside. Then while trying to find his footing, he unslung a PPS-43 submachine gun like the one used by the group's hulking leader, which presumably he would use to murder Dante, Jubal, and Gage.

Dante still was half-blinded by the debris in his eyes, but he could see enough. Growling without forming words, he charged forward, his shoulder out, and bowled straight into the Russian.

His enemy cursed in his native language and stumbled back against the rear balustrade. Dante moved forward again, raising his shotgun, about to fire and send the man over the edge to join his comrade. The man was faster than Dante would've guessed. His foot lashed out in a solid front kick that knocked the Ithaca from the physician's grasp. It landed on the table, then *clattered* to the floor and skidded back toward the glass door.

Then there was nothing but impacts, force, and flashes of

chaos. The material of the Russian's coat intermingled with glimpses of the walls and the gloomy sky as the two men grappled and tussled. Gage was still trying to hold off the last two assassins from within the room. His rifle *cracked* every second or two.

Dante's hands madly sought something to grab, something on the man he could hurt. His eyes were full of tears from the dust, and his vision was only half-functional. The Russian was slightly smaller than he was, but he possessed a lean and frantic strength. He was gradually pinning Dante to the floor, where he could crush his throat, cave in his skull, or simply shoot him.

Dante felt what had to be the man's thigh. From there, he punched him hard in the groin. As the man grunted and doubled over, Dante surged forward and up with his whole upper body, tossing the Russian off him and freeing both his arms.

His hand went to his belt and found the hilt of his baton. He pulled it free. Not as good as a gun...but it would do. And his vision was mostly back.

The Russkie stood straight and fell into a boxing stance. He'd dropped his gun at some point in the commotion, but Dante didn't know where it was. He didn't appear to have a melee weapon. He was near the rear corner of the balcony. Dante had managed to remain near the door, blocking the man.

"Now you will die." The man spoke in a thick Slavic accent. A small knife appeared in his hand, probably from somewhere in his sleeve.

Dante frowned and drove the baton forward into the man's armpit, taking him by surprise. He dropped the knife as his face contorted in pain.

"No," Dante snapped. "Because I'm a fucking doctor and saving lives, especially mine, is what I *do*."

The Russian tried to twist away, but Dante struck him over and over again with thrusts from the truncheon. He drove it mercilessly into nerve centers and targeted muscle groups, anywhere he could find where it would cause the most pain, damage, and incapacitation. Within two seconds, the Russian was on his knees, paralyzed with locked up muscles and general agony.

Dante raised the baton and brought it down in a lateral roundhouse stroke against the side of the man's head. It made a *thunking* sound, and the Russian collapsed—unconscious at the least, maybe even dead.

"Yeah," Dante muttered. He retrieved his shotgun, glanced at the adjacent balcony for any more unwanted visitors, and plunged through the sliding door back into Jubal's room.

CHAPTER TEN

Gage struggled to hold off the remaining attackers. He'd sprung up into a kneeling position beside the bed, making himself into a bigger target for the sake of having more freedom of movement and a better vantage from which to shoot. The last two Russians seized the opportunity created by their diversion on the outdoor balconies. They advanced on Jubal's room in a tight and aggressive pattern, each supporting the other with a short burst of gunfire while the other dashed forward a few steps, then repeated it.

Gage could tell what they were doing, but, at first, he couldn't see them. He certainly appreciated the large magazine capacity of his new rifle. Still, with how difficult it was to hit his enemies from within a room, he would rather have had eighty rounds than twenty.

By the time a pair of legs became visible through the many holes in the wall, someone was able to fire a burst of three or four shots that came dangerously close to perforating Gage's groin and legs. They splintered the wood floor beneath the carpet. He leapt to his feet in time to see the door crash open and the last of the four henchmen charging into the room, his rifle shouldered.

Gage shot him. Two times, then three. The .308 bullets blasted clear through him and created a vast spray pattern of crimson droplets behind him that glistened in the bright light of the central area.

The man didn't fall. He seized up, stumbled, and his rifle's barrel swept aside as his arm started to fail, but the gun went off all the same, spewing rounds into the floor and side. He still came. He stepped into the room, using his other hand to pull the rifle up toward Gage's face, determined to squeeze off a killing shot before expiring himself.

Gage pulled the trigger again and heard only a click. Then pure instinct took over.

Screaming enough that his voice went hoarse at once, Gage dropped the rifle so it dangled by his side from its sling and, in the same motion, drew one of his kukris and charged the Russian. There was no time for a carefully chosen strike. There was only the mad rush to hack into him, to cut him down by any means necessary, before the AK-47 was level enough to kill.

The blade flashed down. It clove through the Russian's chin and jaw and buried itself in his chest, shearing his collarbone in two, splitting ribs and sternum, severing the lower windpipe and the artery beside the heart.

The man fell at last. The light went out in his eyes a third of a second before his rifle could take Gage's head off. The kukri stuck in his chest, pulling Gage's hand down as his body tumbled. He yanked up but couldn't free it. So he let it go.

As the kukri left his hand, the entire space in front of him where the dying Russian had stood filled up. A figure blotted out the light. The gigantic man Gage had nearly killed earlier was the only one left.

Gage went for his rifle. The huge Russian snarled and kicked it aside as though it were a twig, and the force of the sling dragging against his arm nearly dislocated Gage's shoulder. Then one of the massive hands smashed into his chest in a chopping motion, knocking him straight back so he fell to the floor. His head struck the edge of the bedframe.

His vision blurred, but in the clearer instants, he saw the ugly, mutilated face twist into a savage smile, heedless of the pain it must have caused the man after what Gage's knife had done to him previously.

The giant raised his submachine gun, the barrel's mouth opening right in front of Gage's face. "*Suka,*" he grunted.

A door opened behind them, and a shotgun roared. The huge man fell back, bellowed like an angry bull. The gun dropped from his grasp as buckshot slammed into his armored vest. It didn't appear to penetrate, but it hit hard enough to stun him, driving him back a step.

Dante snarled, "Fuck off!" as he advanced, pumping the Ithaca and firing again, then again. The giant stumbled back, out through the ruined door and into the hallway, while Dante moved forward and blasted away.

Gage pulled himself up into a sitting position, ready to spring to his feet if need be, as he watched. The Russian thrashed in pain. Some of the pellets tore into his limbs and hip area, but mostly Dante was unloading shells straight into the man's chest in a blind rage. Each shot drove the Russian farther back toward the railing that overlooked the first-floor lobby.

The shotgun clicked. Dante stopped, dumbfounded, about two paces from the door. Their last opponent was still alive.

Gage jumped up. Again he let out his high-pitched, ragged war cry, and with all rational thought pushed out of his head, charged straight at the stunned assassin.

Dante stammered, "Hey! What are you doing, pal?"

Gage couldn't hear him. He plunged straight toward his enemy, focused solely on him, crossing the hallway in what seemed like a single bound.

The colossal man's back had struck the railing, and he'd begun to arch backward over it, unable to get his bearings after being pummeled with half a dozen 12-gauge shells. That made Gage's task a little easier.

Operating on pure adrenaline, the small Gurkha seized the giant's legs beneath the knees and somehow lifted them. By the time the Russian realized what was happening, he was already pitching over the edge, his enormous weight dragging him into the void.

The man bellowed again as he fell. He crashed into one of the decorative pillars and scraped against it for a second, then plummeted the rest of the way to the lobby floor next to the fountain. A *thud* rose, the impact practically shaking the floor, and everything fell silent.

Gage turned back toward Dante, gasping, wheezing, and shuddering. His friend stood in what remained of the doorframe, mouth slack and shotgun hanging from his right hand. Then he started to laugh.

"Ha, ha—holy shit. We *did* that. What are the odds, pal? Ha!"

Gage managed a weary, nervous smile. He wasn't sure he wanted to know the odds. They'd probably been slim. Still, the two of them had pulled through. Gage walked back across the open hallway.

Then Dante abruptly stopped laughing. "Oh, Jubal. Damn." He turned and hustled back into the room with Gage in tow.

Jubal was still breathing, but he'd finally passed out. He didn't look appreciably worse than he had a couple of minutes ago, but he looked no better, either. The bullet had created a nasty mess.

Dante observed, "He's lucky to be alive, but luck alone isn't going to save him at this point. Help me get him up. We need to get to a hospital with proper facilities. I don't have enough stuff on me to treat an injury of this magnitude."

Gage nodded, asking no questions. The two men carefully lifted the young man, bearing him between them by the shoulders, and trudged out into the hall. When they reached the landing on the stairs and passed close to the railing, both stopped in their tracks.

Below them on the lobby floor near the decorative column and fountain, there was no one. No broken, lifeless body. Nothing indicated that a seven-foot-tall man had fallen three stories to that very spot.

"Oh." Gage sighed. "That is...bad."

Dante stared, awestruck enough that he momentarily forgot his haste to help Jubal. "Who the hell *is* that guy?" he marveled. His face paled with almost superstitious dread. "Who, and *what?*"

CHAPTER ELEVEN

No one accosted Gage or Dante as they carried Jubal out of his place of employment, which doubled as his home. No one poked their head out a door or ran around a corner in a panic. Not a single soul was anywhere to be seen or heard. The staff and clientele had all fled once the shooting had started.

Unless some few of them were still hiding in their rooms. Gage had to pray that stray bullets hadn't injured anyone. He doubted it, but it was difficult to be sure, and they had no time to check the building thoroughly. He mentally noted that it was his responsibility to find someone else who could do so and clean up the worst of the mess.

Since the mess did *not* include the Russian colossus, it seemed relatively safe to assume that he would remain Gage's and Dante's problem. Gage kept his right arm free and held Jubal with his left. If their nemesis reappeared, he could draw his revolver or one of his kukris with speed and ease.

He was beginning to wonder if anything short of an artillery cannon could kill the hulking bastard. The skin on the back of Gage's neck crawled. His experience at the dig in the ancient ruins in the hills only a month and a half ago had made it abundantly clear that there were more things in heaven and earth than he could fully understand, scientist though he was.

As they crossed the ground floor lobby and made for the front exit, Dante flicked his gaze to the side, catching Gage's eyes. "Do you know where Atlantica General is? It's our only viable option for medical care since there aren't any other non-exclusive hospitals on the island with the facilities we need. Everything else is either an elite clinic or operating theater set up for the usual select group of wealthy clients. The peons mostly have to make do with homegrown medicine or the long waits at General."

Gage confessed, "I don't know where it is. It's somewhere in the middle of downtown, is it not?"

Gage racked his brain as his friend kicked open the door, exposing the gentle steps outside that led down to the pavement. The air was cool and damp, and the day's light was starting to fade.

"Yeah." Dante had to keep modulating his stride to match Gage's shorter legs so he didn't get ahead and pull too badly on Jubal's arm or shoulder in his haste. "A little southwest of dead center. So we can mostly head due west. You'll have to drive. Once we get into the truck, I'll need to keep an eye on Jubal. I can't remember all the street names, but I'll know them when I see them. Let me know once we get past 10th Street, okay?"

Gage agreed. He began repeating the street's designation in his head, fixating on its importance.

Laboriously and trying to be gentle despite their desperate urgency, the two men hustled across the pavement, moving around the corner of the faux temple toward the parking area. It occurred to Gage that the Autocutioner made for a highly visible and obvious target. It wasn't damaged in any obvious or noticeable way, but, he wondered, what if the Soviets had disabled it in some way? What if they had rigged it to explode when he turned the key in the ignition?

His gut clenched in half-nauseated horror at the idea. With

Jubal potentially dying in their arms, there was no time to find another way to cross the city. They would have to take the risk.

No. That was wrong. *He* would have to take the risk.

"Stop," he declared in a sharp, clear voice. Dante did stop, probably assuming that Gage had been overwhelmed with pain from one of his lesser injuries. "Wait here. Hold Jubal. I will start the truck by myself. If they tampered with it, it would not be right for you and Jubal to pay the price."

Dante stared at him bug-eyed, unable to think of anything to say on the spot. While he stood there holding the wounded young prostitute, Gage hastened across the rest of the lot, taking longer strides with his good leg to make up for the shorter hops of his bad left ankle.

He reached the vehicle, sucked in his breath, and opened the door, climbing into the driver's seat and brandishing the keys. After a second's hesitation, he decided that if this was the end, Dante was at least smart and capable enough to find other means of getting to the hospital without him. The thought was strangely comforting.

Gage put the key into the ignition and turned it. Nothing went wrong.

Gage exhaled, closed his eyes, and allowed himself two or three seconds of relief. Then he looked out the windshield and saw Dante gradually hauling Jubal the rest of the distance toward him.

Frowning, he clambered down, met the pair halfway, and aided them in getting to the vehicle. They lifted Jubal and carried him into the back, where they laid him down on a makeshift bed of canvas sacks with a rolled-up vest for a pillow.

Dante knelt with his eyes on the younger man. "Gage, I'm going to stay back here with him. Get us moving, and move fast —but try not to crash, all right?"

"Of course." Gage returned to the driver's seat, focused on

which route would take him due west as quickly as possible, and piloted the armored truck out of the lot and onto the street.

There wasn't much traffic. The entire neighborhood had turned into a virtual ghost town in response to the cacophony of violence at the brothel. Everyone had either fled or was lying low. Within an hour, though, Gage guessed that things would be bustling once again. Cities were strange like that.

However, after half a mile, the streets became crowded with other vehicles, noisy and chaotic. Something occurred to Gage—the Russians would likely trace them to Atlantica General with ease. Their hit squad had failed, but it seemed preposterous to assume they didn't have other agents waiting in the wings to finish the job.

"Dante," he called. Once his friend responded, he added, "They will send more men after us. We must have security at the hospital. I'll call Eleanor Cervantes. Please tell me anything else you can think of. If she can get it for us, she will."

The physician's only reply was, "Yeah, good idea. Nothing else comes to mind, though. Do it."

Since Dante was occupied with watching Jubal and intervening in case the young man's condition grew worse, Gage realized that he would have to drive and operate the radio simultaneously. The quirks and vagaries of operating a large truck were coming back to him quicker than he would've assumed, but still, with traffic growing thick and haste being of the utmost importance, it might prove difficult.

He glanced at the radio long enough to flick the "On" switch before finding the receiver by hand, unhooking it, and letting it hang loose with the microphone facing him. He would have to hope that Eleanor could hear him without him needing to grab it and hold it to his mouth.

As it turned out, his timing was impeccable. No sooner had he let the receiver hang than some idiot in a sports car zipped out from behind a tall building next to an intersection, completely ignoring the "Yield" sign that an enterprising businessman had put up to discourage traffic accidents next to his establishment.

Gage's breath hissed between his teeth as he stomped on the brake. Both hands clutched the steering wheel, veering sideways to increase the distance between his truck and the sports car's driver. Fortunately, the only other vehicle in the immediate area was a sedan that chugged along a few hundred meters behind him.

Both the sports car driver and the sedan's operator honked at him. Gage stabilized the truck's course, narrowly avoiding driving over the sidewalk as the truck fishtailed, then sped past the intersection. He gritted his teeth.

The radio crackled at the same instant that Dante exclaimed, "Hey! Watch it, pal. We don't need Jubal getting thrown against the wall back here."

"Yes, I'm sure," Gage grumbled. "We don't need him getting crushed in an accident, either."

Sighing and muttering, Dante admitted, "Good point. Be careful, okay?" Next to him, Jubal moaned in pain and delirium.

The fuzzy noise on the radio gave way to the voice of Eleanor Cervantes. "Hello, this is Eleanor. Is that you, Dr. Gurung?"

"It is," he replied, louder than he would've spoken normally. "Can you hear me? I cannot hold the microphone now." The receiver had begun rocking around and occasionally banging into the dashboard, which drew an extra crackle of static each time it happened.

There was an awkward pause, then Eleanor's voice stated, "Ah, yes, I can, but there is some interference. So unless you can improve your reception, I cannot promise that I will hear everything you say. Please, tell me how things are going. Do you need help? There are reports of a gunfight in the southeastern district."

"We have a wounded man with us." There was no time for polite formalities, so Gage stuck to relating the facts, and only the facts, as quickly as possible. "He's a friend of Dr. Costa's and has given us helpful information.

"The same people who tried to kill us the other day wounded him. We're taking him to Atlantica General Hospital for emergency care. However, we believe the assassins will try to strike again. We must have security people to guard him while he recovers, and Dante and I complete the investigation."

Ms. Cervantes responded with a low sound in her throat. "Mm. I will do what I can, but I don't think we have enough personnel to provide a full security detail for this man of yours, in addition to the people we have guarding Janet Feng. Additionally, the Executives and their assistants have many other things to worry about across the island. We're spread too thin right now. There's only so much we can do. Over."

Gage let out a sharp and grating breath, not bothering to hide his frustration and exasperation. Normally, he was more polite and restrained. The present circumstances weren't normal.

"There's no one at all? The Executives have completely run out of trustworthy people they can afford to pay? Over."

Dante had overheard and shouted, "We barely came out of that alive, and we were lucky. I got a feeling that guy's going to come back next time with even more heavy hitters. We need a fucking army if you want the truth. Hire anyone you can get."

Eleanor's tone was one of a level-headed adult trying to remain patient while explaining something to a youth. Gage found it mildly infuriating, but he forbade himself from overreacting.

"Executioner Gurung, and Dr. Costa. Money isn't a problem for our mutual benefactors. Time and trust *are*. We could hire random people off the streets, but would they be dependable? We could bring in more people we *can* trust from the mainland, but would they arrive in time?

"The ferry from Nova Scotia might take up to two days, and even a private plane could be several hours. However, let me see what I can do. We might have one or two good men available. Over."

Gage nodded, mostly to himself. "Thank you, Ms. Cervantes." It sounded like she would be a minute or two, so he glanced back at Dante after checking to see that the road was clear. "How is Jubal?"

Grimacing over the mostly-still body of their passenger, Dante opined, "He's doing about as well as could be expected, for someone with a bullet hole through his chest. He's holding on, but he could worsen at any minute, frankly. If he does, it had better happen at the hospital. If it happens while we're still in this damn truck... I don't know if I can save him."

That reminded Gage of something. "I believe we are almost to 10th Street."

"Good."

Before Dante could offer more, Eleanor came back. "Gurung? Yes, I can spare one man. Perhaps that doesn't sound like much, but he is skilled and loyal. You two will be there also, yes? The three of you, plus hospital security, should be able to protect your witness adequately. This is Atlantica, after all. Over."

By that, Gage understood she meant that even the lowliest security guards tended to be grizzled individuals who carried a significant amount of firepower. With nothing on the island technically illegal, people could only keep what they could defend with force or the threat of force.

Before Gage could accept Eleanor's offer, Dante shouted from the back. "What? *One* man? That isn't good enough, goddammit. Goliath is still out there, even if he has two broken arms and a dislocated hip or something. Based on what we saw, we'd be lucky if an entire *team* can slow that monster down!"

The volume of his voice echoed in the enclosed space, and it disturbed Jubal, who groaned and squirmed on his crude bed.

"Sorry," Dante muttered and put a hand on the young man's forehead.

Gage paused, searching for the right words to bridge the impasse between his partner and his benefactor. Both had legitimate views and raised good points. It came as a relief when Eleanor offered a proposition.

"Gurung, Costa. I understand your concern. Allow me to suggest that instead of splitting our limited resources between different areas, we simply have Ms. Feng moved to the hospital. That way, we can combine the security team watching her with the extra man I can send to Atlantica General, and they can all guard her and your witness at once. Over."

Gage still had his doubts, but up ahead he saw a building that looked like a hospital. He glanced back at Dante, who nodded and rapidly pointed out the fastest route to get to the emergency room.

Navigating two quick turns and pulling into the hospital's lot, Gage let out a ragged sigh. "Eleanor? Yes, although that's not a perfect option, it's the best one that seems to be available to us. Have Janet and the people watching her come here at once. We'll remain until they arrive. Over."

"Very well." Eleanor sounded a bit pleased with herself for coming up with a halfway decent solution. "I'll handle it immediately. Focus on keeping your man alive, and I'll take care of the rest. Over."

Dante muttered something, probably of a cynical or obscene nature, but Gage ignored it. "Thank you, Ms. Cervantes. I will call you again if I must. Out." He hung up the receiver and switched off the radio as the Autocutioner barreled into the nearest available spot by the E.R. entrance.

Once they ground to a stop, Dante immediately lifted Jubal and tried to move him toward the rear of the truck, on the presumable grounds that it would be easier to get him out that way than to shove him between the seats in front.

Realizing what he was doing, Gage climbed out the door and

locked up the truck, then hurried around to the rear. He opened the back gate as Dante and Jubal reached it.

"Here," Gage offered. "I can keep him upright while you help him down."

Dante swung Jubal's feet around to dangle over the edge. "Yeah, just don't twist him or anything. We don't want to aggravate the wound. I mostly stopped the bleeding, but it could tear back open without much effort."

It took them half a minute to get Jubal into a braced standing position on the ground. He was still mostly unconscious. Then, after Dante jumped down from the truck, they picked him up and held him horizontal between them, moving as fast as they could without the risk of dropping him or yanking him too hard from either end.

Dante's foot lashed out and pushed the double entrance doors open. A woman within sat behind a reception desk. She glanced at the battle-ravaged pair and the half-dead young man in their arms and pointed to the right, not bothering to ask questions.

Dante nodded. "Much appreciated. Call a doctor, or a couple of nurses, whoever's available. Gunshot wound."

The emergency room's lobby only had five people in it, and Gage estimated that none of them was in the same level of danger. Part of him felt faintly guilty for skipping past them, anyway, and bulling through the doors leading into the hospital proper to demand instant attention—but that was perhaps the only course of action that might save Jubal.

As they barged into the hallway beyond the lobby, another pair of doors opened to disclose three nurses, two women and one man, all of whom stopped in their tracks at the sight that confronted them.

The lead nurse's hand went reflexively to her upper chest and throat. "Oh my God. Is that a gunshot? Keep pressure on the bleeding!" She turned and shouted, "*Hey!* We need a gurney out here, *right now.*" She pushed back through the swinging double doors, waving wildly, while the other two nurses rushed forward.

Dante told them, "I'm a doctor. He's stabilized for now, but he needs immediate treatment. He took a rifle round through the chest. Broke a rib, damaged the lung but hasn't collapsed it yet, and I'm pretty sure there's some internal bleeding, although it looks like the bullet missed his heart and major arteries."

They reached out and gently took Jubal from the two men, nodding acknowledgment of all that Dante had said. Gage gathered that they were professionals. Despite Atlantica General being the supposed dumping ground for the poor, it seemed to have nonetheless been able to hire people who knew what they were doing.

The head nurse returned mere seconds later with a doctor, the two pushing a gurney between them. Dante sprang forward and helped them all lift Jubal into place. The young man was mostly unconscious again. His eyes fluttered open for a second or two as he shifted positions, then he winced in pain and passed out once more.

Gage watched as the medical professionals carted him off, babbling about technical things beyond his understanding. He'd learned some basic medicine over the years. It was hard not to, between fighting in a war and performing scientific investigations in far-flung corners of the globe. However, he lacked the advanced knowledge of people who saved lives for a living.

Dante started to go with the others beyond the swinging doors, but one of the nurses stopped him with a hand on his shoulder. "We'll take care of everything, Doctor. It looks like you need to rest and see to yourself and your friend in the meantime."

He stood there, baffled for a second, and the nurse ran off. Then he shrugged and turned. "I guess she's right," he said. "We got the shit kicked out of us back there, didn't we? I'm not used to sitting on the sidelines when someone needs saving."

Gage gave him what he hoped was a sympathetic smile.

"You've done much already, Dante. He probably wouldn't have survived this long without your care."

The tall physician let out a long, exhausted sigh. "Yeah. You're right. When he pulls through, I get half the credit. You get a sliver of it too since you stopped him from being blown away." His expression hardened. "We need to rest, but we can't rest too much. Have to stand watch 'til the other guys get here. Along with Janet."

"Yes," Gage conceded. "I don't think they'll try to kill us again so soon, however. That giant man couldn't have recovered so quickly. I'm sure the rest of the team will be here soon."

He wasn't so sure of that. Saying it out loud made him feel better. More importantly, it probably had the same effect on Dante.

The taller man drew a long, deep breath and let his eyes drift closed for a few seconds. "Okay. I think we're okay. For the time being." He opened his eyes again. "Let's go lean against the wall, hey?"

"That is a most excellent idea."

They let their bodies slump, staying within the hallway until someone specifically demanded that they sit in the lobby with everyone else. It might've been for the best that they didn't. The other patients might've been unnerved by the sight of the two bloodied, gun-toting men. One of whom furthermore wore the skull-and-sword insignia on his shoulders.

After they'd had a minute to rest, Dante looked down at Gage's feet. "All this excitement can't have been good for your ankle, bud. Want me to take a look at it?" He allowed himself to slide down the wall and fell into a sitting position on the floor.

Gage did likewise, going slower for the sake of his leg. "No, thank you. I believe it will be fine." He waved to disguise his uncertainty on the subject. "We both simply need to rest. There has been almost no relaxation for us since two days ago. Plus, we've taken more than a fair share of bruises and bumps. Simply being able to sit or lie down would be the best thing."

Dante shrugged. "Yeah, you might be right about that. As your physician, I *should* tell you to shut up and let me examine it anyway. Especially if Katakura will pound the crap out of me if it has another fracture or something. You know what? As a personal favor, I'm going to let it slide. For now."

Gage smiled again but said nothing. His friend mirrored the expression.

Then Dante's face grew serious once more. "Shit. We can't rest yet. The security team isn't here yet. We have to stand guard. Well, I can do the 'standing' part for the first hour or so. As long as you can shoot from a sitting position, you can stay where you are."

"Thank you." Gage felt for his rifle and determined that swinging it down into his hand would be easy. He also patted himself to ensure that he had at least one spare magazine still loaded with bullets. "Firing from the seated or prone position is preferable to firing while standing. However, it is better to have support, such as a bench rest. I will make do."

Dante chuckled. "I'm sure you will. You seem to be good at that."

CHAPTER TWELVE

Janet sat on the bench within the back of the truck, feeling alone, although there were three other men around her and another two up front. The vehicle rumbled and shook as it moved down the streets toward the general hospital in the city's southwestern district.

The men guarding her refused to tell her exactly what was happening. All they'd given was a vague promise that she would get to see Dr. Costa and Dr. Gurung again and that they would fill her in on the details when they arrived.

She knew—*knew*—something was wrong. That there had been a new development and not a good one. The already dangerous and chaotic situation had worsened, and they moved her to keep her protected from the growing threat. It was the only explanation that made any sense.

One of the guards, a British man named Jim Pelham, looked up at her and caught her eye. "Are you doing well, Miss Feng? We should arrive in about five minutes." He was generally the most polite of the security detail. The others weren't rude, but they weren't very sociable, either.

She inclined her head gently toward him so her bobbed hair

swayed a little in that direction. "Yes, thank you. I would like to know what has happened, though."

Pelham grimaced, but not without empathy. "I'm afraid they haven't told us all the details either. Only that we're all to relocate to Atlantica General for security reasons and that Executioner Gurung will fill us in on the rest."

Janet nodded again. It was odd to hear Gage Gurung, the kind and mild-mannered little man whom she'd spent weeks looking after during his convalescence, referred to now as an Executioner. Someone engaged in grim and bloody business, with authority over other armed and dangerous men.

Still, all this was happening for the sake of her safety. She looked forward to seeing Dante again.

The ride was supposedly almost over, but she wished there was a window to look out, rather than having to stare at the armored truck's metal walls and floor. Atlantica City was beautiful at night with its streetlamps and tall buildings glistening in the moonlight and starlight, at least on clear evenings. Even when cloudy as it often was, the dazzling display of modern progress had a certain grandeur to it.

Her parents had, by their accounts, come from a small village deep in the hills in Shanxi Province. She'd grown up on the outskirts of San Francisco and had always enjoyed visiting the city despite the hassles involved.

From the front seat, Senior Officer MacLeod, a doughty old Scotsman who ran most of the Executioners' auxiliary security operations, barked, "We're three minutes from site. Hospital staff say all is well so far. We're to meet Gurung and Costa in the emergency room lobby."

Nods went around the truck's rear compartment. Everyone was on edge and looked forward to having an actual building to sequester themselves.

They'd all heard about the shootout at the Temple of Aphrodite. The details hadn't yet unveiled themselves, but the general perception was that it had been a bloodbath. The entire neighborhood's populace had evacuated themselves or hid in their cellars with shotguns, baseball bats, knives, or whatever else they could use to defend their lives and homes.

Whoever was responsible for the violence, the buzz so far was that at least some of them had escaped into the streets. Although well protected, their armored truck was an obvious and tempting target.

It had been less than an hour ago when they'd received the calls. Janet had been reading and sipping tea, trying to relax. The men on guard were decent enough to mostly leave her alone, focusing on their job or joking among themselves.

The first call had been from MacLeod, warning them about the fiasco at the brothel. Then the phone rang again, mere seconds after Pelham had hung up. It was Eleanor Cervantes, instructing them to gather up Janet and relocate to the hospital. Minutes later, while Janet had struggled to control the sinking sensation of fear and despair that descended through her gut and seemed to have no bottom, they'd hustled out the front of the hotel.

The security team had sent two men out first to do recon before the other two brought Janet out. Then the armored truck had pulled up, driven by none other than MacLeod himself. He'd personally taken charge of the mission. The first thing he'd said, dispelling some of Janet's awful terror, was that Dante and Gage were still alive.

Janet's attention snapped back to the present. The truck turned and slowed. They'd probably arrived at Atlantica General. After it stopped, the team repeated their usual procedure of having two men head out on point, checking for threats and securing their perimeter, before the rest of the crew and Janet could emerge.

Pelham stood on the pavement as they opened the back doors. "All right, Miss Feng, it's safe to come out. On you go, then." He offered his hand, taking hers and helping her as she stepped down to the ground.

Officer MacLeod had gone ahead into the emergency room. The four men with him formed a column spanning the short distance between the vehicle and the doors. Janet walked into the lobby. MacLeod stood there talking to a stocky black man who wore the same blue clothes and black combat armor as the other security guards.

She glanced past them, looking for Dante and Gage, and saw neither of them. Her heart skipped a beat. There were a handful of patients waiting for treatment who cast lazy glances at the security officers and the young woman they escorted.

Janet walked up to MacLeod, hesitant to interrupt him but *needing* to know where her friends were.

"...originally going to be only me," the fifth guard said, "but then they said you guys and the woman would come to the hospital to make things easier since their personnel are stretched too thin across the island lately."

MacLeod gave a sharp nod, then turned to Janet. "Miss Feng, looks like we've got some extra help, then. This is Sergeant Simms. Now, let's find the good doctors."

The woman seated behind the reception desk pointed at an internal pair of double doors. "They had a man with them with a bad gunshot wound. They went through there and haven't come out. I guess the staff let them stay there while their friend gets his operation."

Janet sighed with relief. MacLeod thanked the receptionist, then went outside and brought two of his other men inside. The remaining pair, including Pelham, were to remain outdoors and patrol the building, keeping an eye out for any threats until further notice.

MacLeod and Simms went first through the doors to the interior hallway, with Janet behind them and the other two men in the rear. No sooner had the doors swung open than the two point men halted. Janet froze, fearing the worst.

"Oh." MacLeod grunted. "There you are. Why the hell weren't you two sitting out in the lobby like normal people? Bloody daft. I almost drew a gun on you."

Dante was standing, but barely. He leaned against the wall, his legs only half able to support his weight in his exhaustion. It looked as though he'd been about to use his shotgun as a crutch of sorts but then thought better of it.

Gage, on the other hand, sat in the corner, also braced against the wall, with his short legs splayed out. His ankle must have been hurting him again. Janet hoped he hadn't re-injured it.

Both men were still wearing their combat gear, and both looked as though they'd been in a war. Dust, dirt, and dried blood covered their skin and clothes, and they reeked of stale sweat, gunpowder, and blood. She could tell at once that both were wounded, but probably not too seriously.

Dante's eyes briefly flicked over Janet. Then he looked at MacLeod. "Yeah, yeah, Officer. Sorry about that, but we didn't want to scare the normal people out there. They didn't permit us to follow them into the operating room." He sniffed. "Even though I'm a doctor."

Gage smiled and added, "Yes, we've been standing watch this whole time. Or sitting watch, in my case. My ankle is somewhat sore. We were having a historical debate. So far, nothing bad has happened."

"Right," MacLeod acknowledged them. "I have five men here as promised. We'll scope out the situation. Could you debrief us on what happened? Gurung, we'll let you handle that. Dr. Costa, why don't you take care of the lady?"

Dante turned and looked into her eyes. "Of course. With pleasure. I'll take her out to the lobby."

Groaning as he forced himself to move again, Dante took a step forward, supporting his own body once more rather than relying upon the wall, and reached out to take Janet's hand. Before they left the hall though, he looked back over his shoulder at Gage.

"*Yes*, the construction of St. Peter's Basilica in Rome *was* the event that *really* kicked off the Protestant Reformation. It was the catalyst, bud. Some people couldn't handle that much beauty and talent, so they figured they'd bail on Catholicism and start their own more boring version of Christianity. That's how my dad always explained it, and frankly, I don't see or hear any other explanations that make sense."

Gage sighed. "You must always have the last word. Selling indulgences was what offended Martin Luther so much. It was the corruption, not the aesthetic extravagance. This is not to say that Luther was correct about everything, either. But—"

"Doc," MacLeod interrupted him, "or Executioner, beg your pardon. We have important matters to discuss."

Waving Dante off, Gage turned away to fill the senior officer in on the details of the situation. The other man, Simms, stood awkwardly near the doors leading back into the lobby, unsure who to remain with.

Dante ignored him for now and took Janet to a bench in the farthest corner of the E.R., where they could talk in relative privacy. He did a quick visual scan of the other patients. A mother with a child and a handful of older adults. *Probably* not anyone likely to be an informant for the Russians.

Still, how could he be sure?

Janet didn't ask questions yet. She burned with curiosity, and part of her was annoyed and resentful over the fact that everyone had kept her in the dark this whole time. They assumed that they didn't require her input. Still, she'd grasped that much of what happened were things that lay far outside her areas of expertise.

Dante had retained hold of her hand as they settled into their seats. His was dirty and rough but curiously comforting in the way he held her so firmly but with such gentle intent. "Janet. I'm sorry we couldn't tell you anything, but they advised us earlier to avoid divulging too much information over phone lines. Somebody could've tapped them. The same people who tried to kill us could be listening in."

She gave a slow nod. "I suppose that makes sense. I'm only glad that Officer MacLeod told me that you and Dr. Gurung had survived."

He laughed in a low, grim way, looking off into the distance. "It was close. I'll say that much. Damn, damn close. I took Gage out to the temple to see Jubal. Icarus. You remember him? I think I mentioned him before. He had a relationship with Pietr, one of the gunrunners I used to work for, so I thought he would have some information for us. He did, especially since Pietr stopped by to beat the shit out of him and demand his money." He shook his head.

"Oh, I'm sorry to hear that." Janet had never met Jubal, but it seemed that Dante had a lot of sympathy for him and was always trying to help him. Part of it was simply his Hippocratic Oath, of course. Still, it seemed to go beyond that. For all his cocky and cynical attitude at times, Janet had always believed that Dante was sincere in his desire to serve humankind through medicine.

"Anyway," Dante went on and told the rest of the story. He described the remainder of their conversation with the male prostitute, which was sad but productive since it had produced a lead—Pietr's brother Vlad, whoever he was.

Then he came to the part that she was desperately curious about but was almost afraid to hear. It turned out to be as bad as she'd imagined and worse.

"...and guess who was leading the bastards." Dante clenched his jaw. "Our old bud, the not-so-jolly, not-so-green giant. His face looked like someone stitched it back together with fucking piano wire after Gage split it open the other day." He blinked. "Sorry, you probably don't want to hear all that."

The mere mention of the huge man who'd stormed into the

cottage sent a wave of cold through her body. She went still and vaguely felt like throwing up but tried not to show it. That would've been embarrassing in front of Dante. Not to mention that giving in to her fear like that seemed like giving power to the man who inspired it.

Dante related how a firefight had broken out, with himself and Gage trying to protect Jubal and only half-succeeding. A stray bullet had slipped under Gage's arm, pierced the young man's side, and damaged his lung. Dante had struggled to keep him alive while Gurung blasted through the walls at the attackers and two of them had snuck around to the rear balconies. They'd nearly killed Dante until he'd been able to toss one to his death and kill or severely incapacitate the other.

Meanwhile, Gage had taken out the other two henchmen. When they came up against the towering leader, even multiple 12-gauge blasts to the torso and a three-story drop had failed to kill him.

Dante concluded, "I'm sorry to report that the hulking son of a bitch—uh, pardon my language—is still out there somewhere. I don't know. After how much damage he's taken, maybe he limped off into a dark hole and died of his wounds. Lucky breaks can happen, right?

"Still, until we know for sure, we have to assume that he'll come after us again. Next time he might have even more of his goddamn comrades with him or thugs he hires locally. It makes no difference. I'm not trying to scare you, Janet. I want you to be fully aware of the situation. We brought you here so the security team can watch over you and Jubal at the same time."

She looked at the floor, trying not to think too hard about what might happen if the monstrous Russian attacked the hospital with a small army of flunkies. "Yes, I understand. Thank you for trusting me enough to tell me everything. What happens next? Will you and Dr. Gurung—Gage—stay here? You need medical attention yourself, and so does he. I don't think it would be a good idea to go back out there and—"

Dante cut her off. "Good idea or no, we have to. We have to find that bastard. We need to find out what the Russians are doing on Atlantica and what it has to do with the people I used to run with. If not, they'll run roughshod over this whole island and turn it into another fucking Hungary or Mongolia or Cuba. We can't let that happen."

Or China, Janet thought. Her parents had been supporters of Chiang Kai-shek and the Kuomintang. They'd fled the country before the end of the war, once it seemed that Mao Zedong's victory was inevitable. Her views were...somewhat different than theirs. They had their reasons. It was useless to try to change the past.

"Dante, I understand. Still, why can't Tyler or Daria deal with it? You're not an Executioner. You're a doctor." She couldn't help admiring him for his ability to fight alongside a soldier like Gaje Gurung. She didn't want him to get himself killed, either.

It looked like he was about to answer her when the internal doors flew open and MacLeod strode out, making a beeline for them.

"Dr. Costa, Miss Feng. They say you can come in and sit in the waiting area outside the operating room. They've started on your boy and are taking care of him. Gurung's there. My men will keep an eye on the place. If there's any trouble, do as they say. I need to speak to the Execs about a few things, so if you have no objections, I'll take my leave."

Dante raised a hand and flourished it. "I think we'll be all right, Officer. The more men we have here, the better, but seven guys with guns isn't too shabby. Thanks for all you've done. Keep in touch."

MacLeod grunted a response that Janet couldn't really understand under the man's Scottish accent, then he turned and marched out the door. A moment later, the armored vehicle pulled away.

Dante frowned. "I didn't realize he meant he'd be taking the truck. Well, we still have Gage's 'Autocutioner,' as they call it. That thing would make a nice getaway vehicle. Heh, heh. Let's see how Jubal is doing. I'm curious if the scrubs they employ here are doing the job right."

Groaning a little, he hauled himself to his feet, and Janet stood beside him. She could tell that he was profoundly fatigued. A kind of strange, wired energy animated him when he had something to focus on, but his body was in dire need of rest, and his mind wasn't far behind. She hoped he didn't plan to do anything as stupid as to try to go after the Russians tonight.

A nurse met them on the other side of the interior hallway. "Hello. Follow me, please." She beckoned and turned, her white shoes *squeaking* on the floor tiles. She led them to a broad dead-end hallway between two rooms.

"Your friend is undergoing his operation in there. Please, don't disturb them. They need absolute concentration. He was pulling through last I heard, though. We'll update you on how things progress."

"Good," Dante quipped. "Jubal is tougher than you might think. He was in a fight before he got shot. You probably noticed how bruised and battered he was."

The nurse made a sour face. "Yes, that concerned us, but not as much as the gunshot wound. Oh, there's your other friend, the little Indian man."

"Nepali," Dante corrected her. "Yeah, good, I wondered what he'd got up to. About what I figured."

Rather than sit in one of the available chairs, Gage had sprawled out on the floor and was snoring in a deep, steady cadence. There was a definite peacefulness about the whole thing. Janet envied him, in a way, and she suspected Dante did as well.

Her day had been far less eventful than theirs. The long hours of worry still ate away at her and made the passage of time feel more taxing than it was.

Dante settled into one of the chairs and pushed another out to Janet, who accepted it and slowly lowered herself into the seat. She glanced past the tall physician's shoulder, through the glass window into an empty room with several open hospital beds.

"No one is in there," she observed. "Dr. Costa. Maybe you should sleep? I don't think they would object to you taking a hospital bed. It would be more comfortable than the floor." Not that Gage seemed to mind.

Dante shook his head. "No, there's no time for that. We can spare a few hours to rest a little and make sure Jubal's going to make it, but that's all. With that monster still out there and probably planning to strike again soon, we need to get on this case as soon as possible.

"Gage and I have to find this Vlad guy. It's our only lead, so basically our only hope." He seemed about to say more but yawned instead.

"How do you know that anyone else knows about this man?" Janet protested. "It's not as though *everyone* is looking for him. The city isn't too big yet. He won't be going anywhere, will he? You almost died. Please, Dante, get some sleep. Gage has done the smart thing."

Dante waved in defiance, but there was a noticeably feeble, flagging quality to it, like a machine with an almost drained battery.

"No. No, there isn't time." Judging by the way he slurred his words, he was on the verge of delirium with sheer fatigue. "Pietr. He's our only hope. If he gets the money he needs from his cousin, he'll be able to flee Atlantica. Then everything falls apart. No leads, no way to find out what the Russians are up to. We don't..."

As his voice trailed off, Janet tried to get comfortable on the narrow wooden chair with its cheap cushion but never quite succeeded. It felt as though each time she shifted her posture, she noticed some other flaw in the chair's construction. A minor thing that she might've been able to ignore otherwise now seemed unbearable.

She stood instead, took Dante's arm, and tugged on it. He rose beside her, surprisingly, offering as little resistance as if he was a child and she was his minder. She guided him into the adjacent room with its fresh and welcome line of beds.

"Sshhh, Doctor." She planted a kiss on his mouth, which caused his eyes to drift all the way open in surprise before they sagged shut once more. She gave him a gentle push and he more or less toppled over, catching himself with one arm, but still ending up on the mattress where he should've been. She allowed herself to fall beside him.

Dante's head shook weakly again. His eyes were mostly closed. "Can't stop... He's still...still out there."

Janet ran her fingers through his dark hair and over his brow. "Rest now, Dr. Costa," she whispered in his ear. "Lie here with me for a little while. Only a few minutes."

"Okay." His voice was barely more than a halfhearted sigh by this point. "Just a...little bit. Little..."

He drifted off to sleep, his head resting in Janet's lap. She stayed where she was, holding him.

CHAPTER THIRTEEN

Dante was helping his father tend the counter at the flower shop. Except that his father had been dead for four years. And he was a grown man now.

"This has to be a dream." His voice sounded the way it had thirteen or fourteen years ago.

His father turned toward him with a critical squint, his big mustache bristling, his jowls turning pink as they often did for no particular reason. "Finish wiping down the counter, Dante. The game doesn't start for an hour. You can work until then."

His friends were playing baseball at six, as they always did during the summer. By then, the humid heat that always seemed to grip New York through its warmer months would begin to slack off as the sun sank toward the horizon, and sometimes, if they were lucky, the fire department would come by and open up a hydrant for the kids to play in the resulting stream of water.

This had to be a dream, though. Nonetheless, Dante got back to work.

He was halfway done cleaning the counter when the door opened, and the little bell rang. When he looked up, the flowers were wilting, and the light from outside dimmed since the man who forced his way through the door was so big that he blotted out the sun.

Then it seemed that everything was moving slow, too slow to be real, and far too slowly to accomplish anything in time. His father sensed danger at once and reached under the counter to grab the double-barreled shotgun he kept there, his thick fingers fumbling on the stock.

Time had not slowed down for the intruder, who was little more than a huge dark mass raising a World War Two-era Russian submachine gun in one massive fist.

Dante's eyes flew open and his hands clenched in the air. He gasped, staring up at the blank white ceiling, noticing the blank white walls around him, feeling the bright lights shining into his eyes and the soft bed below his body.

"Okay." He breathed, then gulped. "Okay. Yeah. I was right. Just a fucking dream." Beads of sweat lined his brow. He wiped them off, then sat up, groaning. He'd passed out while still wearing his armor and all his gear. Someone had at least taken off his boots and removed the shotgun from his shoulder, leaning it against the bedframe beside him.

Someone else was coming into the room. It was a clean room in a hospital. Atlantica General, he recalled. He remembered most of what had happened, but his memory fuzzed out when he tried to recall how he'd ended up in these particular quarters. The last thing that was clear in his mind was following a nurse into the back area of the hospital and hearing that Jubal was doing well.

The people who came in were a nurse and an orderly, pushing a gurney on which none other than Jubal himself lay. Dante's eyes fixed on the young man. He was unconscious, but the proper color was coming back to him, and his chest and stomach rose and fell a little every three or four seconds.

The nurse, the same one who'd convinced him to stay behind when they'd first handed Jubal over, noticed him. "Good morning, Dr. Costa. We're glad you got some rest. Jubal made it this far. Dr. Harlin will be here in a minute to discuss things with you. Would you like some coffee?"

Dante opened his mouth and found it gummed up as though he'd been drinking last night. Once he cleared it, he said, "Yes, please."

The nurse and the orderly carefully moved Jubal onto an empty bed, two down from the one Dante had passed out on, which was the closest to the wall. Then they excused themselves, with the nurse promising to bring coffee in a minute or two. Dante nodded his thanks and wondered if he should try standing yet.

Then, squeezing around the departing nurse, in came the doctor, presumably Harlin. He was engaged in conversation with someone behind him, who turned out to be Gage.

"...settle with your employers promptly, I'm sure. We're accustomed to billing our patients after the fact and having to wait to get paid, particularly since our funding is largely from a handful of wealthy philanthropists."

The doctor, a tall but hunch-shouldered man with thinning gray hair not unlike Gage's, turned and saw Dante sitting up and looking at him. "Ah, Dr. Costa, you're up. Let me have a look at the patient, and we'll talk."

"Good," Dante quipped. "Gage, how are you doing? Also, how the hell long was I asleep? I don't remember coming into this room, or passing out here, or much of anything."

A trace of memory wiggled around in his brain, something he *should* have recalled but didn't, trying to make itself felt, seen, and heard. He struggled to perceive what it was.

Then, as though the hidden memory had stimulated something else within his mind, he realized that Janet was nowhere in sight.

He sprang to his feet, his limbs stiff and his head swimming with dizziness. "Where's Janet? Is she all right?"

Gage held up a hand. "Yes, she's fine. She has gone to get us food, is all. The security men are still with her, and everything has been peaceful. I'm not sure when you fell asleep, but it's now eight-thirty in the morning. So you were probably out for at least ten hours, perhaps longer."

Dante rubbed his eyes. He wanted to rush out of the room and look for Janet himself, to be certain she was safe. But he trusted Gage's word.

Dr. Harlin examined Jubal briefly and turned back to the pair, his hands in his pockets.

"Well, it was a rough surgery. The bullet lodged under his opposite shoulder blade. He was lucky that it missed his other lung, heart, and spine, but it still did a fair amount of damage. We managed to remove it. I expect him to make a full recovery, but he will be bedridden for quite some time. You did a good job of stabilizing him, Doctor. Without your on-the-spot care, he probably would've lost too much blood or gone too deeply into shock."

Dante exhaled. "Yeah, thanks, don't mention it. It seems like Atlantica General has good staff, after all. No offense, but I've heard people say that the best people go to private clinics. You know how it is here. Money is everything."

The older physician's face fell into a deep frown. "I do know. Still, someone has to treat the general populace, and as long as the place is supported, I'm willing to be one of the ones who do. Although between you and me, I had a drinking problem. Back in Canada. I cleaned up since then, but my reputation might not have recovered if I'd stayed home."

Dante grinned. "I used to have an organized crime problem. Atlantica is truly a land of new beginnings, isn't it?"

Harlin waved and pivoted toward the door. "It is that. Well, I have other patients to attend to, and I need some sleep myself.. finally. The rest of the staff will be able to see to whatever you need in the meantime. Also, please tell those security men to do as the nurses say. There's been a bit of a territorial struggle between our staff wanting privacy to do their jobs and your guys wanting to prowl around everywhere to sniff out threats."

Gage reassured the doctor that they would talk to the officers about respecting the hospital's boundaries, and the aging man left them behind.

Dante patted himself down, ensuring that all his gear was still in place. It all seemed to be. "One nice thing about this damn island is that nobody thinks twice if you bring a gun with you everywhere." He pulled his 1911 from its holster and did a quick brass check.

His friend nodded. "It's strange and sometimes disconcerting. Still, people must be able to protect themselves." As though inspired by Dante's fastidiousness, he drew his Webley revolver and checked to ensure it was full before reholstering it.

Dante wondered when Janet would be back. He wanted to double-check the exact procedures the security guys were using. They had to be sleeping in shifts, which meant there probably weren't more than three of them on active duty at any given time. He trusted MacLeod's and Eleanor's judgment, but the guys assigned to them were only human.

Their colossal nemesis, though...Dante wasn't so sure about him.

Footsteps approached, at least two pairs. Then the door opened and Janet walked in, dressed casually and carrying a big tray. Two plates piled high with mostly breakfast fare were on it.

"Good morning," she greeted them. "Dr. Costa, a nurse said she was bringing you coffee, and I intercepted it. So there is an extra cup of tea here if anyone wants it."

Behind her was one of the security guards, his rifle slung at low ready, safety on, and his eyes reassuringly bright and vigilant.

Dante smiled. "Morning, Janet. Why don't you have the extra tea yourself? Or offer it to that gentleman. I'll have the coffee, and I assume the other tea is for Gage, right?"

As the smell of food wafted throughout the room and reached his nostrils, he realized how incredibly hungry he was. He'd eaten nothing since a light lunch yesterday. No dinner, even after the strain of everything he'd done all afternoon and evening.

Gage raised a hand. "Yes, I'll have a cup of tea, thank you very much."

Janet set the tray down on a folding stand, and each man took a plate, along with forks, knives, and a napkin. Scrambled eggs, sausage, fried tomatoes, and toast with fruit preserves stared back at them, and Dante found it hard not to drool. He forgot to request salt or pepper for the eggs and dug in, seemingly vaporizing half of the repast in the space of a minute or two.

Washing it down with coffee and looking up, he saw that Gage had eaten his meal nearly as fast. Both of them were in definite need of refueling.

"Oh, my," Janet remarked. "I think I might have to get each of you a second helping. Perhaps you should finish your plates first and let the food settle."

Through a mouthful of bread and preserves, Dante mumbled, "Sure. Sit and drink your tea."

Janet did so at the foot of Dante's bed. She offered the cup to the guard, who shook his head, then she sipped.

"Hey," Dante called. "Did you eat anything yet, pal? Don't want the guys protecting us working on an empty stomach."

"I'm good. Had breakfast a little over an hour ago. A *light* breakfast. You can't fight on too full a stomach, either." He was a fairly beefy man so Dante suspected he ate well when off-duty, but he had a point.

Gage swallowed a mouthful of food. "Yes, this is true. During the war, we ate only small rations before a battle. Some men tried to do the opposite, thinking it might be their last meal. It's easier to move quickly when not weighed down with a great deal of food. Plus, stomach wounds are more serious when a man has eaten recently. Although..." he let the thought trail off and dug back in, clearing his plate.

Dante shrugged. In the back of his mind, the knowledge that they *should* be charging out the door to find Pietr, Vlad, and the towering Russian, continued to gnaw at him. Realistically, it would be an hour or more before they could begin the hunt. They had time to digest a nice big meal. Or two.

Once both men finished, Janet stood and collected their plates. "Yes, I think you both need another helping. You didn't eat much yesterday, so it would be good to have your nutrition replenished for the day. Please wait here. I will get it."

Dante's hand shot out and snatched her by the wrist. She stopped, looking at him with an expression of mild but growing alarm.

"Janet, take an extra member of the security team with you if you're going any distance at all." He looked past her to the guard. "There's at least one more man available, isn't there?"

"Yeah," the guy said, "he's doing a patrol, but we can pull him off it for a minute or two."

Dante nodded. "Do it, then. Also, Dr. Harlin said something about not barging in on the nurses while they're working. You know, respect their turf, that kind of thing. This is their place. Of course, if you have reason to believe there's a legitimate threat, then ignore what I said."

Rolling his eyes toward the ceiling, the man quipped, "Yeah, we do our best to keep everyone happy."

Janet looked at Dante. "This man does a good job, and the others are keeping an eye out for things elsewhere in the hospital or outside. I will be fine with just him."

He sharpened his gaze while Gage looked on in concern. "Janet, I insist. All right? As soon as you two leave the room, find someone else to watch your back. Then he can go back to patrolling once you're back here with us."

She sighed. "Fine, we will, as long as you sit and finish your coffee. Relax, and prepare yourself for the day. Stress is bad for digestion."

He relinquished her wrist, and she took the tray and plates away. The security officer nodded and followed her. He shut the door on his way out.

Dante settled back on his bed. It occurred to him that he was filthy with all the blood, grime, dust, and sweat from his ordeal yesterday and could use a shower. The thought of such trivia passed quickly. He kept turning over scenarios in his head about how the Russians could break into the hospital and get to Janet.

Gage noticed his unease. He flashed a wry smile. "Dante. For a man who says he doesn't intend to get involved with a woman, it seems you are being most possessive."

Irked, Dante snapped his eyes toward his friend and scowled. "Possessive? For God's sake, I'm only trying to keep her safe. Wouldn't want any innocent person to get mixed up in all this unpleasantness. It would be the same if she was anyone else."

He doubted that was *entirely* true, but it was close enough that he could say it out loud in good conscience.

Gage shook his head and waved that off. "No, no. I'm talking about how the two of you were curled up together on the bed. It was a cute sight."

Dante's jaw dropped, and he was too aghast to respond for a good ten or fifteen seconds. "*Cute?*"

Gage shrugged. "You are fortunate and should be grateful. Nobody offered to, what is the word, ah, *cuddle* with me when I fell asleep in the hallway. Although one of the nurses was kind enough to help me into one of the beds when I woke up in the middle of the night."

Snorting, Dante shot back, "Yeah, well, you passed out too soon. Next time, we'll let you join. All three of us can collapse together, in unison, and do nothing all night except sleep in the same general vicinity as one another."

Gage chuckled, and after a second, Dante laughed too. The mood in the air between them softened. They sat in comfortable silence a moment or two, finishing their respective caffeinated beverages of choice. Then Dante found his eyes drawn to Gage's leg.

"How's your ankle, bud? You should let me take a look at it. Yesterday we were kind of preoccupied with keeping Jubal alive, but now that he's probably okay, might as well move on to the next order of business where injuries are concerned."

The Nepali couldn't help a wistful frown. "I almost would prefer you did not. That way I can assume that any pain is only minor, and I will be fine in another week or so. If you look, perhaps I am afraid of what you will find. I'm not sure I want to know the truth."

"Understandable, but stupid," Dante scoffed. "If you broke it again, we need to know so we can treat it and get you back to one hundred percent. If it doesn't heal properly, you could be walking with at least a slight limp for the rest of your life."

Sighing with obvious reluctance, Gage shifted his position so that his leg was sticking far out from the edge of the bed and pulled his pant leg halfway up the shin.

Dante got down on his knees, removed the brace, and looked it over, touching it gently at first, then prodding and massaging it more thoroughly. Gage winced a tad here and there but otherwise didn't react much.

"Well," Dante reported, "as we can both see, it's swollen, but not badly enough to assume any serious damage. You had *mostly* healed by the time this whole business started, after all. Might've set you back a few days, and we should get an X-ray to be sure, but I think you'll be all right. As long as we can keep you from having to do too much overly physical and dangerous shit."

Gage cleared his throat. "That reminds me. We're going after this man Vlad today, yes? How do we approach him? Do you know what to expect?"

Dante chewed on the question as he rubbed the ankle, working out a couple of minor knots in the surrounding muscles and taking note of the best positions and level of tightness he should apply when re-fastening the brace.

"Well, we know the guy's a major drug dealer, and with friends like Pietr Urlicht, he's probably not a very nice person, right? You're the closest thing we have to law enforcement on the island now. So he's probably not going to welcome us with open arms. It'll be hard to go in and pretend we're his friends."

Gage gave a single nod. "Yes, it is as I'd feared. We'll have to move in fast and prepare to hit them heavy and hard. I would rather it were not so. If we can talk to him, that is what we shall do. However, we must assume that things will go badly."

Dante strapped the brace back into place, readjusting it slightly to provide better support for Gage's ankle in its current condition. "What if Pietr's already gone, I wonder? Or if he bit off more than he could chew, and Vlad decided that family ties don't mean shit and put him in a ditch somewhere with a forty-five caliber hole in his head?"

Wincing as the physician tightened the brace, Gage declared, "I don't know. We have to hope that hasn't happened."

"Bud." Dante sighed. "Hope isn't a plan. Don't they teach that in the military? Have a plan for everything? If Pietr already skipped town, or if he's dead, what do we do?"

It appeared, based on the sour twist of his mouth, that Dante had finally succeeded in aggravating the stoic Gurkha.

"Then, in that case, we tie you up like a goat baiting a leopard," Gage offered. "You would make fine bait. That great Russian monster would sniff you out with ease."

Dante stared at him. Then he burst out laughing. Gage resisted at first, but soon he was cracking up, too.

Janet returned with the tray loaded with two more plates of

food. She stared at the two warriors snickering and giggling like a pair of schoolboys who'd gotten away with pinning a nasty sign to the back of their teacher's dress.

She set the tray down between them. "Please, eat. Don't bother to tell me what's so funny."

CHAPTER FOURTEEN

The man stood leaning against the alley wall, his coat pulled up over his shoulders and around his face, and his hat yanked down in front as well. Doing so had caused the cap to split at the back, but the person he was meeting would have no way of knowing that.

Plus, it was dark. No electric lights penetrated this particular corner between buildings and the structures blotted out most of the sky's light. There were few windows. It was the perfect location, a place where *anyone* could hide and remain invisible.

No matter how visible they would've been under other circumstances. No matter how easily they would've stood out among other people, under the light of day.

The man's ears were unusually sensitive. He heard the rats scrabbling around in the discarded garbage that lined the alley, the roaches moving through the cracks in the cheap concrete. Much of the city was new, but parts had aged quickly.

He heard the noises of cars rushing by in the street beyond, out in the light. Footsteps, too. Most of them were simply average pedestrians passing. Then came the odd, interrupted cadence of the set of steps he sought. They were the footfalls of a man who was frightened, hesitant, and uncertain of his course. He slipped out of mainstream society and into the alley.

The huge man in the coat and hat waited, making no sound or movement as the smaller man approached.

Money would be involved in what was about to happen—a transaction geared toward profit.

Just like everything else that happened on the wretched island of Atlantica, a haven of capitalist decadence so loathsome and shameless that it made the United States look tolerable by comparison.

The island's faults would be its undoing. A place that so gluttonously reveled in the old and obsolete ways of the bourgeoisie was, in a way, ripe for a revolutionary transformation into something more...forward-thinking.

Such visionary endeavors weren't the big man's area of expertise. He'd left his country, exiled to the foul capitalist world, and had to survive on its terms. The business of perpetual revolution had to remain with others who might benefit from his baser-minded pursuits.

The small man came around the dumpster to the darkest portion of the alley, far at the back. He didn't see his contact until he was nearly on top of him. When he approached the gigantic bulk, he must not have realized he was looking at a human being.

"Holy shit," he muttered under his breath. "Are you, ah, the guy who needs the, uh, stuff?"

The big man took one step forward. He moved with a limp, given the damage he'd taken in his recent tumble. "Yes. Show me merchandise." His voice was so deep it sounded like it was being processed through some sort of electronic device, bringing a normal bass down to the level of grinding rocks.

The dealer nodded, glanced around, and opened his coat. A dizzying profusion of drugs lined the interior—mostly painkillers of various sorts. "What do you need, friend? How much? If you're looking to sell, I can get you bulk, but then I get a finder's fee, okay? And you got to go through my contacts. No cutting out the middleman."

The buyer extended a hand that was like the claw of an industrial crane. "Give me all."

Blinking, the smaller man repeated, "All? Shit, man, I can do that, but it's gonna cost you. There's a five percent markup for the hassle I gotta go through to go back and resupply since I was hoping to sell to a few different—"

The huge hand moved with astonishing speed as it snatched the man's coat and tore it off him. The dealer spun backward and aside, his arm screaming with pain at having been nearly dislocated, and he half-fell to his knees. By the time he got his bearings, the giant had stripped some of his wares off the garment and was consuming them in a virtual frenzy.

He cracked open a bottle of pills, upended it, and poured half of them into his mouth. Then he tore the top off a bag of cocaine and snorted a billowing cloud of it into his oversized nostrils. Sighing deeply, he folded up the coat with the rest of the drugs packaged within it.

Then he reached into his pocket and produced a wad of cash, dropping it on the ground as he turned and walked away.

The dealer stared in amazement at the spectacle he'd witnessed. He scampered over to the clump of bills. It appeared to be Soviet rubles. He was slightly fuzzy on the current market value of Russkie money, but he was pretty damn sure the giant man hadn't included the markup fee.

Or bothered to compensate him for the loss of his coat.

"Hey!" he shouted, staring after the ungrateful customer. He reached into the waistband of his pants and pulled out his .22 revolver, thankful that he'd ignored a couple of guys' advice to carry his gun in a shoulder holster. "Hey, dickhead, I'm *talking* to you! I said there was a markup. And nobody steals my fucking coat!"

The giant stopped and looked back without turning around. "Be quiet." Then he kept walking.

The dealer hesitated in indecision. He looked at the gun in his hand. Normally, holding it gave him a sense of power. Made him bold enough to take on guys he otherwise wouldn't have messed with. It wasn't a very large caliber, but nobody wanted to get shot with *any* bullet, even a .22.

Yet staring at the buyer's elephantine back and recalling the way he'd downed enough drugs to kill some men as though he were snacking on a bag of candy...

He looked down at the dirty pavement, his face burning with shame, and returned the weapon to his pants. "Fuck you," he muttered. When he looked up again, the titan was gone. With any luck, he'd never have to see him again.

CHAPTER FIFTEEN

Although eager to get out on the street and pound asphalt—to take the fight to the enemy and get things resolved once and for all—Dante almost regretted it when his long-postponed shower ended. Still, he couldn't languish under the stream of warm water all day.

He turned off the water, shook out his hair, and let some of the steam dissipate before stepping out of his stall to towel off and get back into his sandals and robe. The staff was laundering his clothes, and he hoped to get them back soon.

Fortunately, it didn't take long. Gage had gone to the laundry room to check. He returned to where they'd eaten breakfast with both of their outfits folded over opposite arms. "Here you are, my friend. Let us get ready quickly. There isn't much morning left."

"Right." Dante pulled on his clothes, followed by his armor and gear. "Too bad the security guys aren't around. We could've given them a drag show with those robes."

Gage chuckled. "I don't think they would've enjoyed it very much, but yes." He gritted his teeth as he pulled his pants on over his braced ankle. He considered asking Dante for help but decided it would be better to do it himself, if possible. After a moment of careful effort, he managed. "Will I be driving again?"

Dante chuckled. "It's your truck, bud. If I crash it, the Execs will probably try to take it out of my pay or something. Besides, with me riding shotgun, I can do all kinds of helpful stuff, like give you directions, man the radio, or fire an actual shotgun at bad guys. Whatever the situation requires."

As the mass of his equipment, including the Ithaca 37 and bandolier's worth of shells for it weighed down on him, Dante groaned inwardly. He was stiff and sore, and his long sleep and double-sized meal had left him feeling sluggish. His mind was eager to hit the road. His body was far less enthusiastic.

He thought of something. "Gage, I'm going to check on Jubal. Technically he's Harlin's responsibility now and the nurses', but he's also my friend, and I'm the one who got him accidentally involved in all this, anyway."

The Gurkha shrugged, then went back to loading rifle magazines with 7.62 x 51mm NATO rounds. It looked like he intended to bring along as much ammo as he could carry. It was a good idea for the most part, but Dante wondered how his ankle would handle the extra weight of all that brass and lead.

At least they could rely on the Autocutioner to act as their beast of burden for most of the day. Still, there was no guarantee they wouldn't end up having to run and gun on foot, relying only on the strength of their bodies to support whatever they brought with them.

Dante walked over to the third bed. Jubal was still asleep. Given how dire his condition had been, he would've needed a great deal of rest no matter what. Plus the medical team that operated upon him had followed up the anesthesia with plenty of sedatives.

The young man's dark golden skin looked a little more normal, more hale and healthy than it had in the immediate aftermath of the rifle round he'd taken through the side. His body was replacing the lost blood with the help of a little rehydration by the hospital team.

His heavily bandaged wound needed redressing soon. Most of the bleeding had stopped, but it looked like he'd rolled over at some point during the night and broken open part of the gash since a small portion of the gauze had turned a deep reddish-brown. Dante contemplated opening the dressing himself to examine things, but that might cause serious rifts in trust with the hospital staff.

He would have to rely on them to care for Jubal while he was gone. Thus far, the younger man was recovering pretty well. Dante clamped down on his professional urge to meddle and focused instead on the major task ahead—infiltrating cousin Vlad's headquarters and finding Pietr Urlicht.

Dante turned away from the bed. He was about to start telling Gage how to get to the scrapyard that the drug outfit used as a front when someone knocked on the door. A small figure was hazily visible beyond through the frosted glass window.

"Come in," he said.

The door opened, and Janet stepped in. "When will you be leaving?" Her eyes were wide with concern. Not blatantly so, but Dante knew her well enough that he could parse out the subtleties of her expression, the sharp pangs of emotion that barely showed under her usual veneer of serene beauty. "You said before that you were in a hurry."

Gage had finished locking and loading. He gave her a mild smile. "We're ready to go. Your timing is most excellent."

"Yeah," Dante agreed, moving closer to her. "We had to get all our stuff together and recover. I suppose it's for the best that you convinced me to...to get some rest instead of charging out last night. Uh..."

His voice trailed off as the fog over his memories cleared. He recalled it, now. Janet had been the one who guided him into the room. Before he'd collapsed and passed out, she'd kissed him.

The very notion made it hard for him to think straight. He was glad he no longer wore only a bathrobe.

If Janet noticed, she didn't show it. She kept looking at him with the same expression, a curious mixture of calmness and intense focus.

Dante looked away and made a show of checking on Jubal again before scanning the room for any necessary items he might've dropped. As he went about the charade, he divulged a little of what was on his mind.

"Janet, thank you again for helping us get through this. I know you probably don't think you've done much, but you have. It's the small things that make a difference, sometimes. As for what I'm about to do, I can't say for sure how it will turn out. It will be dangerous. That's the nature of this stuff. We have a plan."

That was *half* true. They had the rough outline of a plan and would have to fill in the details later once they had a better idea of what Vlad's setup was like.

"So," he went on, "I don't want you to worry too much about us while we're gone. We'll have radio contact with Eleanor the whole time, which always helps, and we have our body armor, plenty of firepower, and a vehicle that will stand up to almost anything short of an anti-tank rocket. You be careful, though. Don't go anywhere alone. Ask the guards to escort you if need be, and tell them about anything you see that might seem suspicious."

Janet put her arms around herself and rubbed her shoulders as though she were cold, although the room was comfortably warm. "Yes, I know. Thank you, Dr. Costa. The team has been good to me so far. Maybe the man you threw off the balcony died after all. There's a chance he won't bother us again. Isn't there?"

Gage piped up. "A chance, yes. We must be sure before we can relax, I'm afraid. It would be foolish to let our guard down if he's still out there."

Dante glanced at his friend, then back at Janet. "Yeah, he's right. That's a big part of what we're heading out to do. If we can find Pietr, we might be able to nail this guy once and for all. Then, no more innocent bystanders will get hurt."

His eyes drifted back over to the third bed. Still speaking to Janet but no longer looking at her, he added, "If Jubal wakes up, Janet, please tell him I'm sorry. I apologize for my part in this and regret the whole thing. I led the Russians right to him. Maybe they meant to take him out anyway, but either way, he shouldn't have been in the crossfire. I ought to have thought of that before I made a beeline for him and was so obvious about it."

Janet let out a deep sigh that had a note of frustration in it but was mostly full of sympathy. "Dante. That's not true. You're being silly."

Gage, who seemed embarrassed by having to stand around and listen to their conversation, quietly excused himself. He took his bag of extra supplies and walked out the door, waiting in the hallway a few paces beyond the threshold while Dante and Janet finished speaking their pieces to one another.

Dante noticed, of course. He knew they should get going as soon as possible. But...

"What do you mean, it isn't true?" He figured she was trying to make him feel better about the situation, but he'd never seen much use in little white lies. The truth was better, even when it hurt.

The slender young woman took a couple of steps closer to him and laid a hand on his arm. "You aren't responsible for what happened to Jubal. You aren't the one who shot him, after all. That was the work of other people. You saved his life. You're carrying enough heavy things on your shoulders without having to carry other things that don't belong to you.

"What put Jubal in danger was being involved with someone like Pietr. He should've known better. You tried to counsel him away from that man. Do you understand?"

Dante swallowed and looked up at the ceiling. Janet's words

were like oversized vitamin pills—probably healthy but hard to get down.

"Maybe that's the case," he conceded. "Maybe. But... Ugh. I can't shake the feeling that it wouldn't have happened if I hadn't been there. Besides, my Catholic guilt isn't about to let anything as rational as that stop me from feeling bad about myself."

Janet laughed softly, and after a second, Dante cracked a smile as well. The remark had come so naturally that at first, he didn't realize he'd made a joke of sorts.

Janet's hand moved up his arm and came to rest against his jaw. "Well, you must go. Good luck. Here's something to take with you, which I hope will serve you better than all that guilt." She leaned forward and kissed him on the mouth.

He froze at first, then responded for long enough to savor the moment. He made himself pull away. Otherwise, he would've preferred to linger there all day.

"Well," he breathed. "I think it *will* serve me better. At least, it's a lot more pleasant. Take care of yourself, kid. I'll be right back."

She blinked as though not fully grasping his humor at first, but she nonetheless was subtly smiling as he turned away and marched to the door. There was a spring in his step, something he wasn't sure he would have after how badly sapped his energy had been all morning.

As he opened the door and shut it behind him, Gage was still standing there, waiting and looking at him with half-lidded eyes. "Where is my kiss goodbye?" he grumbled in a tone of mock disappointment.

Dante laughed. "No idea. Also, the usual phrasing is 'goodbye kiss,' but at least I know what you meant, right?"

Gage waved it off. "It's as I said earlier. You're so greedy with this relationship you say you don't want."

CHAPTER SIXTEEN

Since Dante had seemed distracted by his goodbye to Janet, Gage hadn't bothered to raise the issue of exactly where Vlad's base of operations was or how they might best approach it. They would undoubtedly be able to figure it out after they left the building.

Despite his shorter legs and bum ankle, Gage was out in front as the pair walked through the hospital. The security team nodded at them. One man even saluted, which Gage found mildly embarrassing. He returned it all the same.

As near as he could tell, they were good men—vigilant, conscientious, and well-versed in the tactical minutiae of their profession. Still, he didn't know any of them personally and had to trust the judgment of Eleanor Cervantes and Officer MacLeod. Neither of *them* had ever given Gage any reason to doubt or distrust them.

The hospital staff glanced at the two men and looked sheepishly relieved that they were departing. Hosting the security guards was one thing. An Executioner was another.

They passed through the lobby, drawing similar looks of fascination and dread from the civilian patients waiting for treatment, and Gage reflected on what this would mean for the rest of his life.

He'd never thought of himself as a man whom other people were inclined to fear. Yes, he'd fought in a war and killed people when necessary. His people had a long martial tradition behind them and were famed as fierce warriors. This had always been something he'd regarded as peripheral to his primary existence, as a kind of emergency protocol that only applied in situations where everything else had gone wrong.

His self-image was of a farmer who'd become a scientist. People who knew only that side of his personal history seemed to think he was a nice and pleasant man. Harmless, even.

Now, with the skull-and-sword on his shoulders, he wouldn't be able to partake of such small comforts. He was obliged to take responsibility for his position and accept that people would regard him as a bringer of death.

Dante seemed afflicted by no such troubles. Then again, Gage had overheard much of his self-flagellation regarding Jubal. He had problems of his own. On some level, the two men approached the world from extremely different perspectives and filtered their experiences through thoughts and emotions that were little alike.

Such a disconcerting thought. Still, it inspired Gage to focus on what united them—the ways in which they were similar.

"Inalchuq of Otrar, the Khwarezmian governor," Gage said. "He captured the Mongol caravan and had them all executed on suspicion of being spies of Genghis Khan. A wise and shrewd man who suffered poor luck?"

Dante perked up, blinking as they pushed through the hospital's front doors into the parking lot. Both men scanned their surroundings for threats and saw nothing. It was a sunny, pleasant day, the island's frequent slate-colored rain clouds having dispersed overnight.

"Nah. He was a greedy idiot and not much of a host. You can

see why Genghis invaded and poured molten silver into the prick's ears. Too bad about the other, uh, tens of thousands of people who died in the process."

They strode toward the Autocutioner, and Gage once again worried that someone might've tampered with it. However, MacLeod's men had assured him that they hadn't seen any suspicious characters near the vehicle all night or morning.

"Hmm." Gage readjusted his rifle on its sling. "That may be, but perhaps he'd heard the rumors of what the Mongols had done to other nations and had reason to be concerned about espionage, yes? He and his men resisted the Horde until the bitter end. They fought far harder than many other cities of Khwarezm."

Dante shrugged. "Credit where credit's due, in that case. Inalchuq himself didn't fight hard enough at the end, though, if they managed to take him prisoner and do the thing with the silver."

"It is easy," Gage observed, "to judge what other people have done in desperate circumstances. Although I've seen you fight, so I suppose that were you in his position, you would've gone down with a sword in hand. So would I, although I do not like fighting very much."

Dante stared at him, then laughed. "You're awfully good at it for supposedly disliking it. Anyway." He exhaled raggedly. "This little operation today might be the kind of thing we can accomplish without necessarily massacring all the bastards. We'll probably need to throw our weight around and put the fear of God into them, yeah. If we do it right, it doesn't have to be a bloodbath."

Gage's smile was grim, even wistful. "Yes, that would be nice."

He clambered into the driver's seat, noting that his ankle was mostly functional but slightly numb with the echoes of pain. When he turned the key to start the engine, he'd almost forgotten about the unlikely danger of the engine exploding.

Instead, it started normally, and he closed his eyes in relief once more. "I shouldn't worry so much. The truck is almost completely tamper-proof," he mumbled.

"What?" Dante seated himself and pulled the door shut. "Worry about what?"

"Never mind. I was, as you say, thinking out loud. Now, where are we going? Jubal told you, but I'm afraid I don't remember the details of this location." He frowned. "Now that I think about it, it would be a good idea to ask Eleanor if she knows anything about these people."

Dante nodded. "Yeah, do it. If she doesn't know, she can find out. Vlad's place is, from what Jubal was saying, a scrapyard and auto shop near the southwestern edge of town. I basically know where it is, but I haven't been there myself so I can't say what exactly we're looking for."

Gage considered the implications of that. They would have to find a secure vantage point to scout the place before they barged in. He turned on the radio and waited for someone to answer.

The voice that responded was female but higher-pitched than Eleanor's and lacking her distinctive Mexican accent. "Hello, is this one of the Executioners? Eleanor is busy, but I can take a message and give it to her as soon as she gets back."

Gage hesitated. He didn't know how common it was for Eleanor to be away from her radio, and there was no way to be certain that someone hostile hadn't infiltrated the station or intercepted their frequency. The knowledge that the Soviet Union was trying to subvert Atlantica to its purposes had thrown up a miasma of suspicion that overlaid everything.

He exchanged a glance with Dante, who sensed his thoughts and nodded.

"Very well. Please ask Eleanor to look into an auto shop or a scrapyard, run by a man called Vlad, in the southwestern outskirts of Atlantica City. We wish to know everything about it and the people who own it that we can. Thank you. Over."

The young woman on the other end said she would pass on the message, and Gage heard her jotting it all down on a pad of paper. Then she said goodbye and the radio went silent.

Dante shrugged. "As I understand it, the Executives' inner circle is pretty tight. Katakura trusts Eleanor and everyone who works under her. So does Barruk, from what I hear."

"Yes, of course." Gage shifted into gear and drove onto the street. Since Atlantica General Hospital was in the western part of town, he didn't anticipate the drive would take too long.

Still, something worried him. Katakura trusted the security of the Executives, as Dante put it. What about the Coven of Miracles? The secret society Daria Barruk had mentioned, whose members might include some of the Executives themselves?

He decided it was useless to overspeculate and focused instead on driving.

Dante gave him directions, pointing out how to navigate the streets. After about fifteen minutes, they reached the correct neighborhood. It was a sparsely populated, somewhat industrial area, transitional between the city and the countryside. Brand-new manufacturing plants were going up alongside a smattering of houses and sheds that were among the earliest buildings erected on Atlantica.

To Gage's annoyance, Dante asked him to drive around more or less at random. They passed a couple of blocks before they came to a sort of fenced-off compound at the literal edge of civilization with only scrubland beyond it, which caused the physician to sit up straight and point.

"That's it. It has to be. Circle and park beside that building over there. We'll be able to watch the place without them noticing us while we wait for Eleanor."

Gage did as his partner suggested. The truck came to rest beside a bare concrete wall whose color acted as decent camouflage while also casting a shadow against the noonday sun.

The Autocutioner came equipped with a pair of binoculars.

Dante removed them from their hitch on the wall and adjusted them to fit his eyes, aiming the lenses at the scrapyard and turning the dial to focus them. His eyesight was extremely good, and whoever had used them last wasn't so fortunate, so it took a moment.

Then the scene before them came into view. The wire fence surrounding Vlad's compound was a good ten feet tall, with poles supporting it about every ten feet. At the top were coils of barbed wire. Atlantica being the kind of place it was, anything that wasn't for sale was ripe to be stolen if left unprotected.

The scrapyard proper, a veritable graveyard of dead cars and rotting mechanical parts, was in the northeastern section of the compound. Probably, it was there so the buildings would offer a small amount of shelter from the moist and salty sea breeze that blew in from the west, slowing the pace at which all that metal rusted into uselessness.

The garage was the main building, located in the compound's center and readily identifiable by its three loading bays where cars or small trucks could drive in. Each bay also held a lift. Attached to it was a nondescript jumble of rooms that probably constituted an office of sorts.

In the southeast was a smaller outbuilding, perhaps a miniature warehouse or toolshed. Dante also faintly discerned what looked like a storm cellar entrance and exit adjacent to the office building. He wondered how much of the operation took place underground. It would certainly make more sense to store drugs and other valuable merchandise in a deep, hidden cellar than in a file cabinet next to a window or some such.

A pickup truck with a tied-down blue tarp covering its load drove through the main gate and stopped. A man out front with a shotgun openly slung from his shoulder closed the gate, while another man in a suit coat questioned the driver. The suit-coated guy wasn't visibly armed...which likely meant he had a handgun somewhere on his person.

After a short interview, Suitcoat Guy waved the truck through, and it drove into one of the garage's open bays. Then the man who'd questioned the driver strolled around the perimeter of the main structure. The gate guard lounged in place, glancing at his surroundings every minute or so but otherwise not seeming to take his duties too seriously.

Dante lowered the binoculars. He was about to report his findings to his partner, but Gage had switched on the Autocutioner's radio and held the receiver. Static crackled before giving way to Eleanor's usual polite greeting.

"Good day, Executioner Gurung. How can I help you? Over." It occurred to Dante that she'd hesitated for a second after being patched through to speak so Gage could've immediately requested aid in an emergency without having to talk over her.

Gage held up the receiver. "Good day, Eleanor, thank you. We're at the garage that houses the drug operation of this man, Vlad, according to the intelligence that Dr. Costa gathered from Jubal. Did you receive my question earlier? Over."

Eleanor replied, "Yes, I did. I wanted to make sure you weren't in trouble before I began reading these things off. If you're in a secure location, I can begin. Over."

"We are," Gage told her. "Please, go on. Read us everything you have. Over."

Both men sat and listened as Ms. Cervantes regaled them with the pertinent information on Vlad's shop. She began by briefly summarizing the basic, publicly available stuff such as its founding date, the services it advertised, and so forth.

"Since Atlantica has no codified laws to speak of," Eleanor explained, "his dealings in narcotics aren't technically illegal. Old habits die hard, as the saying goes. Some vendors have taken to selling drugs openly. The problem they've encountered is that there are no laws to protect them, so walking around with highly lucrative products in plain sight, they've frequently been robbed or murdered by others who then seize their wares to resell."

Dante grimaced. "Sounds about right. Even some of the worst parts of New York could learn a thing or two from the way we do things here on Atlantica, am I right?"

Ignoring him, Eleanor continued, "Therefore, many drug dealers have taken to operating in secrecy as they did in other countries, or at least, they tend to be as discreet as reasonably possible. Having a front business, as Vlad does, means that his competitors are left guessing how much stock he has. They're never sure when customers are coming in for legitimate automotive services or when they're coming in for morphine, cocaine, hashish, or amphetamines instead."

Gage nodded. "Yes, I see. Would you say, then, that it's safe to assume they would not give us a particularly warm welcome?"

"Most likely," she confirmed. "Again, they aren't breaking any law simply by selling drugs, but when the Executioners show up somewhere that sees a large amount of illicit activity, people tend to get hurt or killed. That by itself might be a problem. Or they might mistake you for simply business rivals conducting a raid."

Dante chortled. "If we *wanted* to give that impression to put on an act, I'm pretty sure I could handle it. Don't ask me how. Or why."

"Yes, Dr. Costa." Ms. Cervantes acknowledged him for the first time. "Based on what Katakura has told us, we have little doubt of that. Don't underestimate these people, however. Vlad isn't one of the major players in the drug trade, but he's large enough to be somewhat visible to those who look for such things. He has various connections to the gangs and crime outfits from Eastern Europe—those that operate primarily within Atlantica, as well as those based back in the mother countries, but are seeking to expand upon the island."

Gage scratched his chin. "Does that mean they might be working with the Soviets?"

"It's doubtful although not impossible. Most of the modern organized crime in the Slavic countries has spawned from petty gangs, mutual aid societies, and black market dealers who formed within the Soviet gulags. As such, there is little but hatred between the criminals and the government servants who put them in such a dire situation to begin with. If you believe there's a connection with the USSR involved in the attempts on your lives, it's more likely to be an *indirect* one than a true alliance between Communist agents and Slavic mobster types."

Dante rolled his tongue around his teeth. "Small mercies..." He raised the binoculars again and examined the gate as Eleanor regaled Gage with things like the usual coming-and-going times of the place's heaviest customer traffic.

The gate, Dante saw, had a noticeable hitch in it. The guards had to slow the opening and closing at a certain point to keep it from binding up. "That's interesting," he remarked under his breath. He had an idea but opted to wait to blurt it out until Gage finished speaking to Eleanor. They'd been sitting here for too long, but so far there was no evidence that anyone had spotted them.

Gage finished his radio conversation. "Thank you once again, Ms. Cervantes. We appreciate your help. Now, we must go in. We'll radio you again if things go poorly and we require further aid. If we're, ah, able to do so. Out."

"Good luck, Executioner. Out." Her voice faded out, and Gage switched off the radio, hung up the receiver, and looked at his partner.

Dante didn't waste time and launched instantly into explaining his observation about the hitch. "If we wait until the gate is in the process of being closed and charge right through it during the slowed-down part, we'll almost certainly be able to slam right through. I think. We wouldn't want to speed up when *it's* speeding up, or the gate will bind, and we'll end up trapped, possibly with a crunched front end and your fancy Atlanticore engine spilling out in front of a bunch of gangsters."

Gage frowned. "Yes, I see. Actually, I do not. May I have those field glasses?"

Dante handed them over. Gage had to adjust them substantially to suit his relatively poor vision, but after a moment his mouth opened in a silent Eureka moment. "There it is. I think you're right, Dante. We should wait for another vehicle to seek entrance into the compound and follow it." He lowered the binoculars and grinned with uncharacteristic mischief. "Then we'll be ready to make a most noisy entrance."

He gave the binoculars back to Dante, who hung them up and pumped his shotgun once, chambering a round. "Knock, knock, assholes."

CHAPTER SEVENTEEN

Sergiu frowned beneath his heavy mustache as yet another truck rolled up to the gate. Rather, a pair of trucks. Out in front was a semi towing a half-sized trailer, and tagging along behind it was what looked almost like an old, repurposed military truck. That was strange. He'd seen stranger. All sorts of different people tended to show up to do business with Vlad.

He had a Winchester 1897 pump shotgun hanging from his shoulder. The weapon was old but still formidable and reliable—it was one of the World War I models and could be slam-fired by a man who knew what he was doing—and the sling from which it hung was new. People tended to respect him when they saw the weapon in his grip. Thus he let the stock fall into his hand, holding it at a low ready position as he walked up to examine the first driver and open the gate.

Though Sergiu didn't recognize the truck itself, the man behind the wheel was familiar. A fat pale guy with a heavy five o'clock shadow who always wore a yellow cap. He was a regular buyer and courier who came in about once every two weeks, purchased merchandise in bulk, paid in cash, and drove off without any problems. Sergiu had seen him with three different vehicles over the month, and he never came back in the same one twice in a row.

They locked eyes, and Sergiu nodded. There was no need to interrogate or warn a trusted, longtime customer. So he simply opened the gate, observing the speed differential as usual and allowing the semi to rumble through. He waited until the vehicle was clear and within the compound before he began the process of re-closing the gate.

It almost seemed like a waste of time. It had been three months since the last time anyone had dared to attack them or otherwise try anything stupid, which by Atlantican standards was impressive. It meant that their operation was gaining respect.

The previous raid attempt by one of their business rivals had failed miserably. Vlad had been ready for them, along with everyone else, and Sergiu had personally blown the head off one of the thugs. They were pretty sure the gang who hired them was a Brazilian outfit, but their lackeys in the raid were a mishmash of people hired from across the island.

Sergiu stepped forward as the gate began to close, once again holding his Winchester one-handed and ready to be brought up to his shoulder in a flash if necessary. The military-style truck advanced. *A little too fast.* He peered toward the windshield to get an idea of who the driver and passenger were while he debated whether to call for backup.

Behind the wheel was a short, dark-complected older man, balding and bespectacled, dressed in what looked like combat fatigues. Next to him in the other seat was a taller, younger white man with wavy black hair. Both of them were grinning like maddened teenagers on a joyride.

Sergiu's inner mental alarm went off. Something was seriously wrong, especially since the truck was still accelerating.

"Stop!" he shouted in English. The gate was already closing, and he was fairly sure it would shut before the truck could barrel through. Even if it crashed against the perimeter, the resulting mess wouldn't reflect well on his competence as a guard.

The passenger was leaning out the window with a shotgun.

Sergiu raised his weapon, but he wasn't fast enough. The younger guy fired a blast of buckshot that kicked up dirt at Sergiu's feet and ricocheted off the metal beside and behind him. The guard grunted, stumbled, and fell back as he squeezed off a shell. It *dinged* harmlessly against the truck's armored hull.

Then the vehicle slammed into the gate—right as it was slowing down, and thereby overcoming the hitch. The gate screamed, and metal *crunched* as the impact flung it aside. The truck barreled into the compound, slowed and knocked mildly off-course by the collision, but that was all.

Sergiu cursed madly in his native Romanian as he climbed to his knees, raised his shotgun again, and fired two shells at the rear of the invaders' vehicle, although he knew it was useless. The armor easily repelled the buckshot. Even the wheels had metal shroud-flaps hanging in front of and behind them, protecting the tires from damage.

"Fuck." Sergiu sighed. It was one of the English words he was most intimately familiar with.

Within the truck, Dante laughed as the wind whipped his hair back. He'd ducked back in when they slammed open the gate, but as soon as they were clear of it, he leaned out the window again, Ithaca in hand, working the pump and spraying buckshot at random across the compound.

There weren't too many guys out and about yet. Undoubtedly, Vlad would have some muscle waiting in the wings. By laying down suppressing fire right at the beginning, he hoped to scare them into keeping their heads down, shocking them with his miniature blitzkrieg while he and Gage got into position on their terms. If they intimidated the bastards enough right from the get-go, they might be able to acquire what they wanted without having to kill anyone.

Gage stomped on the gas and spun the steering wheel, tapping the brakes here and there when he threatened to overshoot his mark or swerve too much on a turn, but otherwise observing almost no safety measures, restraint, or common sense whatsoever.

Up ahead, two guards were converging on one another while also getting into position to open fire on the truck. One had a pistol, the other a submachine gun. They likely wouldn't have been able to penetrate the truck's armor with their weapons unless they managed to blow out the windshield, and even it was reinforced well enough that it could probably withstand pistol rounds.

Both were moving toward the upper shell of a junked car mounted on cinder blocks.

"Hold on." Gage pressed down on the gas and swerved right toward the obstacle.

The guard with the submachine gun squeezed off a short burst that *pinged* uselessly against the side of the truck. The vehicle veered to the right and swiped the gutted car from the side, knocking it violently off the blocks and sending it rolling toward the two men on the ground.

Dante pulled his upper body back in through the window barely in time. "Hey!" he protested. "I was *busy* there!"

Metal crashed against metal. The half-car raised clouds of dust and gravel as it tore up the ground, and the two gunmen dove and rolled, narrowly avoiding being crushed or cut in half. The guy with the submachine gun dropped it as its strap caught on a smashed chunk of cinder block. By the time either regained their feet, the Autocutioner was already racing toward the compound's other side.

Dante was trying to load more shells into his shotgun. He dropped one as the truck rocked and careened around, spouting off a series of colorful four-letter words until Gage nodded at him and righted their course again.

Now they were heading straight toward the main office building. Dante aimed out the passenger's side window and fired two more booming volleys of buckshot, deliberately missing a guard who'd frozen in panic. It was enough to shock the man out of his stillness. He jumped behind a cluster of steel drums.

Dante's second round kicked up a spray of mud from a lower, moister area of the ground in front of what looked like an outhouse. The door had been opening, but it slammed shut again as the blast struck in front of it.

Gage pressed on the brakes. The big truck slowed and screeched to a halt about three or four yards from the office's front door. He and Dante exchanged a glance before hopping down, guns in hand.

Someone fired at them, possibly the guard who'd been at the gate. Gage retaliated with three rounds of suppressing fire, almost certainly hitting nothing but buying them time. Then he turned to the entrance as Dante moved in beside him.

Gage held his rifle aside with his left hand, then drew his revolver with the right, leveled it at the door, and fired once. The slug blew off the latch and left the knob hanging, but the door itself stayed in the same position.

Fortunately, Dante was already advancing from Gage's flank. While the Nepali holstered his handgun and turned to squeeze off a couple more blind-fired warning shots with his AR-10, the physician pressed forward and kicked the door open. Or, rather, kicked it *down* since the hinges snapped. With the latching system destroyed, it simply fell inward to *clap* loudly against the floor, raising a suspicious cloud of white dust.

Within, the office was sparsely furnished. It had to be to make room for all the product lying around. Crates and boxes were full of plastic bags that contained various forms of amphetamines and heroin. A single, solitary-looking white brick could only be cocaine.

Hastily trying to gather up the drugs and stuff them into more containers were five men. A shotgun rested on a small table of warped wood next to one of them, but none had a firearm in his hand.

Of course, neither Dante nor Gage was such a fool as to assume that there weren't at least two or three pistols concealed in their waistbands.

Everyone froze, more or less. Two guys turned their heads from side to side, checking the reactions of their compadres, but that was their only movement. There was one other, a muscular individual in the rear corner who was slowly moving his arms as though he were feigning the beginning of a hands-up gesture.

Dante noticed it and pointed his shotgun straight at the man's chest. His arms stopped instantly. At the same time, Gage stepped in and leveled his rifle at the others. Confronted with heavy fire-power and with the intruding pair having the drop on them, they didn't dare try to shoot back.

Since Gage and Dante had shown no indication they were about to open fire and murder them all regardless, the gangsters seemed to be wrapping their heads around the fact that they could still get out of this alive...if they cooperated.

Gage was the first to speak. To the virtual shock of everyone else present, he used a casual voice, in a normal register, as though he were asking the host if he would be so kind as to spare a cup of tea. "We're looking for Vlad. Has anyone seen him, by chance?" He slowly turned his head from side to side, scanning the room with wide yet calm brown eyes behind his spectacles.

Nobody spoke except a man near the center of the room. He was of average height and had lean, bony features with sharp cheekbones. He'd slicked back his dark hair with grease of some sort, and across his knuckles were tattoos that neither of the intruders could identify or translate.

Trying to keep his cool but obviously afraid in a way that bespoke a deep familiarity with fear, the man stated, "Just take drugs." He waved vaguely around him at the treasure trove of addictive substances. His thick accent was almost certainly Romanian.

Gage glanced to Dante, but the tall physician kept his eyes on the gangsters. He allowed a small, faintly evil smile to creep across his face and took a pair of heavy steps forward.

"Thanks for the offer, bud." He advanced another step, pausing when he could level the muzzle of his shotgun about a foot from Vlad's chest. "That's not what we're here for. We wanted to talk to you about something involving your cousin Pietr."

The dark-haired man squinted, and it turned into a pair of quick blinks as though he was genuinely confused. "Pietr?" He hadn't expected the question.

Dante was suddenly aware of music playing throughout the compound at a low volume. He hadn't noticed it until now, and his mind was too busy to identify it.

Outside, some of the compound's guards were recovering from the chaos. Dante noticed them out of the corner of his eye and confirmed it with a rapid, furtive glance out the window. They were getting back to their feet and forming into pairs and trios, surveying the office and talking in low voices to one another. Conferring on how best to retake the building from the invaders, perhaps, or at least speculating about what Dante and Gage wanted.

They were smart, though. Dante had to credit them for that. All of them stood outside Gage's immediate line of fire. The Nepali had repositioned himself within the doorway, where he could watch the men inside and out. A quick pivot would allow him to shoot at anyone. His eyes were bright and alert behind the thick lenses of his glasses.

Gage addressed his abrupt comment to Vlad, though.

"Tell us what we wish to know, and quickly, please. I'm not looking to shoot anyone, but I promise you that your men will die if they don't stand down. It's not my concern if you value their lives. But surely you must value the time and money it would take to hire new men and how difficult things would be for you without them in the meantime. Yes?"

Dante stayed where he was, his Ithaca still poised to blow Vlad's heart out of his chest, and smiled. The Gurkha had made an even more convincing case than his shotgun had.

The Romanian looked back and forth between the two men who threatened him and his operation. The calculating expression on his face was one that Dante knew well. It was the look of someone trying to evaluate the strength, will, and seriousness of the men he dealt with. He needed to know if they were bluffing before he decided.

Then the moment of their test passed. The tension melted away from Vlad's stance and body. His face took on a slightly slack, disgusted look, and he made a lazy flapping gesture toward a microphone sitting atop a radio.

Dante nodded. "Yeah, do what you have to do, bud."

Vlad reached out a knobby finger and flipped a switch. The music, which Dante now recognized as either a Jewish klezmer dance or a comparable piece of Eastern European folk music, stopped mid-note. In the ringing silence that replaced it, Vlad spoke into the microphone. His voice echoed from the speakers around his property and filled the compound.

"Stand down. Do nothing until I tell you to go back to work." Then he repeated himself, presumably in Romanian.

Or, he'd lied to them in English before relaying a more sinister message in his native tongue, Dante thought. There was no way to be sure. With people like him, suspicion was eternal. Yet the physician was too intrigued by the possibility of success to worry overmuch, as long as the Slavs cooperated.

Gage took a step deeper into the building.

Both watched as Vlad's narrow face appeared to grow larger around a slowly expanding Cheshire Cat grin. He had at least four gold teeth, and they glittered under the electric lights within the room. "So, you want to talk to Pietr. Eh? I can take you to him. Heh, heh."

Around him, the others fidgeted, but not enough to draw too much suspicion. They'd grasped that their boss wanted to cooperate with the intruders, at least for now.

"Yes." Gage looked past the other side of the long table that housed the radio equipment. "You may lead the way."

Bobbing his head in agreement, Vlad turned, stepped toward the exit, and made a beckoning motion.

Dante inhaled. They were probably fools to trust a person like the drug dealer to keep his word. But what other choice did they have?

CHAPTER EIGHTEEN

Vlad led them out of the office building while his thugs stood by, glowering with subdued malevolence at the pair of interlopers.

Gage and Dante ignored their stares. When the two of them had broken into the compound, they *could* have killed them. They'd chosen instead to merely create chaos and get in and out without a body count. Dante thought the men ought to be grateful.

Across the compound was a shed. Within it was virtually nothing, aside from a door with wire grating over it. Vlad slid a key into the padlock that held the grating in place, swung it aside, and revealed a tight, narrow staircase leading down into the earth.

Dante smiled. "You first, friend."

Muttering to himself, Vlad started down the steps. Dante followed. Gage kept an eye on the compound guards and brought up the rear.

They stopped in front of a heavy iron door with a lock above the knob, probably a deadbolt. Despite the place's relative newness, rust was already forming around the edges due to the damp Atlantican climate.

"This," Vlad announced, producing a ring of keys from his pocket and waving his hand, "is the place."

Dante stepped in and pressed his shotgun forward so the muzzle was only a hair's breadth of space from the back of Vlad's shirt—close enough that he was sure the Romanian gangster could feel its sheer proximity, despite not quite touching him.

"If anything happens, if you try any shit," Dante said in a voice barely over a whisper, "I'll blow a couple of the vertebrae of your spine right through your cardiac cavity and out your sternum. You understand? Your rotten heart will be on the floor. In pieces."

Vlad chuckled. "Yes, that is fine. Very many details, you describe."

Gage also appeared to be biting his tongue. "I suppose that's the kind of threat I would expect to hear from a doctor."

Dante glared at him. "Shut up, Gage. Keep watch behind us in case any guys come down. And in front of us in case they got any other guys in here, waiting."

The Gurkha brought his rifle up to his chest. "I will do my best to look in both directions at once." It was tough to tell if he was joking since his eyes shot left and right at rapid speed.

Vlad raised the jangling ring of keys, selected one after an instant's consideration, and inserted it into the lock. As he turned it, Dante heard the bolt shoot back and *clack* into place. Then the Romanian turned the knob and pulled the door open.

Beyond was a large storage area, at least the same size as the front half of the entire office building, if not bigger. Although it was difficult to tell its exact dimensions given how much clutter there was.

In addition to the expected tables, crates, shelving, and so forth, there were also a few old bathtubs and cheap industrial vats, some filled with noxious chemicals. Drums of the same substances, both full and empty, lined the walls and aisles between the shelves, along with boxes and bags of other substances. Neither Gage nor Dante knew much about manufacturing illegal drugs, but it wasn't difficult to guess the purpose of most of Vlad's inventory.

Vlad warned them, "Be careful, do not touch vats, or breathe air that is close to them."

As they wove between the vats in question, Dante wondered how much sense the gangster's admonition made. "There is no ventilation down here, from the looks of it. Any fumes would've already spread through the air. If it's that dangerous, shouldn't we have gas masks or something?"

Behind him, Gage made a low humming sound to indicate that a similar thought had occurred to him.

Vlad only chuckled and waved. As they pressed deeper into the cellar, the odd, unpleasant smell grew stronger. It reminded Dante somewhat of a hospital and somewhat of an industrial waste disposal facility. He tried to breathe as shallowly as he could, lest he pass out or a coughing fit seized him. Or become hazardously intoxicated.

At the back of the drug kitchen was another door, secured not merely with a conventional lock but a state-of-the-art electric one with a numerical keypad. They paused in front of it as Vlad punched in the appropriate code.

"This is bunker. We are keeping Pietr safe here." His laugh had a distinctly nasty, grating quality to it.

The door *beeped*, and Vlad unlatched it and pushed it open. When neither of his guests moved to go ahead of him, he shrugged his left shoulder and went himself, holding the door open as Dante, followed by Gage, came through.

Beyond were short hallways going to the left and the right and a slightly longer one that stretched straight ahead. Weak sodium lights were set into the walls about every ten or twelve feet.

Since Vlad hadn't instructed them on what to do about the door, Gage allowed it to fall shut. He was wary about what could happen if it locked them in with whatever or whomever Vlad had waiting for them but possessed no real alternatives. The door latched itself again, and the *clicking* sound echoed once or twice in the stuffy little corridors.

The gangster led them through a surprisingly confusing series of turns in a labyrinth of sorts. The bunker's layout made so little sense that Dante and Gage assumed it must be intentional to confuse any hostile invaders trying to attack the gang in their last refuge.

They passed no fewer than three doors leading to small rooms contained amid the jumble of hallways. There were no knobs, only locks. Dante was all but certain that they circled past one of them twice.

At last, they came to a door in a corner. Something about it, and its distance from the feeble, half-flickering lights on the walls, had a noticeably forlorn quality.

Vlad found another key on his ring and opened the door. The room was bare aside from a small nightstand and a little shaving mirror mounted on the sidewall. As well as a chair in which a man sat chained with a cloth sack over his head.

On either side of the prisoner were two men standing guard. Both became instantly alert at the sight of their boss and the two men standing behind him. They started to raise their weapons—a sawed-off shotgun for the one on the left and an MP 40 submachine gun for the one on the right.

Vlad raised a hand. "Stop!" He added another short string of words, barked in Romanian or perhaps another regional language. The men kept their guns at low ready before relaxing and moving aside to stand against the sidewalls. There was barely enough room for the three newcomers to enter and stand before the figure in the chair.

They did. The door hung open, and Gage left it that way as he occupied the threshold, still keeping watch from the rear. Dante was about a pace inside the room, and Vlad had moved in to circle the prisoner.

He grabbed the sack and yanked it off the seated man's head in one motion. With his other hand, he smacked the back of the guy's head, which drew a startled, sputtering, wordless cry of alarm.

Gage leaned in to get a better look at the captive. He was of stocky build, but his skin had an unwholesome slackness to it, as though he'd lost a significant amount of weight in a short time. His hair was shaggy, and his facial features were surprisingly fey and delicate. They didn't seem to go with his body. He also looked nothing like Vlad.

Bruises and scratches covered his face. Some were probably a few days old, whereas others were fresh, likely put there earlier this morning.

Gage caught Dante's eye, and the physician nodded before looking back at the man. "Hi, Pietr. Nice to see you again."

The captive gunrunner's eyes drifted toward Dante. Pietr seemed dazed, probably due to his imprisonment and abuse, and perhaps also lingering injuries from whatever other ordeals he might've been through recently. His attention was on Dante, but he didn't appear to recognize him yet.

After a quick scan behind him to assure that all was well and no one was sneaking up on them, Gage looked at Vlad. "Why would you do this to him?" It made no sense. They were family.

Vlad laughed in the same harsh, unpleasant fashion he had a moment ago before they'd awoken his cousin. "Why, you ask? Pietr has always been bully. That is your word for people like him, yes?"

Frowning, Gage nodded. Based on everything he'd heard from Dante and Jubal, Vlad's assessment at least sounded accurate. Still…

Vlad went on, "He had good deal, working with men who sell guns. Very profitable. But all of it failed. He was failure, but *still* he was…what is word for one who is too proud?"

Dante wasn't sure if he was looking for an adjective or a noun. He decided on the former. "Arrogant," he offered.

Vlad snapped his fingers. "Yes, arrogant. He comes into *my* place, as though it was his place and owned by him, yes. Demanding money and help. His friends were not with him. Without all his villains and killers behind him, why should I have reason to listen to him? What good is there to work with this *lou* of a cousin?"

He slapped Pietr again on the side of his face, grazing his ear. The heavier man flinched and gasped. His eyes were clearing as he slowly emerged from whatever delirium he'd sunk into.

"I have reason to beat him," Vlad stated. "Like bad child he is. And keep him here until I can decide what is to do with him. Yes, Pietr? You arrogant stupid. I cannot kill him because he is my cousin. But other people want him to die. He has made many enemies in his life. Sooner or later, someone will come to look for him. Then my problem will go away."

Dante arched his eyebrows. He was used to dealing with ruthless people but still capable of being surprised. Still, he could see how Pietr might inspire sentiments of that sort. Even with family.

Gage, on the other hand, was aghast. "You would sell your cousin to those who wish to kill him?" he marveled, the words coming slow and deliberate.

Vlad circled the back of the chain-wrapped chair to Pietr's other side, glaring at him. "He is never good for anyone. But now, at least, he can get Executioner to leave me alone. Yes?"

Dante narrowed his eyes. The family trouble between the two men was ultimately not his business and certainly not why he and Gage were here. He took another step closer so Pietr's face was less than an arm's length away from him.

"Pietr," he began, staring into the man's pale eyes, which finally focused on him and came to full alertness. "Talk to me. I need you to tell me something, and I'm not taking no for an answer. You hear?"

There was a flicker of recognition on the slack face, and Dante pressed his advantage.

"I need you to help me find the Soviet agents that are coming after us. You know who I mean, don't you? Don't pretend not to. I can smell that bullshit half a mile away. Where are they? What are they planning next?"

The man's mouth opened, and another vague gurgling sound gave way, at last, to speech. In a garbled accent that sounded like a mixture of Austrian and Romanian, he said, "You must help me, Dr. Costa. I can help you, but you have to help me. You owe me!"

Vlad chuckled as though he'd expected his cousin to say something like that and found it sardonically amusing.

Pietr went on. "I watched out for you. None of the other men in the ring harmed you because of me. I was your friend, Dr. Costa. You owe it to me to get me out of this. Do that, and I can—"

"*Bullshit,*" Dante snapped, cutting him off. "You were no better than the rest of that gang of lowlife bastards. I don't owe you a damn thing. If I help you, it's because I'm doing you a favor out of pity. You got that, smart guy? Don't get on my bad side. Give us the information we want, or I'm throwing you to the wolves."

Pietr's heavy body writhed with obvious anger. His face flushed, his jaw clenched, and his eyes rolled. "No—no! You get me out of here first. I will give you *nothing*, wop! Stupid pig, we let you live but should have killed you. That was my doing! You owe it to me to get me free. Then *I* will be the one who takes pity on *you*, and then, then..."

Almost before he knew what he was doing, Dante raised his leg and lashed out with his foot. The sole of his boot planted itself against Pietr's chest and knocked him over backward in his chair, drawing startled reactions from Vlad and the guards. They tensed but did nothing else. Pietr struck the floor with a *thud*. The chains holding him to the chair *clanked* and *rattled*.

Dante pounced as Pietr gasped and gurgled. Heedless of the way the guards watched him and readied their guns, the tall doctor straddled the prisoner, aiming his shotgun at the center of Pietr's face.

The smuggler's eyes bulged in horror as he looked up at the face of the man over him. They both knew what was going through Dante's head. The full roster of horrors and humiliations the physician had suffered while the gunrunners held him hostage. They'd forced him to work for nothing save his barely adequate room and board, like a slave or indentured servant, casually insulted him, and exposed him to terrible danger on a regular basis merely by being their associate.

Vlad said, "Do not kill him yet. I would lose money, yes? Ha, ha. Then I would have to take it from you. You would owe me even if you do not owe him."

Ignoring the gangster, Dante instead looked at his friend. Gage was grimacing in a way that suggested almost fatherly disapproval.

"Right," Dante breathed. He tried to calm himself, shouldering his gun and reaching out his hands. One he put on the back of Pietr's chair, and another he looped under one of the lengths of chain. Then he heaved him back up, standing the chair back on the floor and returning its inhabitant to a more comfortable position.

As the heavyset man twitched in nervous anger, Dante focused his thoughts on what lay ahead. The future, now as always, was more important than the past.

"Pietr. There's a monster of a Russian out looking for me. Gage too. Huge, ugly, vicious son of a bitch. We both thought we killed him twice, except we didn't. He's not someone to play around with.

"If you don't help us and point us toward the way we step

these goons at the source, I'm going to do the worst thing to you that I can think of. I'm going to leave you here so you can wait, safe and sound in your little chair until the monster shows up."

The captive's pale face turned paler.

Dante continued. "If you give us good information, we'll see about getting you the hell off Atlantica. Then you can do whatever you want. I don't really care, as long as you don't hurt me or mine. Until then—until you cut the shit and help us—you're meat for the beast. Understand?"

Staring into the smuggler's eyes, Dante struggled to comprehend what was happening in his mind. Then it struck him. Pietr was even more scared now than he had been a moment before with a shotgun at his nose.

"You see?" Pietr rasped. "That is why you must free me. You have to get me out. I have to escape before *Koschei* shows up! I can tell you what you want later. Get me free now, you idiot!"

Dante smacked him across the face to shut him up. It was too difficult to contain his disappointment that Pietr didn't seem to get the message.

In a way, though, he *had* revealed something interesting.

Dante's nostrils flared. "Koschei. Who's that? Tell me."

Pietr looked at the floor and clamped his teeth together although his lips stayed open. A shudder went through his body, causing the chains to rattle. "Arkadi Zorin! He is called Koschei, after a monster from some old Russian bedtime story. He is the man who comes when everyone else is afraid, when everything else is too good for them. He is the worst thing they have. I have to get off Atlantica! He is out there..."

Midway into Pietr's half-panicked rant, Vlad threw up his hands in aggravation and turned away, swearing in his mother tongue as he looked at the wall. His two guards looked nervous but were trying not to show it.

Dante felt something cold forming in his gut and spreading

up his spine. He glanced at Gage, and the Nepali didn't look any more confident than he did.

"Okay." Dante turned his eyes back to Pietr. "So he's a Soviet agent?"

To his surprise, Pietr shook his head furiously, so his shaggy hair flew around in a stringy mop. "No. He is a Russkie but is, how you say, an independent contractor. A mad killer for hire." He twisted in place, straining against his bonds and hoping, in vain, that they might loosen. "There, I have told you. Now get me out of here. We have to get the hell out of here!"

Dante frowned, and the beginnings of confidence he'd felt earlier that they might finally be about to put together the last pieces of the puzzle faded. "Why is a Russian hitman coming after us?"

Somewhere up above came a sharp yet muffled *crackling* sound. Gage fell into a fighting stance, and the two guards did the same, raising their guns and looking at the ceiling.

Dante muttered, "Shit."

Pietr's eyes rolled up as well. He scanned every crack in the ceiling as though looking for something that might be lurking there. "He came after you to get to me, maybe?"

The sounds increased in volume and frequency. It was no longer possible to pretend that they were anything other than gunfire. Vlad was trembling with rage—and probably fear—and pounding his fist against the wall as he cursed up an incomprehensible storm.

"The Soviets could not send one of their own," Pietr explained. "Not even to Atlantica to remove an Allied agent. Do you see? They are greedy enough to want Atlantica to themselves, but they cannot make it clear that they do. They are both the same. The Communists always do this. They disguise their true intentions until the time for the killing stroke has come."

Vlad ignored his cousin and looked at one of the guards, the man with the MP 40. "Go seal the door to the bunker."

The man hesitated. The implication that Vlad expected the attackers to overrun his men upstairs was perhaps too clear.

The gangster reached into the back of his pants and drew a gun, an old Luger. "Go! Get moving!"

Properly motivated, the guard nodded and rushed out the cell door, his footfalls quickly disguised by the many walls of the maze beyond.

Dante had kept his eyes on Pietr the whole time. "What are you talking about? *They are both the same.'* Who?"

As though someone had poked him hard in the side and he'd been holding his breath, the words burst out of Pietr's mouth. "The Chinese!" His terror was unpleasant to watch. "Along with the Soviets, I moved a Chinese agent to Atlantica. They said they, uh, needed a person who could meet with some cult, or coven, something like that?"

Gage had fixated on the growing sounds of combat above them. He abruptly swiveled his face toward the captive and took a step into the room.

"Coven?" His voice, usually so soft and pleasant, was the sharpest Dante had ever heard it. "The Coven of Miracles. That must be what they mean."

Pietr rolled his broad shoulders. "Maybe." Then, noticing the intense expression on the Gurkha's face, he changed his tune. "Uh, yes. Yes! It is the Miraculous Coven, or whatever it was you said. Get me out of here, and I will tell you all about it!"

Dante was confused by the sudden discussion of the occult but retook control of the interrogation. His hands gripped and regripped the stock of his gun. "How did the Soviet find out you were double-dipping? Playing for two teams?"

"How should I know?" Pietr snapped. He was close to hysteria. "When things fell apart for us something must have come loose. The Soviets found out when they picked up the pieces. Now Koschei is looking for her."

For a second or two, Dante could neither speak nor think. His attention was consumed by the sinking, twisting feeling in his gut—the premonition of doom and bad tidings.

"Her?" he asked.

"Yes, yes." Pietr groaned as his whole body shivered uncontrollably. "Pretty thing, she is, except for a scar along the left side of her face."

Dante began to wish he'd never come here. He wished many things, and all of them collided in his mind forming an awful, tangled mess. As he reeled back, his line of sight passed Gage Gurung's face, which held both sympathy and concern.

And understanding. They both knew. At last, it was clear.

Arkadi Zorin, the hulking Russian assassin, had been sent to kill Janet Feng. The two of them had simply been in the way, at first. Then he'd come after them in the hope of getting to her.

His mouth felt like it had dried out and filled with ash, but Dante somehow managed to speak. "We need to get back to the hospital."

Somewhere down the tunnels, perhaps in the drug lab beyond the bunker, they heard more gunshots and a scream of pain.

CHAPTER NINETEEN

Heavy footsteps jogged down the corridors toward their position.

Gage looked at Vlad. "We must unchain him." He gestured at Pietr. "We must be able to move him away from here. They will find us soon."

Dante agreed with a sharp nod.

Someone shouted in what sounded more like Romanian than Russian, and three of Vlad's goons—men who looked familiar from up above when Gage and Dante had first stormed the compound—stomped around one of the corners and into their sight through the open doorway. A pair of gunshots echoed somewhere behind them. Closer and louder.

The guy out in front, who looked stunned by something and had trouble focusing his eyes, relayed a couple of sentences to Vlad in a disturbingly monotone voice. His boss responded with a short, snappy statement. The three men turned and went back into the labyrinth, with two of them taking up positions around one corner and the third crouching beside the other.

Dante glanced sharply at Vlad. "What'd they say? What's going on?"

Wiping the back of his hand across his mouth as he stared toward the doorway, Vlad snarled, "They did not stop Russians from getting into bunker. It will take them time to find how to get through maze." He kicked the leg of Pietr's chair. "If we leave him, we can take emergency exit tunnel and have time to escape."

Gage wasn't surprised by Pietr's reaction. The stocky gunrunner immediately spouted curses, pleas, and threats in a garbled mixture of different languages before settling on English.

"No, Vlad, you fool! I know more—much more! I can help you. You will get many business opportunities out of this. My contacts, my knowledge of the island, my skills. I can set up deals for you back on the mainland. You need to keep me alive!"

Vlad waved in disgust. "Never mind. I will keep myself alive instead." He looked at the guard with the shotgun, the one who had remained in the room. "Ion. Make sure Pietr stays in chair while I open door." He repeated it in Romanian, then rushed to the back of the room.

Ion, the guard, brought his gun up, aimed vaguely at a point an inch or two over Pietr's shoulder, which also put the two barrels between Dante and Gage. His face was drawn and trembling.

The Executioner and the physician responded in kind, raising their weapons and falling into tense combat stances. With a two-shot weapon, the guard was clearly at a disadvantage, but simply blowing him away would've meant that Vlad would shut the secret exit behind him. They held their positions, knowing that violence was a hair's breadth away, but waiting.

Ion didn't seem to be in any hurry to get himself killed. He stood still while his eyes darted around the chamber and beyond to see what was going on in the hallway. Sweat rolled down his forehead in bulbous, glistening drops.

Vlad had found a lever or something hidden by the little end table at the back of the room. It revealed a panel with a keypad, not unlike the one that protected the bunker labyrinth itself. He punched five buttons in sequence. Then a section of the wall in the rear corner next to the table came loose.

Outside was another volley of gunshots, still closer, and the sounds of more men shouting and screaming in pain. Booted feet continued to pound the floor as they tried to navigate the bunker's confusing layout.

Vlad came back to the center of the small room, standing directly behind his still-helpless cousin. He seemed unfazed that Ion and his guests were on the verge of a shootout. He pointed at Gage and Dante. "You two do not have to die. Come behind me, and leave bait where it is."

Pietr sobbed, gnashed his teeth, and spat insults in German and Romanian until Vlad struck him in the back of the head with the base of his pistol and spat in his hair. Gage was disgusted and suddenly wanted to put a 7.62 round through Vlad's skull but knew it would do nothing to improve their situation.

Dante was about to say something but noticed Ion's shoulders jerk. He glanced sideways through the doorway. His position made it difficult to see much, but someone was approaching down the hallway to the right.

"Down!" he shouted. The instant he opened his mouth, the shots rang out.

The Russians had finally bulled through the maze. They blasted away as soon as they saw Vlad's henchmen posted at the corners and the open door of Pietr's cell. The Romanians fired back. The entire underground space became painfully, oppressively loud with the merciless thunder of automatic weapons, the *clanging* of spent brass, and the agonized shrieks of dying men.

Dante dropped to his knees, then to his stomach. Gage did likewise, but at twenty years Dante's senior and with a bum ankle as well, it took him nearly a second longer. Cracks appeared in the walls around them, then holes. Whatever material formed the corridors, it had *some* resistance to bullets. But not enough.

Ion tried to get down as well, but luck wasn't on the guard's side. A stray round blew a red hole through the middle of his left thigh. Moaning in pain and jerking backward, he collapsed onto the floor, lying in an awkward position where he would only have been able to return fire on the Russians through the narrow space between Pietr's legs.

Vlad had already retreated again to the rear of the chamber, intending to make his getaway then and there. Whether anyone else was able to follow him didn't seem to concern him much. He fired a single round from his Luger into the hallway, then backed toward the threshold of the secret tunnel.

While Dante kept his eyes and shotgun trained on the door-way, where he could see flitting dark shapes but nothing yet good enough to shoot at, Gage traced the pattern of bullet holes in the wall with his eyes. His rifle could probably penetrate the mate-rial, but he was reluctant to fire blindly and risk hitting Vlad's men. Morally, they might've been no better than the Russian hitmen, but they were also the only thing standing between those same hitmen and the room where he lay.

It sounded like they were losing the battle.

Then someone ran by the doorway, firing an assault rifle on full auto through the opening and not stopping to witness the results of his handiwork. Dante blasted at him but missed. Then he was gone.

The volley of fire he'd unleashed did its job. Pietr screamed as three or four rounds perforated his torso, sending up a vapor spray of blood and cutting through one of the chain links. The rest of them loosened as his heavy body sagged in the chair. In a final twist of cruel irony, his bonds fell away as he fell out of the chair, free but dead when his face struck the ground.

His body also blocked Ion's line of fire. The guard cursed and propped his sawed-off shotgun on his elbow so it aimed over the corpse at the doorway.

Dante's brain had momentarily frozen during the anarchy,

but then his thoughts grew clear once again as Gage motioned toward the secret exit. "We must go," the Nepali insisted.

His partner nodded. They both got to their hands and knees and launched themselves toward the back of the room, keeping their heads and upper bodies down as they moved.

Another short burst of rifle fire, about three rounds, came from behind them. Dante felt one of the bullets graze his back, perhaps losing some momentum before it redirected its course straight into Vlad's left arm.

The drug dealer bellowed in pain as blood erupted from his mangled bicep. His other arm came up by reflex, holding the Luger and squeezing the trigger wildly. He ignored how close Dante and Gage were as his eyes focused on the doorway and what lay beyond.

Gage swore in his native tongue as one of the pistol's 9mm rounds sailed past his face, close enough that he felt the whistle of air on his lips. Then Vlad was gone. He'd ducked into the secret passage, but not before he did something within that made the hidden door automatically begin to close.

Dante grabbed Gage's sleeve. "Come on!" Hauling on his friend while Ion gibbered pitifully on the floor behind them, Dante heaved himself through the rapidly narrowing opening. Gage slipped past it with barely enough time to avoid having his arm pinched off by the mechanism. Then it ground shut.

The pair paused for a second or two to catch their breath and assess their surroundings. Beyond the secret door was a narrow corridor no more than five feet long, followed by a larger but still cramped room. There were no lights in it, but there appeared to be a wall-mounted sodium lamp embedded in another wall around the corner. A hallway branched off from the room to the right. Judging by the floor's angle, it looked like a ramp that led gradually up to the surface.

Far in the distance, Vlad's rapid footfalls faded as he ascended. Gage bitterly reflected that the gangster would probably make good on his escape, given how quick he'd been to abandon everyone else caught in the mess.

Dante was about to start after Vlad and get to safety but stopped as voices became audible on the other side of the hidden doorway. Gage held up a hand, noticing it at the same time. "Wait," he whispered.

Men were filtering into the cell, at least five of them, maybe more like seven or eight. Two spoke in Russian. It was unintelligible, but the duo distinctly heard the name "Pietr" mentioned twice. The goons must've reported that the crossfire killed their primary target.

There came a groan of pain from somewhere lower in the room. Ion, no doubt. The guard started in Romanian, but the Russians must not have known his language, so he switched to broken English instead.

"Please. Do not kill. I know where she is. Chinese agent! One you want. I can tell. Do not kill."

Dante flung his arms out in exasperation, cutting and striking the air in his sudden fury. He bit his lip to keep from cursing himself out loud and resolved to do it silently in his head instead.

Ion had overheard him when Pietr first revealed that the Russians were looking for Janet. Dante had mentioned that she was at the hospital. Catholic guilt or no, he would've felt terrible about it either way. His face flushed with shame in the dim light.

The cell fell quiet for a moment, then the deepest human voice either of them had ever heard spoke in response. *"Where is she?"*

Dante's spine tingled. There was no question whatsoever to whom that voice belonged.

In the pained silence that followed, someone reloaded a magazine and pulled back a charging handle. The guard, who'd probably been trying to hold out until he could get a guarantee that they would spare him, finally cracked.

"They said hospital. Only hospital. Maybe Atlantica General? Do not kill! I give what you want."

One of the other men, with voices appropriate to normal human beings, relayed what the man had said in Russian. A couple of people muttered in acknowledgment.

Then two sharp gunshots broke the brief spell of relative peace. Ion's voice turned into a gurgle and faded out. For his cooperation, the poor bastard had earned nothing but a quick death.

Gage wrapped his hand around Dante's arm. "We must move," he whispered.

The physician nodded. Both advanced around the corner toward the light and started up the sloping, ramped hallway. The tunnel was similar to the bunker, aside from the constant upward angle.

Behind them, the Russians beat feet back into the bunker labyrinth, leaving the small chamber of death behind. The one mercy fate had shown them, Dante decided, was that it hadn't occurred to their enemies to look for the secret exit.

In their haste and brutality, the Russkies hadn't paused to consider that the fire returned on them from within the cell was more than one man with a double-barrel could've laid down. They'd probably confused it with the shooting from Vlad's other men out in the hallways and hadn't deduced that there'd been more people in the room.

Climbing the long slope, which bent around to the left in one place, seemed to take an agonizingly long time. The angle was sharper than it had seemed at first, and fatigue was catching up to both of them. Gage's ankle pained him so he tried to favor the leg. Dante was helping him walk when the exit finally came into sight.

Gage observed, "I think we're moving in the opposite direction of the Autocutioner. I might be wrong because that maze was most confusing, but I believe this tunnel ends at the compound's far side."

Dante grunted. "Yeah, that would be just our fucking luck, wouldn't it? And Zorin, or Koschei or whatever you call the son of a bitch, is already on the move. This isn't going to be easy. Or fun. Or pleasant. Hell, it might not even be successful."

Despair wasn't in his nature, but neither was telling himself fairy tales to keep up his spirits. He was a realist. They were at a definite disadvantage.

The end of the tunnel leveled out, transforming from a ramp into a simple hallway. The walls here were no longer whatever plastic-like substance the bunker had used. They were simple stone and concrete and were damp with mold. A rectangle of thick golden lines showed at the end—sunlight leaking through the outline of a door.

Gage panted from the lengthy exertion but quipped, "I don't think we're still within Vlad's compound. We've come a long way."

"You're probably right." Dante loosened his hold on his friend's shoulder now that they were on flat ground. "Just a question of *how* far away it is and how long it will take to get back to the damn truck."

When they reached the door, it was unlocked and unlatched. There was no knob on their side, so they simply pushed it open. Beyond it lay an alley between two buildings, somewhere in the city's exurbs, which would put them a good four blocks from the supposed auto body shop and scrapyard operated by the Romanians.

Dante clenched his jaw. "Dammit. Too far. Those pricks have a head start on us, to boot."

They emerged from the alley onto the sidewalk of a street, not far from where they'd initially parked the Autocutioner when scoping out Vlad's headquarters. They could see the compound in the distance. If they'd had a vehicle, it would've qualified as "close." On foot, and with both of them tired…

Gage frowned and rubbed his chin. "There is something else which I've thought of," he declared. "There's a better than good chance that Zorin might've disabled my vehicle. I don't think he would make the mistake of leaving it, especially since he would've recognized it from the brothel.

"This time he wasn't wounded and fleeing for his life. He must know that we're nearby and will follow him if we can. He's probably instructed his men to slash the tires or at least left one or two men behind to slow us down."

Dante's hands rolled into fists. "Yeah. Probably. So what do we do? I could try running over there anyway since I can move faster than you can. If the truck's operational, I can drive it back here and pick you up. If not, well, I don't know."

The two men stood beside the street, frustrated by their situation and seemingly mocked by the eerie quiet in this desolate corner in the city's farthest outskirts. Then Gage spotted a dump truck rolling to a stop at the mouth of the alley. The driver climbed out and joined two other men who appeared from a nearby building before all went inside, leaving the truck where it was. They were probably construction workers and contractors on their way to another job site at the edge of Atlantica metro.

Gage bent and tightened the brace around his left ankle. Then he started into the street, crossing it at a slow jog.

"Hey!" Dante ran after him and caught up a second later. "What the hell are you doing, bud?"

The same rare, crazy smile Gage had worn when they'd first launched their vehicular attack on the scrapyard was back on his face. "Getting us a ride."

CHAPTER TWENTY

Gage fidgeted and looked behind him for the seventeenth or eighteenth time in the last three minutes. "I thought you said you'd done this many times. What kind of criminal are you?"

Dante paused in his labors to glare up at his partner. "Hotwiring a car, or a truck, ain't as easy as it looks in the movies, okay, pal? I didn't say 'many times,' I said I'd done it before. Once, successfully, about three years ago. And, uhh, one other time when I was a kid, except I fucked it up in that case."

He returned to fiddling with the wires beneath the steering wheel as Gage sighed and took his nineteenth glance behind him at the street. So far, the construction guys were oblivious that they were about to become victims of grand theft auto. They must've had a lot to discuss within the building. Or a lot of drugs to snort or inject.

Gage leaned down a little. "When you succeed, let me drive. Trust me on this, please. I will let you use my rifle if you need to make a shot from a longer distance."

"Yeah, yeah," Dante muttered. A tiny spark appeared somewhere in the shadows where his hands worked. Then the dump truck's engine roared to life, seeming to over-exert itself at first before its growl lowered to a steady purr. "Hah! I knew I still had it in me."

Dante pulled his head out from beneath the dashboard and settled into the passenger's seat while Gage sat behind the wheel, pulled the door shut, and set out at once to shift gears, grab the steering wheel, and find the brake and gas pedals. The truck's rightful operators were unlikely to remain clueless much longer given how loud the engine was.

"Go," Dante urged. "I did my part. You do yours. Only fair."

Scowling with annoyance at his friend's statement of the obvious, Gage put the truck in drive and released the brake, allowing it to rumble and roll forward out of the alley.

Sure enough, the three men ran out of the adjacent building as Gage turned the truck into the street. Despite all three being overweight and middle-aged, they were moving with surprising speed.

"Hey!" one bellowed. "Get your fuckin' ass back here, you fuckin' piece of shit!"

Dante leaned out the window and cupped his hands around his mouth as Gage pushed down on the gas. "Watch your language, bud. Besides, we're only *borrowing* it."

A street lamp passed disturbingly close to his head, rustling his hair, and he pulled himself back into the vehicle in sudden alarm. "I need to quit doing that crap. Especially when you're driving."

"Yes, that is an excellent idea. Now help me find the fastest route to the hospital. I remember some of these streets, but I lack familiarity with this part of the town."

A couple of passing cars honked at them for no particular reason. Maybe they'd seen the brief spectacle with the construction workers, who were now receding in the rearview mirror. Or perhaps they simply objected to another large, unwieldy dump truck clogging up the streets that their faster, sleeker vehicles would've otherwise dominated.

Dante directed his partner through the western outskirts of Atlantica City until they progressed deeper into the metropolis. The general hospital wasn't too long a drive from where they'd been, but it seemed to take far too long nonetheless.

Arkadi Zorin and his cronies must've had at least a seven- or eight-minute start on them, possibly longer, given their mercilessly long trek up the sloping tunnel. Not to mention the precious minutes Dante had to spend hotwiring the truck.

They didn't encounter too much traffic and got away with running a red light at a relatively empty intersection, despite the honks of protest from a motorist who was still a good hundred yards away. However, the dump truck was slow to accelerate and didn't have the same maximum speed as a high-end car. Each time they had to turn, it seemed to take a minor eternity to get the rumbling mass of steel back up to an acceptable velocity.

"Fuck," Dante muttered. "I only hope those bastards hit every red light on the way there, not that they probably would've stopped. And that MacLeod's men see them in advance and know what they're doing."

Gage kept his eyes on the road but nodded. "Yes." He paused, wanting to ask something but unsure how his friend would take it. They'd grown to know each other quite well over the last five weeks or so, but the doctor was, by Gage's standards, rather volatile in his emotions.

Still, there was no escaping the fact that an excruciating conundrum awaited at the end of their mission. Gage had to know what Dante intended to do.

"When we arrive, and if we succeed in stopping the Russians, what will you do?" He waited a second for the question's implications to sink in before he added, "About *her*. Since you're now aware that Janet—or whatever her name truly is—is a Chinese spy. I know you don't want to think about it. But we must. It changes everything."

Three times in a minute, Dante opened his mouth and tried to speak but could never spit out more than one or two vague, noncommittal words at a time. Good answers weren't forthcoming. His mind couldn't deal with the question in their haste to rescue her, and he had no desire to tackle the dilemma of how to deal with her.

At last, he managed something. He gulped. "I suppose that since Atlantica, um, has no real laws, we can say she technically isn't breaking any rules by being here. Right? Right? Makes sense to me."

His moment of defiance didn't last, and he swallowed the lump forming in his throat. "But, uh. Shit. There are still all those other fucking laws, the international ones about who can and can't operate here on behalf of their governments. That goddamn treaty. I forget its name..."

His voice trailed off as he tried not to dwell on it.

"Yes," Gage affirmed, but he felt that Dante was still dodging the real issues at hand. "The many world governments seem to be, how does one say, being obtusely literal about this all. By that I mean, the laws about how the governmental forces of an established country cannot occupy Atlantica.

"I would imagine that Red China would certainly disavow Janet if someone discovered her. They would claim to have no knowledge of who she is or say that she acted without orders, against their wishes. Sending spies they can deny allows them to pull a dirty trick and get around the laws."

Dante had been rubbing his chin. For a second or so, the motion changed into covering his mouth with his hand. He closed his eyes and shook his head.

"Let's, uh," he mumbled in a hollow voice. "Let's get to the damn hospital first. After we deal with our old friend Koschei, we can decide what to do about her. I don't want to talk about it until the big Russian prick is dead or fleeing the hell off the island if nothing else."

Gage responded with a slow nod, almost a bow of the head. "So be it. I understand. We're almost there, are we not?"

"Yes." Dante took his hand away from his mouth and opened his eyes. "Yeah, about two more blocks. Keep your eyes open, and I'll do likewise. We don't know how well they're going to be watching their backs. They must've figured we would be along after them at some point."

So far, Gage saw no direct evidence that anything was wrong. However, a sudden flow of cars moved away from the hospital's vicinity. Occasional pedestrians, whether singly or in groups, also tried to hurry away from the place.

That wasn't encouraging.

As Gage prepared for the worst, Dante queried in a rare display of irresponsible distractedness, "So, about the Coven of Miracles. What does that have to do with all this? Why would the Chinese want in on it? You mentioned it before, didn't you? I don't remember much about it, though."

The Gurkha grimaced and made a low sound of disapproval in his throat. He contemplated ignoring the question until the necessity for action drew Dante's attention away from it. Then Dante's mind might chew on it in the hospital while they should stay focused on combat.

Thus he opted to tell his friend the short version of the story.

"Yes. When I was at the archaeological dig in the hills, we discovered an ancient temple or complex that made highly advanced use of Atlanticore as a power source. Daria Barruk and I discovered that Dr. Limbu, the head researcher, was in league with this coven. She wished to harvest the crystal on their behalf, betraying her profession as a scientist for the sake of what she thought was the greater good.

"What is most disturbing is that ancient Atlantica's technology seemed truly incredible. If it could be replicated or built upon, the person or group who controlled it would wield tremendous influence. It would make the internal combustion engine and the modern generator quickly seem quaint and outdated."

Up ahead, the hospital came into view. It was hard to see much yet, but something felt wrong. There were too many vehicles in front of the main building.

Gage added, "Daria suspects these people count among their members many of Atlantica's wealthiest and most powerful individuals. Perhaps the wealthy and powerful of other nations, as well. We have yet to see much evidence of their existence. She is certain that they do exist and aren't to be trifled with."

Dante sighed, but he returned to full alertness as Atlantica General drew closer. "Great. Exactly what we need—a cult of rich weirdos that Russians are trying to infiltrate. I don't know if I can believe this stuff about an advanced lost civilization. I mean, come on. That's like something out of one of those old adventure serials."

He looked at Dante's face. The Nepali's earnest expression, combined with his long history of being honest and trustworthy... "Okay, maybe I do believe it. Before we conclude that little topic, it looks like we're gonna have our work cut out for us here. Take a look at this crap." He pointed in front of them.

Gage saw.

It sounded like Zorin only had around half a dozen henchmen with him when he'd assaulted Vlad's compound, but there must've been other allies or hirelings of his lying in wait elsewhere. By the looks of it, he'd brought *a lot* of his friends with him to Atlantica General.

No fewer than five vehicles consisting of two black vans, a black pickup truck, a red sedan, and a light military truck had formed a blockade at the hospital's front. They'd parked in a crescent shape and prevented any easy entrance through the building's front doors.

Six men with guns stood guard along the blockade. Three faced outward, their firearms braced on the hoods of their vehicles, while the others stood with their backs to the parking lot, watching the hospital entrance and scanning the windows above and to the sides.

"Shit," Dante snapped. "Shit, shit, shit! He's already inside. We don't have to make a plan. We're going to have to—whoa!"

He fell back in his seat as the dump truck's engine loudly digested a fresh infusion of gas and the vehicle accelerated, coming dangerously close to its maximum speed in a matter of seconds.

Gage was staring straight ahead, ignoring the pain in his left foot as he compressed the pedal with his right.

Dante blinked. "What are you doing?"

To his surprise, the Gurkha's face split into another madman's grin. "I'm reliving my days of glory."

The truck rocketed straight toward the barricade.

Dante sputtered, "This thing isn't armored like the Autocutioner! It's not supposed to stand up to serious direct punishment, okay?"

As though eager to prove him right, two of the thugs out front with longer-range rifles opened fire. Some of the shots missed, but those that hit sounded like they were ripping into the truck's body rather than *pinging* off as would've been the case with Gage's official ride. Another punched a shockingly clean hole through the glass windshield about halfway between them, with the projectile sailing through and out the back end.

Gage's smile widened. "The fuel truck during the war. It wasn't armored either. Be thankful that this time, we aren't carting a metric ton of combustible liquid behind us."

Dante slapped a hand over his eyes, leaned his head back, and groaned. "Jesus Christ." Then he winced as a random memory resurfaced of being scolded by Father Lucchese back home for taking the Lord's name in vain.

Of course, the good Lord's help and intervention might be necessary for Gage's ridiculous plan to work.

They'd cleared more than half the distance across the lot. Impact would arrive in seconds.

By now, Koschei's minions had figured out what was about to happen. In a last-ditch effort, all six of them concentrated fire on the approaching truck, blasting with everything they had.

Gage ducked behind the dash, still gripping the steering wheel to keep their course straight. Dante did likewise, spouting off a stream of colorful four-letter words. Bullets slammed into the truck's shell, shattered glass, and raised columns of angry steam from the engine.

Then Gage poked his head back up. They were almost there. Something in his gut lurched with instinctive horror, but he ignored it. The last thing he saw before the collision was the half-dozen men diving for cover as they screamed in terror.

The world split asunder in a cacophony of localized storms and earthquakes. The din of smashing and tearing metal, breaking glass, and shattering concrete overwhelmed everything as the dump truck crashed through. Gage had aimed the truck's front end at the sedan, the weakest part of their foes' makeshift barricade. It tore through and *crunched* the smaller car with surprising ease. It also sheared massive pieces off the two vehicles to either side although they did as much damage as they took.

Gage felt the cab breaking and compressing around him as vertigo tried to rob him of his senses. He cranked on the wheel, trying to intentionally drift the truck sideways to arrest its momentum before it slammed into the hospital's lobby.

It worked...in a manner of speaking. The truck let out a tremendous groan and tipped over on its side, crashing onto the stairs and skidding toward the stone pillars that held up the front portico.

Dante exclaimed, "Fuuuuuuck!"

The columns broke apart under the truck's onslaught, and the roof collapsed, shattering to bits that tumbled over the jagged edges of exposed steel. Dust and smoke were everywhere, but the noise was dying down.

Coughing, dizzy, and with their whole bodies tingling with the possibility of momentary severe pain, Gage and Dante climbed out of the cab. It was badly wrecked by the succession of impacts, but not enough to crush the life out of them.

Dante rose to his feet, staggering around as if drunk. He tried to point at the collapsed structure but vaguely waved. "Good idea," he rasped. "Taking out those pillars."

Koschei's thugs had opened fire on them again from the rear, but the pile of debris with all its heavy steel and concrete did a surprisingly good job of shielding them.

"Oh." Gage dusted himself off and unslung his rifle. "Y-yes. I meant to do that."

CHAPTER TWENTY-ONE

It came as something less than a surprise when Gage and Dante strode into the hospital's main lobby and found it effectively deserted. People's bags and things lay scattered across the floor, someone had overturned a gurney, a water cooler had been knocked over or destroyed, and broad puddles still shimmered beneath the fluorescent lights.

Not a single person was in sight. Gage suddenly felt ill at the thought that if any patients had been present in the waiting area, the Russian might've taken them hostage.

As they trotted toward the front desk and the hallways to the building's interior that led beyond, a woman popped up, hands up and palms out, trembling beyond all ability to control and sobbing. Her face was red and tear-streaked.

"Don't shoot! Please, don't shoot!" she pleaded.

Dante was the first to address her. "Hey, it's okay, we're the good guys. We're not going to hurt you, but you need to get down and stay down. Which way did they go?" He didn't think it was necessary to specify who he meant by "they" under the circumstances.

The woman refused to make eye contact but pointed to the right, toward the swinging double doors.

"Figures," Dante grumbled.

Gage asked, "Do the elevators work?" As the question left his mouth, it occurred to him that elevator access points would be obvious places for Zorin to post sentries. Not to mention if the Russians noticed someone coming up to the third floor where Janet and Jubal rested, they might've been able to cut the lines or simply drop a grenade down the shaft.

Still, they needed to move fast. Haste, shock, and awe might be their best friends against an entrenched and numerically superior foe.

The woman had already sunk back behind the reception desk. She bawled, "I don't know. I don't know anything. They came in and shot the guard, then dragged him away. Everyone ran. I couldn't. I just hid. I don't even know what's going on!"

Dante waved. "Yeah, understandable. Don't worry about it, kid. We'll take care of this." He topped off his shotgun with shells from his pocket and pumped it, the distinctive double-clicking sound echoing in the broad, tile-covered space.

Gage loaded a fresh magazine in his rifle and made sure he had spares. Two extra—not as many as he would like, but it ought to be enough. Especially since they would be fighting at close range. His revolver or his kukris might get the job done if his AR-10 could not.

Dante kicked open the double doors. Both had their guns held ready to fire, but there was no one within the hallway beyond. Footsteps were approaching, though.

A Russian-accented voice barked, "Stop them!" Then two figures ran in front of the windows set within the other double doors at the end of the hallway.

Dante was about to fire, but Gage said, "Wait. We don't yet know that it isn't two civilians trying to get away from—"

A single gunshot resounded, and a hole opened in the door

across from them at chest height. The bullet struck Gage in the chest, *thumping* him but not doing any serious damage thanks to his vest. Suddenly furious, he aimed and fired his rifle at the same instant Dante opened up with his shotgun.

The doors opened as they returned fire, revealing two men, one dark and one pale, armed with cheap handguns. The volley of rifle bullets and buckshot overwhelmed them before they could squeeze off any further attacks, and both went down shrieking and spewing blood. Their bodies toppled back onto a weight scale.

Gage grimaced. "So much for stealth."

Dante observed, "Those guys weren't Russian. Zorin is running low on his people. He must've hired a bunch of random punks off the street."

They ducked into the room beyond the second set of doors. It was empty aside from the pair of corpses.

"Which means," Gage elaborated, "that they'll perhaps be easier foes, but also that they'll lack discipline and pose a greater danger to innocent people."

Dante frowned. "Shit. Let's move." He racked his gun, ejecting a spent shell and chambering another.

They proceeded to the next room, where a nurse lay dead from a gunshot to the head. The sight was so infuriating that Dante failed to notice when a hidden man sprang up from beneath a gurney and wrapped his arms around him from behind, preventing him from retaliating with his Ithaca.

Gage saw at once what had happened and pivoted toward his partner. "Dante!" Before he could return fire, someone else took a potshot at him from a small examination room with the door cracked open up ahead. Making a split-second decision that he hoped was the *right* one, Gage left Dante to his devices for a second while he swiveled his rifle toward the room and fired four times through the door and walls. Someone groaned.

Dante grunted as he struggled against the guy who'd

ambushed him, a tall, lanky individual with an oversized mustache. Dante felt a metal object at the man's hip, probably a handgun, and his lean arms were iron-strong. There would be no breaking out of his grip by direct force. Dante thought of something else.

He bowed his head down and to the side, and with a fast, sharp movement of his hands and forearms, "stabbed" the barrel of his shotgun up and back, striking the lanky man in the jaw. He yelped in pain, and Dante broke free and spun.

Realizing what was about to happen, the man froze in horror and alarm with his hands out, screaming, "No!"

Dante killed him anyway. He fired a single blast at the man's face. His head ceased to exist while the rest of him toppled back against the red-stained, pellet-marked wall.

Instantly Dante felt a pang of awful guilt, a sense that he should've given the man a chance to surrender or flee. Then he thought of the dead nurse, Jubal, and Janet. There was no time for him to do anything except neutralize all threats as soon as they appeared.

Meanwhile, Gage advanced on the room with the snipers. Halfway there, Dante blew the head off the man who'd attacked him. The Gurkha barely flinched. The warrior part of his brain simply acknowledged that it was a variable he no longer had to worry about.

When he was only an arm's length from the barely open door, another shot rang out, punching through the wall and striking the center of his rifle. It *clanged* loudly and was torn from his hands, *clattering* to the other side of the room. He rolled to the side as a third shot followed the second, mentally cursing himself for fully unslinging his weapon.

As he came out of the roll, Gage had already drawn his revolver and kukri. Dante turned toward the scene as the Gurkha fired two shots from his Webley into the space to the left of where the opposing bullets came from.

Silence. Dante whispered, "I'll open the door." Gage nodded.

The physician crept around to the far side and kicked the door open while Gage sprang directly onto the threshold from the other side. A tough-looking woman wearing a shabby cap knelt with a hunting rifle across her knee. She twisted toward them in alarm. At least one of Gage's shots had struck her in the leg, hampering her movement.

Gage didn't give her a chance for a fourth shot. He sprang at her, kukri flashing across her face, throat, and chest, and she fell over in a quivering mass, falling quiet a second or two later.

Dante asked, "Your rifle?"

"No time to properly check it. We must find the stairs or the elevator."

The Nepali reloaded his revolver as they tramped down the next hallway. He could recover the AR-10 later or get a new one if the woman's rifle shot had wrecked it.

Dante topped off his Ithaca. "To be honest, the recoil from this fucking thing is starting to hurt." Then he laughed as though recognizing the absurdity of what he'd said while people were trying to kill him.

"Perhaps a 20-gauge next time?" Gage suggested.

"Pfft," his friend snorted. "20-gauge is for Junior's first duck hunt. I mean, it would probably still work, but back in my neighborhood in New York, it was 12-gauge or bust. By 'bust,' I mean my wrists and collarbone."

No one else assailed them as they came to an area where two elevators waited at one end of the room and a door to the stairwell at the other.

Gage walked to the buttons at the former and pressed one. "For the sake of my ankle, let us *try* the elevators first, and if—"

As the door *dinged* and opened, someone on the second or third floor opened up with a submachine gun or full-auto rifle, blasting the top of the elevator car and likely trying to cut the cables while they were at it. Half of the bullets punched through the compartment and sparked against its interior.

Gage backed away.

"So," Dante remarked, "the stairs."

The Nepali tightened his ankle brace. Dante helped him climb, but it still took longer than they wanted. When they were halfway up the second flight, about three-quarters of the way to the second floor, the structure shook with the tramping of running feet and the doors at the landing above burst open. Whoever had shot up the elevator had reached the same conclusion they had.

"Down!" Dante shouted and shoved Gage out of the way. He raised his shotgun and pumped off a couple of shells.

For whatever reason, his blasts failed to accomplish anything. A silhouette beyond the doors dumped a magazine's worth of automatic fire at them. Dante took at least seven or eight rounds square in the chest. He cried out in alarm as they knocked him off his feet and he fell to the first landing.

Gage's mind tried to process everything at once. He reasoned that the weapon must've been a submachine gun since it failed to penetrate Dante's armor as a proper rifle might've. A few of the rounds hit the steps and railing near him. He raised his Webley, tried to ignore the spraying bullets, and fired once.

Blood spurted from the silhouette's head, and it toppled. Two more silhouettes emerged. One of them threw something a round, dark-colored object.

For the first time since the battle began, Gage nearly panicked. He swung his head back and saw Dante back on his feet and rushing toward him. Together they charged up the rest of the stairs with speed neither would've thought physically possible except through the miracle of pure adrenaline.

They faced their next two adversaries, a pair of men who were probably members of Zorin's circle, across the second-floor landing as the grenade went off.

The *boom* shook the entire wing of the hospital, and the men felt the heat before the fireball bloomed up toward them. The Russians ducked for cover around the edge of the doorway as Gage and Dante threw themselves against the far wall. One of the Russians wasn't quite fast enough. The back of his jumpsuit caught fire and fragments of shrapnel cut bloody lines across his arms and legs.

Then, as though no one was sure who'd started it or why, all four men were abruptly locked in hand-to-hand combat. They crashed into one another, seeking blood.

Dante grappled with the slower man. His face had contorted with crazed anger, he held a knife, and the fire was spreading across his clothes, likely beginning to feed on his skin. Dante held his wrist with the knife at bay and punched the man in the gut to no avail. Then the Russian reached toward his face, clawing for his eyes.

"Fucker," Dante grunted and kneed the man in the groin hard enough to throw him off-balance. The Russian was nearly a foot shorter than Dante. He more or less fell into the physician's grasp. Dante picked him up with a hand on his shoulder and hip and threw him over the edge of the staircase.

The man screamed as he plummeted. The distance wasn't that far, but the small of his back landed directly on the railing near the first-floor doorway. Then he toppled off into a residual patch of flames from the explosion.

Gage stood off against the other man, who was fat but deceptively quick with a knife. The Gurkha had drawn his kukri, and they edged forward and back, circling one another, moving into the hallway beyond the second-floor doors. The Russian's weapon was smaller and lighter, but it couldn't make the same ghastly wounds as the Nepalese machete.

The Russian reached out with a flicking strike, which turned out to be feint, and sidestepped with paradoxical casualness to knife Gage's kidney.

Gage had expected a trick like this. He hopped forward, effectively ignoring the man's knife stroke and swinging his kukri at the man's face. When the Russian stumbled back to avoid it, Gage raised his revolver and shot the man twice in the chest. The Russian's eyes bulged with astonishment and perhaps disappointment at being robbed of a full-length duel against a respectable adversary. He slumped.

There was no time for a fair fight.

"Dante," Gage urged. "Come." He stepped over the man he'd killed as Dante returned from the banister, and they climbed to the third floor.

Once again, Dante kicked open the door. Both men sprang into the hall, guns ready, only to encounter nothing. Up ahead were the sounds of a struggle. They trotted through the hall, rounding a corner to a suite of surgical rooms that looked familiar. The chamber lined with beds where Jubal recovered and where they'd rested was around the next corner.

Their eyes met. "On three," Gage breathed. "One... two... *three*."

Dante inhaled through his nose during the countdown, then swiveled around the corner with his shotgun shouldered and aimed at chest level. He knew he'd have had to do it fast, but every once in a while, he amazed himself.

Right around the corner was another of Koschei's hired goons, a muscular Jamaican holding a long-barreled .357 or .44 Magnum revolver beside himself with the muzzle aimed upward. He'd been preparing to ambush the intruders when they showed themselves. Little did he realize how close they already were.

Dante fired as soon as he saw the man, and the Jamaican's face contorted horribly as the shotgun *boomed*, spitting fire, smoke, and buckshot into the center of his torso. He let out a guttural cry as the multiple pellet impacts blasted him back to fall against the side of a bed. Blood poured from his chest and stomach in shining red rivulets.

As he went down, his finger compulsively squeezed the

trigger of his massive handgun, which thundered and blew a hole through the ceiling. Dante hoped there weren't other patients trying to recover on the fourth floor.

At the same instant the tall physician took out the Jamaican, Gage came around the corner the long way and saw a jowly-faced Russian grappling with one of MacLeod's security guys against the wall opposite where Dante was. Both men had dropped their guns. Now they tried to disable one another so whoever remained on his feet could go for a weapon and end the fight.

Gage pulled his right kukri, the older one he'd had before the Executives gifted him with a second. He screamed and charged.

Both men saw him at the same instant. They briefly froze, stunned at the sight of the small balding man hurtling toward them with a huge, broad-bladed knife. The security man recognized Gage at the last second and went limp, sliding down and out of the Russian's grasp before tumbling to the side. He barely managed to roll under the Jamaican's ravaged body.

The Russian tried to counter-charge Gage, but he tripped against the hip of his erstwhile opponent and stumbled straight into the attack. His hands grasped uselessly for Gage's wrist. Instead, the blade sheared off half of his hand before burying itself at the juncture of his neck and shoulder, splitting his clavicle.

As the man convulsed, Gage ripped the knife free and kicked him in the stomach. He doubled over, which made it far easier for Gage to raise the kukri once more, this time splitting open the back of the Russian's skull. He dropped instantly, straight down, and didn't move again.

It took a second for those who remained on their feet to realize that the fight was over for the moment. Their enemies were dead. It took another second after that to notice Jubal.

The young prostitute had made himself scarce, piling into the farthest corner of the room and barely visible between two beds.

Dante's first panicked thought was that he'd been killed and tossed there to get him out of the way. Then the boy's leg moved, clearly due to living bodily volition.

"Jubal," he gasped and hastened across the floor. "Are you okay? Stupid question, but bear with me."

Jubal's chest was still heavily bandaged. Otherwise, he wore only cotton pants. He looked at Dante as though staring through him, his jaw slack. "It's so loud." His deep voice was soft and oddly childlike.

Dante nodded and extended a hand to help him up. "Yeah. Nobody ever thinks gunshots will be that bad until they hear them in real life. Especially indoors. For Christ's sake, my ears are still ringing. I'll probably end up with tinnitus. Did you get hit? Any gunshots, knife wounds, punches, kicks, anything?"

Jubal shook his head. "No. I hid when it started. They didn't care about me. They were after the woman."

"We know." Dante helped him to the nearest bed and supported him by the arm while guiding him atop it. "Lie down and rest. Stay here until help arrives. I think it's almost over, okay? We only have to deal with, um, probably a couple more at most. And the big guy."

Jubal shuddered, knowing who he meant.

Meanwhile, Gage had gone to check on the security officer he'd helped. "And you, sir? How are you?"

The man grunted. "Mostly fine, thanks to yourself. You boys trying to stop that huge Russian? He already got past us. I'm sorry. Janet ran off, the other thugs pinned us down, and the big guy ran past after the girl. We tried our best. Goddammit, we tried. One of the guys went after them. I don't know what happened to him."

"It's all right. Do you have a radio? Walkie-talkie? Phone?"

The man sighed. "We tried raising someone on the radio but couldn't get through."

Dante had seen to Jubal. Now he turned to the guard. "Keep

trying. Stay here and watch Jubal. Which way did Janet go? And the Russian."

The man pointed at the other hallway. It stretched in the opposite direction from where they'd entered the room. Then he fumbled over to the corner table, where a radio set had miraculously survived the general carnage.

Dante's and Gage's eyes met. "Come on," Dante said.

"Yes," Gage agreed as they hustled out and down the corridor. He called back to the guard, "Tell Eleanor Cervantes everything, and have her send help."

A couple of paces ahead of him, Dante growled, "Time to finish this."

CHAPTER TWENTY-TWO

Dante was out in front. Bodies lay across the hallway. Three of them, to be exact, none belonging to the two people he was most interested in. One was undoubtedly the security trooper who had gone after Zorin, based on his blue uniform. He'd taken a couple of bullets to the legs and had a broken neck.

The second was another of the street thugs the Russian had hired to help him, a bedraggled but otherwise average-looking man with holes riddling his torso and whose dead hands still clutched an empty sawed-off over-under shotgun.

The third was a male nurse who must've tried to intervene. The massive hole in his chest suggested he'd taken a barrel from the thug's shotgun at close range.

Dante was sorry for all of them, but there was no time to dwell on their fate. He jogged down the corridor, stepping over or dodging around their bodies as needed. His objective was the small sitting room at the end, which lay in the windowed north-east corner of the third floor. Gage kept up about three paces behind him.

Voices were shouting up ahead, a woman's and a man's, the latter deep and ogrish. Dante and Gage reached the mouth of the hallway and stopped in surprise at what they saw in the room beyond.

Janet Feng stood in front of Arkadi Zorin, the latter motionless, for the woman pointed a pair of pistols at his face—a Browning Hi-Power in her right hand, and a snub nose .38 revolver in the left. Both Dante and Gage had begun to wonder if it would take an elephant gun to deal with Koschei, but even someone as invincible as him wouldn't be able to survive a volley of medium-caliber bullets through the brain.

It looked like Janet was about to pull the triggers. The Russian towered over her, but she seemed only cursorily afraid. Her posture was that of a wolverine forced to fight a large dog and determined to win through sheer viciousness.

"Tell me," she demanded. "*Tell me now.*" Neither Gage nor Dante had heard such harshness in her voice before. A trace of Mandarin accent crept in as she lost her composure.

Zorin's twisted wreck of a face sneered in defiance. He responded in English. "Fuck you."

"I'm not asking you again!" Janet raged. Her slim fingers were curling around the triggers of the two guns.

Koschei only grinned.

In a flash, Janet's left hand adjusted its aim, moving downward and spitting fire as she put a round in the giant's leg above his kneecap. He snarled and dropped to one knee. Even lowered as he was, it was easy for him to look her in the eye, and his unbroken demeanor remained.

"Do it, *suka*," he dared her in his thick Russian accent, his lips drawn back from his massive teeth.

Janet raised the revolver back up alongside the Browning and pressed both an inch closer to the man's face. "*Tell me!*"

The two were totally focused on one another, locked in their battle of wills. Gage and Dante moved into the room while they were distracted. Dante took the longer route to the right flank while Gage moved in on the left.

Zorin's eyes darted from side to side. He'd seen them both. His hideous grin only widened.

Nothing in Janet's posture or attitude changed, but when she spoke next, it was to the young doctor. "Dante," she began, in a lower but still steely voice without taking her eyes off the Russian. "Please give me a few more minutes."

"Why? What is it you want from him, Janet?"

The muscles of her neck tightened. "I don't have time to explain the world of espionage to you!"

Dante brought his shotgun up to low ready. "Do it anyway. I insist."

Zorin's eyes gloatingly drank in the sight as Janet kept him pinned down with her dual handguns.

Frustrated, the woman spat, "I need to know his contacts with the Soviets. I must do some cleaning. You understand, yes? I will let you two help me. We could work together."

Gage saw his opportunity to tease out more of her motivations. "We might be able to reach an agreement if you will tell us about your dealings with the Coven of Miracles."

"That's why I took the job under Dr. Costa. My orders were to listen to anything the Executioners said about the Coven and as a favor to them, to kill you once I'd learned everything I could, Dr. Gurung."

Gage frowned. He wasn't so much angry as simply disappointed. Dante's face, meanwhile, was blank with shock.

Ms. Feng went on, "Perhaps I kept both of you alive longer than I should've. Then I needed protection from Koschei here. The great and terrible Koschei. I needed time to consider what my options were.

"Now I consider leaving you two alive a realistic option. But you must understand I will not turn against the Coven. I will not turn against my country—I don't mean America. My parents chose the wrong side. They were idiots. I will not betray China. Not even for you, Dante."

The tall physician listened with a kind of sick fascination. Although most of what she'd said over these last weeks had been no more than a bundle of lies, he believed all that she told him now. Judging by her tone and the brief softening of her attitude at the end of her short spiel, he understood that she hadn't fabricated *all* her feelings.

She continued, "We can still work together. This is Atlantica, not America, Italy, Britain, or Nepal. The Soviets are all our enemies." Her tone hardened as she again focused on Zorin's leering face. "They do not play nice. They are not living up to the Communist ideal of *sharing*."

Gage took a gentle step closer along Janet's left side. "Ms. Feng. Please. The Coven is nothing to trifle with."

"I know that better than you do," she snapped. "Which is why I will not betray them."

Gage took another step and was about to continue reasoning with her when her left arm swiveled to point the revolver at his face.

"Back up. Do not come any closer."

Dante blinked as a sudden cold rage awoke within him. He leveled his shotgun at the slim young woman. "Stop pointing that gun at my friend, Janet. I'm warning you."

She must not have expected such a forceful reaction from him because, for a second, her focus and resolve wavered. It was all the time Arkadi Zorin needed to spring forward like a charging bull launched from a catapult and knock the much smaller woman aside.

Janet tumbled into Gage, and the two of them crashed into the wall in a tangle of limbs. She dropped both of her pistols upon impact. As her arms flailed, one of her falling guns caught the hammer of Gage's revolver and dragged the weapon down. It stayed in his grasp but now aimed at the floor.

At the same instant, Zorin continued his charge—toward Dante. The physician panic-fired his shotgun as the giant bowled into him. Most of the buckshot went astray as Zorin knocked the barrel aside and engulfed Dante with his huge, strong arms.

Janet and Gage both recovered from their collision at about the same instant. Their hands shot out in search of weapons in near-unison as well. Gage tried to bring his Webley up to bear, while with his left hand he reached for one of his kukris. Ms. Feng fumbled for his gun, trying to seize it to replace hers, while also attempting to trap his other hand from drawing a knife.

Gage moved forward, trying to throw her off-balance to interfere with her efforts. She was fast. She knocked aside his gun hand and snatched the other kukri from his back, the newer one. It came free in her hand as he drew the original. He also raised his gun hand again.

Janet's face was eerily serene. She lashed down with the kukri, opening a cut on Gage's right hand and knocking the revolver from his grip in the same movement.

He stepped back, creating more distance between them as Janet rebalanced herself and hefted the blade. The way she moved and handled an edged weapon...neither was indicative of anything close to an amateur. This, the Nepali realized, was a dangerous opponent with martial arts training, including knives and swords.

She extended her empty hand toward him, index and middle finger tightly pressed together and pointing upward while the rest of her hand curled beneath them. Her black eyes shone with subdued intensity. Then she lunged.

Gage brought up his kukri in time to deflect the blow with the flat of the blade, knocking hers aside and putting his greater body weight into it. She recovered with startling speed and feinted at him with quick licking strikes, trying to make him flinch and reveal an opening in his defenses.

She was faster and more agile than he, at least fifteen years younger and highly athletic. The demure nurse had been a disguise all along for the deadly creature she was in truth. Still, she lacked Gage's upper body strength and combat experience. He anticipated most of her moves, shutting them down with a stout defense even if he couldn't summon the speed to end her yet. She seemed unfamiliar with the kukri—it was an unusual weapon, with its forward-bent and top-heavy blade, much different from the rapier-like Chinese *jian* or the *dao* saber—but she was adapting to its quirks with disturbing ease.

The two remained evenly matched for the time being. As Janet danced toward the rear of the room, where the uncurtained windows showed the eastern sky, the dancing interplay of their knives only became more savage and perilous.

On the other side of the room, a completely different sort of struggle took place. The two pairs of combatants were only about fifteen feet apart, but it might as well have been fifteen miles.

Since Zorin had batted aside Dante's shotgun, he made the most of a bad situation and swung it back upward, bringing the butt into contact with the giant Russian's jaw. It sounded like something cracked, yet Zorin didn't seem to notice. The mad rush of bloodlust had consumed him, and his freakish size and mass absorbed whatever violence Dante could execute.

Zorin's arms clamped down, squeezing Dante's limbs against his torso. The shotgun fell from his grasp, and he felt his adversary breathing on his face as he laughed and gurgled. Suddenly terrified, as much by his sheer helplessness as anything else, Dante tried not to piss himself. Zorin killed people with his bare hands. And it looked like he enjoyed it.

Too much, in fact. Rather than snap Dante's neck or crunch his skull, he lifted the smaller man and hurled him backward so he crashed against a refrigerator and rolled forward.

As Dante struggled to get to his knees, his brain took a second to sort out the chaotic stimuli around him. Koschei was singing. The prospect of crushing him like a bug had inspired the giant to belt out an old Russian folk song with the jovial tone made perverse by his ogrish, basso profundo voice.

He loomed over Dante, raising his foot to step on him. The sole of his boot looked like the underbelly of a small car falling from a cliff somewhere high above.

Dante's hand went to his side and came up with his 1911. The sight of the pistol gave Zorin half a second's pause. Then he simply stomped awkwardly toward the physician's gun hand. Dante screamed as the bones in his arm strained and rattled under the impact. Now Zorin leaned over him, his huge hand moving closer toward his throat.

Dante still had another hand free, though. He seized his baton, flicked it out, and drove it piston-like into the still-raw, badly-stitched scar along Zorin's jaw and neck where Gage had slashed him days ago. The club drew blood, and Zorin visibly flinched, drawing his foot back by sheer reflex.

It was enough of an opening for Dante to scramble free. He got up and whacked the baton into Zorin's injured knee, which again stunned the giant. The massive hand shot out once more, seizing the young doctor by the throat and lifting him. His feet kicked and trailed on the floor, then flailed at nothing but air.

As Koschei's powerful fingers constricted around his windpipe and compressed his neckbone, Dante desperately lashed out at his foe's face, arms, and shoulders, striking anything within arm's reach. Zorin had steeled himself against mere pain. He was *angry*. His horse-sized teeth were clenched within the cavern of his mouth. His free hand shot out, plucked the baton from Dante's grasp, and flung it aside.

"Shit," Dante croaked.

Gage and Janet disengaged after their most recent exchange, both bleeding from long cuts they'd received on their limbs and shoulders. Janet's relative inexperience was becoming more apparent, despite her nominal skill. Gage was growing tired. His ankle, still operating at less than full functionality, hampered his movements.

She'd noticed. He couldn't pivot on his left foot as she could.

Using it against him, she feinted more and more to his left side, dancing out of his reach before coming back against him with flashing strikes, not so much moving in for the kill—yet—as simply trying to wear him out until he made a stupid mistake. Then it would be over.

He had to do something desperate. Something stupid enough that she wouldn't anticipate it.

Gage sucked in his breath and released it, all at once, in the terrifying high-pitched battle cry he'd used so many times before to unnerve opponents who'd underestimated him. Janet flinched as he bowled into her. She reflexively swung the kukri. Rather than try to dodge it, he blocked it with the armored portion of his upper arm. The small plates and thick material stopped most of the edge, though it still bruised his bicep and the recurved tip area gouged the inside of his arm, breaking the skin.

Janet's lovely black eyes widened in alarm. With the same arm he'd used to block, the Nepali twisted the girl's arm around and back, incapacitating and immobilizing it, while his other hand, holding the deadly blade, moved forward.

She cried out, something in Mandarin. She couldn't twist away from him with her arm trapped. However, speed hadn't deserted her. Her hand lashed out and caught his wrist. For a second they strained against each other—Janet was, paradoxically, in a better-balanced and more stable position that evened the odds against Gage's greater bulk and strength.

There was no time to fight fair. So Gage simply kicked the girl's legs out from under her. Shrieking, she fell straight down, *thudding* and bouncing on the floor. The second kukri, which she'd snatched from him, stayed in his hand.

Dante was blacking out. His vision was fading to darkness, aside from the weird pink and green spots that kept flashing in front of him. He *felt* the vertebrae of his neck sliding out of alignment, on course to breaking altogether. Koschei was still singing a fucking Russian dance—and badly out of tune.

He still had a lucid thought or two. He glimpsed the bloody knee with the .38 caliber slug still embedded in it. Summoning what little physical energy remained, he drove the heel of his boot down into the wound.

Zorin's grip slackened. A little. Dante gasped for air and used the sudden increase in bodily resources to repeatedly kick the towering bastard, mashing the injured muscle, trying to loosen or break the kneecap itself. As his arrogant presumption of victory had grown stronger, Zorin lost some of the pain-numbing benefits of adrenaline.

An ogrish growl rumbled and the huge hand spasmodically flexed open, dropping Dante to the floor. He landed hard but sprang back up to his knees at once, trying to see what the hell else was going on as his vision returned halfway to normal.

"Dante!" Gage shouted. The physician perceived a knife sailing through the air toward him, handle-first. Somehow, he caught it.

Stupidly giddy at the feel of a weapon in his grasp, Dante pivoted on his heels and swung the kukri as hard as he could at the quivering bulk beside him. Arkadi Zorin had not yet recovered from having his leg kicked halfway in two, and he failed to block or dodge the thick Nepali blade. It bit deeply into the corded muscles of his bull-like neck, drawing out a torrent of blood and grinding against the bone beneath.

Dante hadn't eliminated Zorin yet, though. The man's long arms rose, and his bear-like hands clamped around Dante's neck again. His muddy eyes, bloodshot with pain and fury, bulged and twitched. Dante gagged as the Russian's thumbs pressed down on his windpipe.

"No," he wheezed. Then he wrenched on the kukri with everything he had left and sheared the edge through the neck vertebrae and out through the flesh on the other side in a red spray.

Zorin's broad face was frozen in a crazed animal smile as his head lolled sideways, dragging against his shoulder as his body collapsed to its knees. The cranium was soon attached to the rest of him by only a few threads of skin and sinew. Blood had soaked his entire coat and spread across the floor. Dante sprang back, holding up the stained knife as the titan crashed to the floor at last.

Gage made the worst possible error. For perhaps a quarter of a second, he allowed himself to be distracted by the grotesque spectacle of Zorin's death. It was as much time as Janet needed for a reversal.

She jumped up and knocked him down with her shoulder, bracing herself from the side with her foot for maximum stability. Her slim hands deftly seized the kukri from his grasp in the same motion.

He barely knew what had happened. Only that he now lay on his back on the floor, unarmed, and the woman who sought his death stood above him, about to deliver him to his ancestors with his knife. Her beautiful face twisted with perverse satisfaction. The fluorescent lights cast a blue-white glare off his kukri's blade and the shiny black hood of her hair.

Death came not with a *whooshing* strike but with a deep thunderous *boom*.

Gage's mind, battle-tempered though it was, couldn't keep up with the pace of events. It took another fraction of a precious second before he realized that he was still alive while Janet had a gaping crimson hole through her chest.

Behind her, Dante stood blank-faced with a plume of smoke rising from his shotgun.

The girl turned slowly toward him, her features going slack and pale in amazement. She made a brief panting, gasping sound as a trickle of blood ran from her lips down the scar on her chin. Then she toppled over, landing facedown next to Gage, where she lay still for all time.

Gage made himself ignore her body and looked instead at his friend.

Dante's eyes were practically invisible behind the sheet of tears, and his shoulders slumped. His arms hung loose so the shotgun dragged on the floor. He dropped it. Then he flopped down onto two adjacent chairs against the wall, treating them as a makeshift bed. Anything to catch him as he fell over in despair.

It was over. That much, Gage had to fix in his mind, to tell himself half a dozen times to ensure it was true. Once he believed it, he began the laborious, stiff, and painful process of climbing to his feet. Then he caught his breath and wiped his brow before moving over to the line of chairs.

He reached down and put a hand on Dante's arm. "Dr. Costa. Dante. Come, we need to get some rest and treatment." He began hoisting him up, despite the younger man's greater size. Dante had gone mostly limp and didn't offer much resistance.

"Where are we going?" Dante asked in a monotone. He more or less slid into a standing position as the shorter man put his shoulder under his arm, supporting him until he felt like walking.

Gage explained, "To get your hurts looked after. We're in a hospital, after all."

They trudged across the open stretches of the floor, avoiding the massive pile of Arkadi Zorin's remains and not looking at Janet Feng's.

Dante inhaled through his nostrils, the sound sharp and whistling, and exhaled through his mouth. "I can tell you as a medical professional," he began. His monotone took on a cryptic undertone of pitch-blackness. "Civilization doesn't yet have a treatment for the symptoms I'm feeling right about now."

Gage patted his shoulder. Together, they limped away, leaving the room behind them.

CHAPTER TWENTY-THREE

Since the Executives had been kind enough to send a team of mechanics to recover Gage's Autocutioner, accompanied by some gun-toting muscle, just to be safe, he was fortunate to have access to a vehicle for the meeting.

Dante wasn't with him. Gage had left him behind at the hospital, understanding completely that the young man needed some time to himself before he would be much good in a serious discussion. Particularly one about the threats posed by foreign agents in Atlantica.

The truck rattled down the streets. Gage wished he'd drunk a second cup of tea. His bladder would probably thank him for abstaining, but he still didn't feel fully alert after his short nap. In truth, his body needed more like ten or twelve hours of sleep, but for the sake of his colleagues, he'd forced it to make do with four. Until later, anyway.

The city was as dark as a large city could be—not very, in other words. Street lamps lined the roads and floodlights shone from buildings. In some places, the illumination was blue instead of white or yellow since the richer of the island's builders had used Atlanticore crystal instead of traditional bulbs and generators.

Gage frowned. Atlanticore. The Coven of Miracles. Everything here always came back to the endless quest for money and power, usually undertaken by people who already had significant amounts of both.

When he stopped at a traffic light, two things occurred to him. One, the truck handled a little differently. Zorin's men had destroyed its tires, so the repair crew had replaced them with new ones that were slightly smaller—they'd had trouble fitting tires the same size as the originals into their vehicle for the recovery trip out to the edge of town.

Two, no laws forced people to obey the traffic signals at intersections, but most did anyway, within reason. Drivers tended to turn in any direction they pleased once it was clear to do so, regardless of what color the light was. But when traffic approached from all sides, most humans allowed the light to decide. It saved everyone from getting in too many wrecks. Even the city's richer inhabitants couldn't afford to replace their cars daily.

Soon, Gage pulled in at the hotel. Off to the side, he saw Tyler's and Daria's Autocutioners parked in a section of the lot where they would be relatively inconspicuous but still easily accessible in case they had to leave in a hurry. He parked between them, noting with a certain amused satisfaction that his truck was almost exactly halfway between the others in size.

After climbing down from the vehicle, he got halfway across the lot before a bellhop from the lobby came out to greet him and offer him an arm to help speed up his progress. "Thank you," he said. His ankle wasn't *too* bad, all things considered. The aid was still appreciated.

Both Ty and Daria were waiting for him in the lobby's sitting room. Ty wore his Executioner's uniform, as he nearly always did, whereas Daria was in casual clothes. She often worked undercover, in contrast to Ty's more direct problem-solving method, so it made sense.

Of course, both were armed. Gage had left his rifle and newer kukri in the truck. His trusty Webley and his original kukri stayed on his person at all times.

Once inside, the bellhop politely excused himself. Daria and Ty stood to greet him, and they exchanged grim smiles and handshakes. At first, it was unnecessary to speak. They'd all been through similar ordeals. All were part of the club—Executioners.

Ty asked, "How's your ankle? Costa didn't fuck it up, did he?"

"Mm, yes," Daria added. "I wondered the same thing."

Gage shrugged. "It needs more time to heal completely, but it's functional. Dante has done everything he could to keep it from getting worse. I feel that he's a good doctor."

The other two chuckled at that. Ty quipped, "Good enough to treat some of the finest people in Atlantica before I found him. But, people can change. I'm glad the two of you get along and that he helped you resolve your situation earlier."

"As am I," Daria assented. "Let's go up to my room and have drinks, shall we? There are things we should discuss in private."

The concierge at the desk tactfully commented as they headed to the elevator, "There is already vodka and bourbon as you requested, sirs and madam. And a pot for making tea, if that's what you prefer."

They thanked the man, waited for the elevator, and rode it up to Daria's usual "conference room" and hideout in silence. Once everyone made themselves comfortable, they poured drinks. Gage accepted a single small glass of bourbon, while Ty had a larger glass of the same, and Daria a still-larger glass of vodka. Tea, perhaps, could come later.

"So," Ty began, signaling that the serious part of the discussion was at hand. "We have a new reality to contend with. This mysterious Coven of Miracles, which Daria mentioned before, is drawing hostile foreign operatives to the island. If that Russian guy is any indication, they might be willing to kill a *lot* of inno-cent people if they think they can get away with it."

He was, Gage saw, sinking into the cold and focused rage that defined his approach to his job.

Daria didn't exactly seem pleased by the notion either. She traced the rim of her glass with her index finger and frowned into the distance, her eyes dark and haunted. "There will always be such people. Atlantica being a place which is wide open to nearly anyone, we knew they would come, sooner or later."

Gage raised a finger. "It was the Chinese woman who was attempting to gain access to the Coven. The Russian man was here to kill her. Have we learned anything more about the Coven? Or are they still merely a rumor?"

Ty shrugged. He'd been busy trailing the missing kids he'd mentioned the other day. He was close to success but had hit a recent snag, which was why he had time for the evening's confer-ence while he waited for the next development in the case.

Daria had come closer to the Coven's affairs and tried to be more proactive. "They must exist if people are willing to do such things merely to gain their favor. I've found no direct evidence of them yet. It's still hearsay and gossip. Perhaps it's all a lie meant as a distraction from something else. I don't know."

She quaffed half of her rather tall glass of vodka at once, swished it around in her mouth, and swallowed. For a relatively petite woman, her drinking abilities were truly impressive.

"What I *do* know is that the threats we face are growing bigger," she went on. "We might need to begin working together more to combat them as a team or unit. What you and Costa faced should've drawn all of us to help you. Had we known how much opposition there was, we might've done so."

Ty scowled at that. "Half of me agrees. You know I would be glad to help. But I'm looking for *children*, all right? Still, you make a good point." He steeled himself as though he didn't want to utter what he was about to say. "We need more Executioners." He took a swig of whiskey.

Daria gave a sharp nod. "You're very likely correct about that, Mr. Katakura. What do you think, Dr. Gurung?"

Gage had wanted to raise the issue anyway, so he did while answering her question. "I would like to invite Dante Costa into the organization."

Daria simply arched an eyebrow, keeping her mouth shut and her expression quizzical, but Ty nearly spat out his drink.

"No way," he insisted once he'd made himself swallow. "Can't trust that guy. He's a recovering junkie, for God's sake. What if we need him to go after some drug dealer and he keeps half the product for himself? That is *not* the kind of example we're trying to set here."

Gage frowned. Ty had a point, yet he didn't seem to understand the depth of Dante's mettle. He hadn't been there when the two of them had gone through so much and only survived because of each other.

He leaned forward and folded his hands. "Mr. Katakura. Tyler. Please, hear me out. Dante saved my life many times. I would've been overwhelmed without him.

"Despite his past problems and his, ah, quirks of personal character, he's a man with more integrity than you might think. He's also a surprisingly good fighter for someone without military training. Furthermore, it's good to have a doctor around, yes? Allow me to explain all that he did during our mission..."

Ty's curmudgeonly expression of resistance faded, albeit gradually, as Gage regaled him with the full story of their mutual exploits. Daria's face stayed neutral aside from the occasional widening of her eyes at the more interesting parts. Gage supposed that as a former smuggler, she was less likely to be critical of Dante's shady past.

When Gage reached the end of his account, Ty sat back, clearly deep in thought. "Well. That's more than I would've expected from him. Maybe I was wrong. Daria, what do you think?"

She ran a finger along the edge of her chin. "I trust Gage's judgment," she proclaimed. "It might be better for a man with temptations to be with us and under our watch. It will make it harder for him to wander off, get bored, and sink back into the abyss of drugs, will it not?"

"Good point," Ty conceded. "I still don't think he's the ideal candidate, but perhaps we can let him in on probation or something. Keep him on a leash while we ensure he can handle the responsibilities. In the future, though, we're going to need some kind of vetting process. And soon. Otherwise, the quality of recruits will decline."

Daria smirked. "How could it go lower when we started with you?"

Ty glared at her, then burst out laughing. Daria followed suit, and so did Gage.

CHAPTER TWENTY-FOUR

A day had passed. Gage had found the bar while browsing the downtown area around Daria's hotel. It was a nice little place, seedy enough to be cozy, but not the sort of place you were likely to get stabbed for the crime of simply being there where other drunks could see you.

A mix of construction foremen, lower-end salespersons, and couples in their thirties and forties frequented it. The decor was generically tasteful without frills, and it showed the latest sports out of New York, Boston, and Montreal on a nice big screen.

He arrived just after dark, sat at one of the corner tables, ordered a beer, and waited. He wasn't wearing his Executioner's uniform. No point in attracting undue attention.

It took Dante about five minutes to arrive after Gage had seated himself. The young doctor strolled in the front, gave the place a quick appraisal, and nodded before looking around for his friend and ambling over to join him.

"Hi," he opened. "Before you ask, yes, I'm feeling better. Not *entirely* better, but it's an improvement."

Gage gave a rolling shrug. "Yes, that's good. It will take time to heal completely from all that happened. I'm glad to see you more like your old self."

They chatted along those lines for perhaps five minutes. The waitress showed up to ask if Dante wanted a drink. For the time being, he ordered a Coke, implying that he might request something alcoholic later but hadn't yet made up his mind.

After he had his beverage, Gage decided there was no use stalling any longer.

"Dante," he began, looking at his hands, then up at his friend. "I wanted to ask you something. You were concerned about what you would do with yourself after you healed my ankle and once we dealt with, ah, recent things. Well. I've spoken to Tyler and Daria. They agree that we need more Executioners." He paused. "I suggested you for the position."

Dante stared bug-eyed at him. "What?" he sputtered. "Why the hell would you do that? Wait, sorry, no offense. I, ah, shit." He looked aside at one of the cheap framed prints on the wall, then cleared his throat. "We handled the same stuff together, yes. I'm flattered. But me? I'm not a cop. I'm a crook. I don't know how I stayed straight during all this."

"Daria was a smuggler," Gage pointed out.

Dante sighed. "Yeah, fine, but..." He rambled away at some length, elaborating all the ways he considered himself insufficient and unworthy until Gage couldn't take it anymore.

"*Stop,*" the Nepali commanded, his voice far harsher and more commanding than usual, and he held up his hands, palms out. Dante shut up at once, stunned. "Stop it, please, Dante. You've earned my trust many times over these last several days. You've even earned my respect. I can think of no one better suited to the job. Besides, it would be helpful to have a physician."

"Ohh." The younger man smirked. "I get it. You're using me for my medical knowledge. And my courageous tough guy tendencies. Since I saved your life and all."

Gage wagged an index finger. "Now. If I remember rightly, it was I who saved your life first. And whose blade took Koschei's head? You wouldn't have been able to do that with any other knife."

Dante snorted, but the sound transformed into a laugh. When the waitress returned, he asked for a shot of whiskey to go with his soda. "Drinking might not be the best thing for my overall sobriety regimen," he muttered, mostly to himself. "I'll make an exception for a special occasion."

After the young woman returned with the shot, they thanked her, then Dante mixed the drink himself. He raised his glass. "A toast, I guess, to me becoming an Executioner. Which my buddies back home never would've believed."

Gage raised his beer. "Yes, a toast. To Atlantica, which is the island of new beginnings."

They drank together. For a moment afterward, they sat in comfortable silence. When that grew boring, Dante piped up with, "So if this place is Atlantis, where does that leave Crete? I was under the impression that the ancient Greeks were pretty clear on Atlantis being somewhere in the Mediterranean..."

"Nonsense," Gage argued. "The very name 'Atlantis' suggests a different body of water. Furthermore, if we look at Hindu and Tamil sources..."

They argued well into the night. Other patrons, watching and overhearing them, wondered which university cafe they'd escaped from and shook their heads, bemused, as they wandered out into the bright night of the city.

The story continues with book four, *No Backing Down*, available now at Amazon.

Claim your copy today!

AUTHOR NOTES MICHAEL ANDERLE

DECEMBER 15, 2021

Thank you for not only reading this book, but these author notes as well!

So the only aspect of these author notes that has anything to do with this story is (I'm thinking) the series title – Justice Begins.

Many of you know I'm a bit of a cynic (so take the REST of these author notes with 'reader beware – cynic writing' warning in flashing neon.)

In my first series, The Kurtherian Gambit, my main character Bethany Anne would always quote the following when she wasn't sure where the bad guys were hiding, "Follow the money, the answer is always at the end of the line."

I happen to be reading a book called Rich Man Poor Bank by Mark J. Quann with Jeff Cohen.

It is an eye-opening (almost blistering) discussion of banking in the United States (versus, say the Credit Unions in the United States) and has me seriously thinking about cutting all ties with the bank I've been using for over 35 years.

To go to a Credit Union.

The businessman in me is tempted to open my own bank. The lazy part of me doesn't want anything to do with the hassle.

I'm presently down in Cabo San Lucas and I haven't the foggiest notion if the Credit Union ATM's reach down here or not. If they do not, that's going to be a right pain in the ass.

I have not confirmed if this books' statements are factually correct in all ways (I know some are, but there is one statement which seems like I either misinterpreted the notion of fractional banking, or the information on the FDIC website failed to mention an aspect of how it works.) I'm not sure which.

I'm hoping it is just me who got it wrong.

Otherwise, I'm about to move all of my money out of the US Banking system and find a solid credit union I can become a part of – hopefully one with international banking capabilities.

We shall see.

That's about as much rant as I have in me at the moment on this subject. I'm just learning about it and who knows, maybe another hour of reading will have me upset that the information in the book is off-base.

If the information is NOT off-base. Well, I hope that Justice comes calling on a lot of the historical and present figures in the banking industry for allowing this to occur.

Have a fantastic weekend or week, and I look forward to talking with you in the next story you read from me!

Ad Aeternitatem,
Michael Anderle

BOOKS BY MICHAEL ANDERLE

Sign up for the LMBPN email list to be notified of new releases and special deals!

http://lmbpn.com/email

For a complete list of books by Michael Anderle, please visit:

www.lmbpn.com/ma-books/

CONNECT WITH THE AUTHOR

Connect with Michael Anderle

Website: http://lmbpn.com

Email List: http://lmbpn.com/email/

https://www.facebook.com/LMBPNPublishing

https://twitter.com/MichaelAnderle

https://www.instagram.com/lmbpn_publishing/

https://www.bookbub.com/authors/michael-anderle

www.ingramcontent.com/pod-product-compliance
Lightning Source LLC
Chambersburg PA
CBHW022128310726
48972CB00007B/2245